THE WILD COAST

ALSO BY JAN CAREW

Black Midas
The Last Barbarian
Moscow Is Not My Mecca
Cry Black Power
Sons of the Flying Wing
The Third Gift
Rape the Sun
Children of the Sun
Save the Last Dance for Me
The Twins of Llora
Grenada: The Hour Will Strike Again

JAN CAREW

THE WILD COAST

INTRODUCTION BY JEREMY POYNTING

PEEPAL TREE

First published in Great Britain in 1958
by Martin Secker & Warburg Ltd
This new edition published in 2009
Peepal Tree Press Ltd
17 King's Avenue
Leeds LS6 1QS
England

ISBN13: 9781845231101

 Peepal Tree gratefully acknowledges Arts Council support

THE WILD COAST: UNFINISHED BUSINESS

JEREMY POYNTING

Few have written more sensually of the rural Caribbean[1] (in this instance, the "wild coast" between the Corentyne and Canje rivers in Guyana) than Jan Carew. His image of Hector Bradshaw seeing the village when the rains come and he is shortly to leave Tarlogie, "as though he was viewing the landscape through frosted glass" (p.214), brilliantly condenses seer and seen, and the descriptions of the spatial dislocations that come with the floods is equally striking. *The Wild Coast* warrants rereading because its prose pleases, its characters breathe, and Carew is always a good teller of tales, but with the hindsight of the fifty years since its first publication (in 1958) it is the novel's early and interesting contribution to the West Indian novel of childhood and youth that deserves fresh attention.

The Wild Coast comes in a sequence preceded by George Lamming's *In the Castle of My Skin* (1953) and followed by Geoffrey Drayton's *Christopher* (1959), Peter Kempadoo's *Guiana Boy* (1960), Ismith Khan's *The Jumbie Bird* (1961), Austin Clarke's *Among Thistles and Thorns* (1965), Michael Anthony's *The Year in San Fernando* (1965) and *Green Days by the River* (1967), Ian McDonald's *The Hummingbird Tree* (1969) and Merle Hodge's *Crick Crack Monkey* (1970). Apart from *Christopher* (which cleaves closely to the boy's point of view) and *The Jumbie Bird* (only in part a novel of childhood), *The Wild Coast* is the only one of these novels that explores the potential of the third-person mode of telling and in doing so offers a different (and often quite astringent) view of the child. In the first-person novels the child tends to function as an innocent camera into memory, or, as in Lamming, a way of seeing into a changing society. We see how the world looks to the child and can sometimes deduce a growing complexity of vision, but what we more rarely get is a focus on the individual child's distinctive personhood, a maturing complex at the heart of biological, individual and social forces. *The Wild Coast* offers a vividly particular portrayal of the childhood and adolescence of Hector Bradshaw, an individual who has as many flaws as good qualities; a moving and exact calibration of the changes in his relationship with his guardian, Sister Smart; and a bracingly unsentimental recognition of the egocentricity of youth. Carew's novel also diverges from the sexual innocence which characterises this first flowering of the Caribbean novel of childhood and adolescence. It is not until novels such as Oonya Kempadoo's *Buxton Spice* (1998) that youthful sexuality is acknowledged as frankly.

Whilst elements of the novel are no doubt imaginative invention, its starting point – the arrival of a sick child in a remote village on the Corentyne Coast – is, as Carew confirmed in an interview, based on his own and his family's history.[2] But in asking what it means to be an individual and Guyanese, in exploring the role of history and landscape, heredity and environment in the shaping of its central character's moral universe, *The Wild Coast* goes well beyond the autobiographical naturalism that provides the foothills of the West Indian novel.

Carew's principal means of realising the complexity and dynamic of his vision is through his repeated use of the device of doubling (in character and episode) and by deliberately embedding a sense of unfinished business beyond the conventional point of narrative closure. Carew did not invent either of these devices (they are part of the inherited topoi of the bildungsroman – the contrasts between the Tulliver children in *The Mill on the Floss* provide one obvious example) but he uses them in a way that adds, firstly, to the novel's depth in tracing the growth of Hector's personhood and, secondly, in a way that gives the novel a trajectory that confounds any acceptance of the "way things are", a limitation of some of the Caribbean novels of childhood.

The Wild Coast is not without flaws. Whilst the portrayal of the black matriarch, Sister Smart, has real depth and insight, other women in the novel, particularly Elsa, become at times cartoonish stereotypes. Of Elsa, we are told at one point, "at heart she had remained a courtesan" (p.163), and elsewhere there are descriptions of Indo-Guyanese and Amerindian characters that make uncomfortable reading (Dela, for example has the "disciplined inscrutability of her people"). However, the novel is sharply insightful about a particular kind of maleness. Carew's men are invariably in pursuit of sexual conquest (self-perceived in the main as a matter of physical discharge), and the novel acknowledges that this goes hand-in-hand with a reluctance to engage with women emotionally. In a scene where Hector and the adult Tengar are romping on a beach, they are described as "boys together enjoying their freedom from women" (p.88). In one of the few moments when Carew does give space to Elsa's independent point of view, she confronts Hector (who wants use of her body in the same way as his father has done) with a demand for access to his emotional life ("What I want to find out is who you think you are at all..." (p.184)), a demand Hector is too immature to understand.

There are flaws, too, of a genre-switching kind, when, for instance, the characterisation of the old hunter, Doorne, suddenly shifts register into Caribbean Gothic (when he is revealed as Elsa's first, abusive seducer) and he becomes a penny-dreadful devil-man. And Carew barely escapes from exoticism in his portrayal of the Wind-dance in Tarlogie. Whilst "Mantop" is a convincing invention, the climactic African rite in the novel is an awkward concoction of scraps of Orisha, Voudun and Kali Mai and Moko jumbie, when a knowledge of Guyana's Cumfa ceremonies would have provided much more persuasive and ethnologically rooted materials.[3]

The other element in the novel that has attracted critical disapproval is the mystery surrounding the identity of Hector's mother, and there is no getting away from the fact that the revelation is anticlimactic. It is clear from an interview that the issue of family secrets had personal relevance for Carew and such secrets can be read as powerful signifiers of the ambivalences built into the racial and social position of the "coloured" middle class. As Denise Harris shows in her novel *Web of Secrets* (she is Carew's niece and taps into the same family history), it is about hiding away family behaviour that threatens the image of respectability, hiding the nakedness of the actual race relations that gave birth to the brown family, and – the fairer the skin, the greater the urge – hiding away all connections with blackness, whether somatic or cultural. So whilst the mystery of Hector's origins is not effectively developed, we need to remember (because Carew does not foreground this fact) that the novel is set in the colonial 1930s when the scandal associated with the "mystery" would have been real for the respectable middle class.

What is more effective is the theme of secrecy in relationship to character. It is a much noticed quality in Hector, and one that connects him to two of his mentors. For Doorne it's a black man's strategy for dealing with a hostile world; for La Rose a means of preventing anyone from peering into his wounds of poverty – until illness loosens his tongue.

At its core, though, *The Wild Coast* delivers the richness and shapeliness promised in the first chapter where all the novel's key themes are set out: the tension between Hector's indeterminacy ("You spirit don't ever burst out from inside you and fill the empty spaces around you," as Sister says) and his potential for self-determination (the adventure of escape from the Georgetown house); between the constrictions of the Tarlogie house with its barbed-wire perimeter, and his scope for growing into a self-aware manhood in a relationship with the natural world (seen in the free-flying flocks of birds rising from the foreshore); in the clues about his capacity for both heartless impulsiveness and regretful feeling in the episode of the stoning of the kiskadee.

In a nutshell, the first chapter asks the bildungsroman's essential questions: Who is Hector to become? How is he to deal with the givenness of his genetic inheritance (shrouded though it is in secrecy) and avoid becoming a man like his father? How realise his unique potential in response to the influences of his adult mentors, and the forces of history and nature? In this archetypal process, there are encounters to interpret, challenges to meet and sermons to store away for future use.

The challenges, whether the ordeal of crossing the swamps to Black Bush, or rescuing Laljee and Dela from the Tarlogie mob, each provide fine examples of the kind of storytelling at which Carew excels. But it is the use of the device of doubling that gives *The Wild Coast* its richness of psychological texture and shape.

Hector is shown as engaged in a process that begins in the perception of opposites, moves to seeing subtler differences and grows to an awareness of people's real complexity. He begins to see that his mentors are not only paired in multiple ways, but are also often divided, within themselves. For instance, when Hector first arrives in Tarlogie, the two characters who stand in a most obvious pairing are his father and Doorne. The latter becomes a surrogate father because he sees potential in Hector where Fitz Bradshaw sees none. Fitz and Doorne stand, too, for the inheritance of the slave master and the unfinished business of the slave. But deeper knowledge of Doorne leads Hector to see that, no less than his father, the old hunter is capable of being an authoritarian bully.

Hector's relationship to history is further located through the pairing of Sister and Doorne. Both are direct descendants of slaves and represent contrary sides of the inheritance of slavery. Sister has a dignity borne of learnt patience and stoic endurance where Doorne bears the strain of resistant rebelliousness; Sister maintains an idealised version of the culture and values of the white master where Doorne is committed to maintaining his Africanness. So it is that Doorne sets out to make Hector aware of his dual ancestry as a brown child when he tells him the story of the slaves who dig a pit to trap and bury one of Hector's white ancestors. When Hector asks why Doorne has told him this story, the old man says:

> "...I wanted you to know that you got the blood of the master and the slave in you' veins. You' papa trying to forget it and acting like he is a white man but you musn't never forget it, boy." (p.56)

This is an aspect of his Guyaneseness that Hector has to confront. But he must also deal with the contradictions he perceives within both these mentors. If Sister Smart is a paragon of tough-minded, loving-kindness and unstinting generosity (she protects Hector in a way that "never allowed anyone to crush his hypersensitive spirit"), she has also denied so much of herself: her Africanness, her sexuality – all the things she spurns as "pagan". We know that both are active self-denials; Sister observes regretfully, "But woman who lie fallow too long en't no kind of woman at all" (p.72). The commenting voice observes: "Sister's prejudices were part of her strength", and her

9

obsession with protocol can be seen as an attempt to impose form on both Tarlogie's and Hector's formlessness. Doorne's doubleness involves by contrast an unambiguous sense of Black pride, and of his sexuality he observes, "Better to be a beggar with good sap in you limbs than to have money and position and a sugar stick with no juices in it" (p.53). But, in contrast to Sister, Doorne has a nihilistic streak of cruelty when he feels threatened. That kind of selfishness characterises much of Hector's behaviour, and it is only after Sister's death that he begins to learn some of her generosity of spirit, particularly in the way he extends sympathy to his broken father.

The pairings are never accidental. Hector's perceptions always relate to what is gradually taking shape in his psyche out of its initial formlessness. His embryonic sense of his position as a child in a brown/mulatto middle-class family, aware of its restrictions (i.e., to keep away from those "ragged, loudmouth urchins" from the "nigger-yard", as Aunt Hanna commands him) is one of the dynamic prompts to both his interactions and his reflections on them.

Beyond race and class, Hector confronts more fundamental ways of being in the world in the doubling of Doorne's sons, Caya and Tengar. At first they seem to exemplify contraries of laziness and activity, living in the head and living in the body. But the more Hector sees, the more he recognises that whilst Caya seems like a lily of the field, he is also, as Sister says, a "sly mongoose of a man", who worms his way into Dookia's favour and the murdered Chinaman's rumshop. Yet over this complex of oppositions overarches the fact that Caya, as drummer and Shango priest, has the spirit of the true bard, and a vision that carries him beyond Tarlogie's mundanity. Tengar, by contrast, appears to be the man of action, but whilst he is described in metaphors that identify him as a force of nature (as a mora tree trunk or coconut palm) there is also truth in Elsa's complaint that he's "like a lump of mud watching time pass by" (p.202). This image and its opposite, of Tengar bellowing like a red howler monkey in "wild, inchoate anger" when he learns that his father is Elsa's first seducer, further connects to what we see developing in Hector's personality, when Sister looks at him and observes, "you see him there looking like butter can't melt in his mouth, he got the fury of a tiger in his heart" (p.75).

Hector, like Caya, lives in his head, a dreaminess he feeds with reading "about boys younger than me doing all kinds of brave things", a Tom Sawyerish observation that leads to an almost fatal recklessness on the expedition to Black Bush when he confuses nature and culture in an anthropomorphic way and attacks the hogs in sympathy with the stricken jaguar. As Doorne complains:

> "Is who tell you you is any hero? All you is, is a maugre, skin-and-bone pickny with a lot of book story spinning confusion inside you' young head . . ." (p.115)

Sister sees the same tension, but she perceives that Hector's urge to live in and through his body may save him from his book-fantasies without cutting him off from genuine learning:

> He was a strange boy, a wild boy, a dreaming boy who often gave the impression that most of his life was being lived in a fantasy world [...] And yet, she had to admit, he had an earthy, physical side to his nature [...] You only had to watch him eating, shovelling his food down as if he was afraid that someone would snatch the plate from before him, to know that he had some of the peasant in him... (p.188)

But if, like Tengar, Hector is at his happiest living in his body, like Tengar he is led by his instincts. As Sister charges: "You got a bad habit of drifting into things and then acting like you not responsible for what develop" (p.186).

One strength of Carew's use of doubling is that he is rarely content to remain with either/or terms and this connects to the novel's dynamic of unfinished business. One topos of the Caribbean bildungsroman is, for instance, the character divided from himself by education. This is certainly true of La Rose:

> His book-knowledge had forced him to live astride two worlds – the world of swamps and forests and wide skies, and the world of the straight lines, the written word, the Faustian conflict. He had tried to link the two but his mind had exhausted itself in the struggle, leaving him with a tenuous foothold in each of the two worlds. (p.101)

For La Rose, personality and experience force him into a

manichean divide. He complains that whilst Hector's class and colour give him real choice, he has only two: "to be ricefield yokel or to try to be a teacher…" (p.174). On the surface this seems true, but when one considers that the ricefield yokels in the novel include Caya (whose complexity has been suggested above), it is clear that La Rose is drawn to a reductive reading of his situation. As he says: "Somewhere back in my small-boy days something got stamped to death inside me" (p.102).

For whilst education is taking Hector away from the village, it is also evident that, for reasons other than his class and colour advantages, he is not destined to arrive at the same soul-destroying sense of division. La Rose recognises this after the incident when Hector challenges him on why Keats's "Ode to a Grecian Urn" has to be regarded as a masterpiece. Hector doesn't know whether it is or it isn't, but he has the instinct not to take this for granted, just because a white "stranger-man say so in a book", and because what Hector has in his head is an image of the village women carrying water jars on their heads (p.79). La Rose tells Hector "that thing that's dead in me is alive in you, and you won't be a failure if you keep it alive" (p.102).

There are countless other doublings, but enough is enough. However, there is another kind of doubleness that deserves attention, and this relates to the narrative voice. Though told throughout in the third person, it is generally clear when the novel cleaves to Hector's point of view and when the narrator speaks in a voice that exists beyond Hector's capacity.

That voice is concerned with two things, firstly with foregrounding the novel's post-departure perspective, and secondly with the theme of unfinished business. We know that Hector is destined to leave Guyana and find himself in a wider world, so the novel keeps asking: What will Hector carry away from Guyana and his years in Tarlogie? This is a question that goes beyond Hector's self-consciousness and the clues to its answer are located in two places: in the various sermons he hears, and in the observations that he is absorbing something from his physical presence in Tarlogie that he will only understand much later in his life.

It is, of course, a familiar topos of the bildungsroman, that it speaks through younger and older selves. There's a predictive voice located in the narrative that invites us to guess a trajectory for Hector's post-novel progress, but there is also a more externalised moral and political voice that tells us what tasks Hector needs to address – whose outcomes remain uncertain.

With respect to what he takes away from Tarlogie it is important to recognise that it is not only Hector who is unfinished, but the village itself. There is no sentimentality in Carew's vision of the African-Guyanese village, as there is, say, in Roger Mais's *The Hills Were Joyful Together* (1953) when his uprooted village people, now in the ghettoes of Kingston, are shown reaching back into memories of a more whole, more coherent world. Tarlogie has scarcely emerged from the dark-ness and deprivations of slavery; time there "was a river trapped in an ox-bow and going round in circles" (p.74); Tarlogians still live in a state of unaccommodated nature and have scarcely begun to enter history to remake their lives:

> The swamps were vast, but people lived huddled together in villages, colliding like tadpoles in small ponds. [...] Explosions of anger were a necessary relief from the tensions of living like crabs in a barrel. (p.195)

That judgement (which looks forward to the dark vision of Harold Ladoo's *No Pain Like This Body*, 1972) connects to Dookia's killing of her abusive husband, to Caya's reluctance to share any of his good fortune in taking over the rumshop with his family – though the comment is also made that when the floods come "life only continued because of the charity of the poor to the destitute" (p.222) – and to the episode when a mob of Tarlogians turn on two ethnic outsiders, Laljee and Dela. But Carew also shows how, in their different ways, Tarlogians such as Sister and Galloway, and Caya and Doorne, show sparks of vision in their struggle to make sense of their world through, respectively, the patterns of European-derived Christianity and the African survivals of the Wind-dance. From both of these Hector derives much. From Sister and Galloway he can take the strength that comes from living according to a belief system and a moral code, even though both are compromised by their colonial roots. This is made clear in the sad irony of Sister singing "Wash me and I shall be whiter than snow" and powdering her usually dignified face to go to church so "it looked as if flour had been sprinkled on her opaque, black skin" (p.92).

What Hector takes from the Wind-dance is altogether more fundamental. Though the portrayal of the rite is not without its ambivalences, there is a movement of imagery through the novel, from Sister's initial comment on the sickly boy when he first arrives in Tarlogie, as lacking in vital spirit, "water with no wind in it" (p.28), to the point where the winds of inspiration at the ceremony enter Hector's spirit and animate it in ways we suspect he will never forget. The event is a climactic moment in the novel, and there is a beautiful description of how Tarlogie is transfigured in the evening light on the night of the Wind-dance. Hector's attendance makes Sister complain that she's only managed to bring up "a young savage who en't no better than the barefoot, good-for-nothing people in this village" (p.159), but she also recognises that, "[h]is rebellion was such a fundamental one, she knew that the whole pattern of authority she had established over his life was broken for ever" (p.160). Sister's context is domestic and within the timespan of the novel, but her comment can be read as predicting Hector's future rejection of the whole ideological structure of colonialism. Carew realistically indicates that Hector's conscious motive is curiosity, but he wants to convince the reader that behind this:

was an unconscious impulse [...] to see which was more valid for him – the abstract heaven and hell about which the white minister preached or Caya's shango bacchanal with its drumming and dancing harking back to the African forests of long twilight. (p.148)

What happens at the ceremony answers Sister's pitying comment on the young Hector's passivity ("You spirit don't ever burst out from inside you and fill the empty spaces around you"):

He only felt a dizzy heat suffusing his body and his limbs turning to liquid. He was released from all that was his life in Georgetown and in the big house in Tarlogie. The disciplines imposed by his father and aunt, by Sister and his teacher fell away. The savage singing of shango drums had exorcised them. (p.155)

The uncomfortable choice of "savage" is perhaps intended to reflect Hector's immature frame of reference, because what he does next is go to Elsa's hut and demand sex from her, repeating his father's sexual rapaciousness at the very moment of potential transcendence. It carries him not to union but to revulsion and separation:

> Elsa, wrapped her legs around him and her animal smell attracted and repelled him [...] When she had drained the sap out of him and he was feeling limp, he rolled away from her and vomited. (p.158)

We have to see this as Carew's honesty about his character, but the sexualising of the Wind-dance episode suggests that the novelist, too, had a further journey to travel before Africa in the Caribbean could be seen in an unsensational way, free of negative colonial stereotypes.

However, it's also possible to see a degree of anxiety on Carew's part about his narrative representation of African cultural practices, because he adopts a distinctive stylistic mode that belongs neither to the consciousness of the character (in this case Caya), nor to the mode of the narrator's commented asides, but instead creates a consciously dignified poetic voice which is given, like the lyric poem, the force of an vatic "external" authority through its rhythms and its music:

> But wherever a man wanders he will find the neighbour-wind, the companion-wind, the messenger-wind howling its welcome, fanning awake the still leaves, lying down and rolling on the grass and the reeds. Neighbour-wind can live next door to a man who is afraid of the strangeness of an alien land. Companion-wind can strum familiar tunes on the harp-strings of trees. Messenger-wind can carry a cry of anguish across continents and seas. The wind was a symbol of absolute freedom [...]. For the descendants of the slaves the meaning and the message of the wind-dance had not changed. (p.96)

This sense of connection with place is the other imprint Hector will carry with him beyond the end of the novel, absorbed by divine possession, as Tojo suggests in response to Hector's question about how you become a Shango priest:

> "... and once you born in Tarlogie don't matter where you go or

where you try to hide the spirit does search you out and make you know, and once you get the message en't nothing you can do 'bout it but take over." (p.152)

Sister's version of how Tarlogie is absorbed is less mystical, but is still rooted in the senses rather than rational thought:

"This coast has already given you something that, wherever you go, you will have strong memory to hold on to – the smell of the earth, the feel of the hot sun, the knowledge that when you stand facing the sea there en't nothing behind you but swamp and forest and the blue horizon – you can never tear them things out of your system even if your restless spirit carry you to the ends of the earth." (p.171)

The other source of a future beyond the novel is embedded in the various sermons offered to Hector. Much goes over his head, but in each instance, Carew's prose rises to a pitch of rhetorical force that suggests that though the young Hector doesn't really understand them now, the words will be embedded in his memory for future reference. For instance, when Sister tries to tell Hector that there are things more important than book-work he could learn from Teacher La Rose, she is described as being in a vatic trance ("the words took hold of her and rocked her thin body and her eyes shone like stars over the rim of a whirlpool" (p.71)) – and then in a state of embarrassment, because she is aware of Hector's incomprehension:

"To be rich and proud en't so hard. [...] But the poor man's pride is the pride that does live in a lair in his heart when his foot reaching through his shoe sole to feel the dust of the road and the mud of the swamp, he can still hold his head high as heaven, and when hungriness scraping his belly dry, he still won't bow the head or bend the knee. [...] Take good heed of that young man's pride because if he can seed your heart with the pride of the poor, the pride that is blind as Sampson's eye and strong as the strength of the wind, then he will give you more than a whole river of words in the white man books." (p.70)

In time, Hector grows to an uncomfortable awareness of what La Rose has given him, but it is with respect to the houseboy Tojo, his companion in age and sometimes adventure, that Carew shows Hector to have the most unfinished business. Hector doesn't mistreat Tojo, but he fails to make any connection with him, fails, particularly, to recognise the inequality of their positions. As the "older" commenting narrative voice remarks: "Tojo and Hector were both nearly sixteen but they were as different as an Eskimo is from a Zulu tribesman" (p.147). This is so important a theme for Carew that he is driven to speak further about Tojo in this extra-fictional voice, pointing to the fact that this perception is utterly outside Hector's consciousness when he describes Guyana's Africans as "a plastic race, a resilient people [who] survived by living secret lives among themselves... disciplining themselves and their children to a point of implacable docility all the time knowing that time was on their side..." (p.148).

It is at this point that Carew speaks most forcefully about a future beyond the boundaries of the novel:

> Tojo was content with his heritage of waiting, but Hector had the blood both of master and slave in his veins and the problems of both to solve. Before him lay the choice of allegiance, the question of loyalty, the need to discover who he was and what he was. Some day Tojo and his midnight people would break out and he would have to take sides.(p.148)

Here, one sees Carew writing a manifesto for the Caribbean novel of the future, though expressed in terms that are very much of its time. The reference to "blood" reads uncomfortably now (as it does in Mittelholzer's historical *Kaywana Trilogy* – and as it ought to do in Walcott's celebrated "A Far Cry from Africa"[4]). There are elements of both Mittelholzer's essentialising racial determinism and Walcott's sentimental mythologising of what is in reality – as it is for Hector – a political and cultural choice. As the novel shows, Hector never sees himself as white or related in any essential way to whiteness. The only white person he knows is the Reverend Grimes and to him he feels no connection at all. Hector's choices are about whether his interests lie with the Guyanese elite (white, brown or black) or with the worker and peasant majority; whether he will remain loyal to the cultural myth of Europe assiduously propagated by sections of the middle class, or embrace a creole vision of Caribbean culture in which Africa (and India – but that's another story) plays a full part.

That kind of characterisation of the choices that Hector has to make lies only a little ahead in the West Indian novel (see Lamming's *Season of Adventure* (1960)), but Jan Carew's rich, flawed, but always highly readable story of a boy who emerges from fragility and sickness to find himself on the wild coast between the Corentyne and Canje rivers remains a lively, rewarding and revealing step along the way.

Notes

1. Before *The Wild Coast*'s publication, only Claude McKay's *Banana Bottom* (1933), Mittelholzer's *Corentyne Thunder* (1941), Selvon's *A Brighter Sun* (1952), Lamming's *In the Castle of My Skin* (1953) and Naipaul's *The Mystic Masseur* (1957) provide any convincing images of the Caribbean village. Of these only *Corentyne Thunder* provides Carew with a model for what he achieves here, and though Carew knew and respected Mittelholzer (a slightly older man), copies of *Corentyne Thunder* were so scarce before 1970 that it is quite probable that Carew may not have read it before writing *The Wild Coast*.

2. See Daryl C. Dance, *New World Adams: Conversations with West Indian Writers*, 2nd ed. (Leeds: Peepal Tree Press, 2008), pp.40-41.

3. In Carew's defence, little was published on the subject until Kean Gibson's *Cumfa Religion and Creole Language in a Caribbean Community* (New York: State University of New York Press, 2001).

4. From *In a Green Night* (London: Faber, 1962): "I who am poisoned by the blood of both,/Where shall I turn, divided to the vein?"

CHAPTER ONE

HECTOR sat on his front porch and watched the sunlight fanning out and cleaning the sky. The sun nudged its way above the dark wall of courida and mangrove trees that stretched along the foreshore, and the wind blowing out of a bellows of sea and sky rolled away the morning mist. Hector had already been in Tarlogie for three weeks but he had never seen the village. The evening his father brought him he had been burning up with fever. He had spent the three weeks in bed and his only image of the world outside had been framed in a square of open window through which he could see a patch of sky and tamarind tree tops. The fever had left him weak but it had also heightened his consciousness of the new environment into which he had moved. With the morning mists vanishing it was as though a veil had been torn away from the face of a primeval landscape. The swamp, carpeted with weeds, buffalo grass, water lilies and saffron, spread out in wide and flat infinites beyond the public road. This burnt brick road with its verging grass had been built up high with a deep ditch on either side and it twisted like a red snake from the unpainted schoolhouse at one end of Tarlogie to the police station at the other end. Between these two institutions were rows of huts on tall stilts, Chinaman's rum-shop, the Congregational Church and the big, hacienda-type house which was owned by Fitz Bradshaw, Hector's father. The wide, barren grounds around the big house were fenced in with barbed wire. It was the dry season and the earth had been grilled a parched brown by the sun. The few clumps of blacksage, ants bush and wild coffee which had survived the heat, looked like leprous scars. A driveway, a hundred yards long and flanked by coconut palms with yellowing fronds, led from the front porch of the house where Hector sat to the public road. Hector could hear the fronds rustling in the wind and the sound was in harsh contrast to the lisping and singing of the tamarind and po-boy trees which surrounded the house.

"You throw 'way the blanket from around you, boy?" his guardian asked from the doorway. He turned and looked at her. She was still a stranger to him and what impressed him was that he had never seen such a tall old woman. He measured her height in the doorway before he replied:

"The sun is hot, Miss Smart, and I'm feeling much better now."

"How many times I have to tell you not to call me Miss Smart, Hector? You must call me Sister, like everyone else does. I'm not nobody's sister, don't have a chick, a chile or a relative but they all call me Sister and I like it."

"I will call you Sister if you want me to," he said, and suddenly she reminded him of the drawing of an old woman in his *Grimm's Fairy Tales,* a tall old woman whose body seemed to be made of plaited lianas, only Sister's face was dark and benign and her eyes had no evil in them.

"You're the dreamingest child I ever did meet," Sister said. "The days can swallow up all the hours they like without you knowing or caring whether is dayclean or night-time. You' spirit don't never burst out from inside of you and fill up the empty spaces around you." She went back inside and he heard her chuckling and repeating "The dreamingest child I ever did meet. . . ."

Hector turned around and looked out on the reefs behind the village. Coconut palms grew thickly there and their fronds interlocked and formed a huge canopy above the massed under-growth. The wind had pressed against their slender trunks so insistently that many of them were bent like old men's backs. Birds were flying from the foreshore towards the ricefields behind the reefs – pairs of curlews and spurwings and screaming parakeets, cranes flapping their bleached wings lazily and above them all the wild ducks and red herons.

★   ★   ★

Hector watched the birds and remembered the singing of a pair of kiskadees in the backyard of his father's house in Georgetown. He had followed the sound of their singing until he saw them perched on the stem of a paw-paw leaf. Watching at their yellow breasts against the blue sky, he had picked up a stone and flung it at them. The birds ended their song and their bright eyes looked alert as they jerked their heads from side to side. He hurled another stone at them and struck the cock full in his breast. The kiskadee fell like an over-ripe fruit. He picked it up and ran to his sisters.

"Look, Ethel, Cynthia! Look!" The two girls abandoned their mud cakes and Ethel, the elder, said:

"Let it go! The poor bird," and her compassion for the kiskadee frightened him. He wanted to drop the bird but his hand would not open.

"God will punish you for that," Cynthia said.

"Let's bury it and put flowers on the grave," Ethel said, and he and Cynthia stood over her while she dug a hole in a rose bed. The kiskadee's mate circled low over them, and looking up at the flambeau's blossoms above him Hector imagined that it was the cry of the bereaved bird that made the blossoms tremble.

"Poor bird, poor bird," Cynthia kept repeating.

"Shut up!" Ethel said. "You can't see that the boy's sorry." Her eyes followed the circling distraught kiskadee, then she put its dead mate into the hole quickly and heaped earth on it. Afterwards they scattered rose and canna lily petals over the spot.

"What all you doing there! You want to make a mess of the garden or what!" They had not seen the gardener approaching and his presence disconcerted them, forcing them to avoid his eyes. "Better clear up the mess all you make before I complain to the master or the mistress." They made no attempt to obey and he left them for a moment and returned with a basket and broom.

"Laljee, I killed a bird and we buried it," Hector said, "leave the flowers alone, please!"

"Chu! People does kill birds all over the place. Some of them does even do it for fun." Laljee swept the petals into the basket and stamped the burial mound flat with his bare feet. "Lord, Master Hector, you look like you see an evil spirit." Hector turned away and walked towards the back-yard. He was certain that the dead kiskadee would fly out of its grave one night and peck out his eyes. He had wanted to ask Laljee about this but was afraid of being laughed at. He would ask Tojo, the houseboy. Tojo was an authority on magic. Hector had already seen him place a humming bird on a red-ant's nest, and when the bones were picked white, Tojo had pounded them into a powder. Tojo said that this powder was good for casting spells over your enemies or for freeing you from spells they had cast over you. He would ask Tojo to sprinkle some of his magic powder over the kiskadee's grave, then perhaps the kiskadee would fly away and get lost in the waste of sky and treetops beyond his garden. He found Tojo spinning tops under the breadfruit tree behind the water-vat. Tojo was a squat, bow-legged boy with a wide smile and teeth as white as tiger orchids.

"Tojo, I killed a kiskadee and I'm afraid it will peck out my eyes at night. . . we buried it under the flambeau tree in the front garden. . . I'll show you where."

"If you give me a penny, Master Hector, I will cast some magic over it and it won't never find you," Tojo said with grave certainty. Hector handed him the penny, thinking that it was a good bargain. "Where under the flambeau tree, Master Hector?"

"In the first rose bed, you will see where Laljee stamped down the earth." Tojo wasn't really his friend and it was because of this that Hector could confide in him. Hector envied Tojo. The houseboy was always wriggling through the back fence and escaping up Parson's Alley to play with ragged, loudmouthed urchins from the nearby tenements. Hector had to stay in his fenced-in garden and play with his sisters.

"What's it like in Parson's Alley?" he asked.

"Nothing much to see there, Master Hector, besides a lot of dead cats and dogs and carrion crows tearing them up." A reckless idea entered Hector's head – he would go and see for himself. His Aunt Hanna was out shopping and she was the person he feared most. His father was seldom around the house, he left for his store in Camp Street early in the mornings and usually returned at night when he and his sisters were asleep. Aunt Hanna was the real head of the Bradshaw household. Hector was a motherless stranger in his father's house – sickliness (he suffered from constant bouts of malaria), silence and fear were his only defences against his aunt, his father, his sisters and the servants. He was only happy when he could shut himself away in the enclosure of his own fantasy.

He was going to run away – to escape into an aloneness that the world outside of his garden seemed to promise.

The cook called Tojo, and Hector watched the houseboy running towards the kitchen, his legs spinning like bent spokes. Afterwards he heard the cook calling him for lunch and he ran towards the back fence, away from the sound of her voice. He crawled through the hole Tojo had made in the fence and headed up the alley past islands of shadow. A gutter ran through the centre of the alley and a viscous moss-green ooze flowed down it and emptied into the big canal which ran parallel to Vlissengen Road. Half-way to this main road, he wanted to turn back but his legs carried him forward. He came upon a cluster of carrion crows tearing at a dog's carcass. He held his nostrils and ran past, hugging the fences on the far side of the alley. He reached Vlissengen and made his way towards the sea wall. The noonday sun, striking the white, marlstone surface of the road dazzled him and when he looked up he saw a dizzy rim of treetops against the white sky. He kept hoping that he would not meet his father or his aunt.

He could smell his rubber soles burning as he walked up Vlissengen Road. When he reached the sea wall he saw a stunted tree on the beach and sat under it. It was low tide and wrinkled brown sands stretched far out to meet a sea that was sheeted white with sunlight. He began to regret having left home without first eating his lunch. It would have been better to escape after his midday meal. But the thought of how upset everyone would be when they discovered that he had run away was almost as comforting as a belly full of food. For the first time in his nine years he had done something reckless, something more adventurous than Tojo playing with the tenement children in Parson's Alley. He remembered how Aunt Hanna had once caught him talking to a street urchin through the hibiscus hedge and how she had scolded him for being low-minded and not having any pride.

"So that's the kind of company you want to keep, eh!" she had said, "Well, let me tell you, Mr. Man, if I so much as catch you saying a word to that kind of nigger-yard boy, I will pepper your skin for you."

Afterwards, he had had to stand in a corner with his face to the wall until he had promised never to commit such an atrocity again. She had to beat him to extract the promise. He feared her but sometimes resentment strangled his fear and he would defy her in the dumb, secret fashion which she attributed to "his mother's bad blood."

A beggarman came and sat beside him in the shade of the stunted tree. An old black man with big, alligator-like eyes. Hector tried to edge away but the beggar reached out a dry, bony hand and held him back.

"Don't 'fraid of me, young master, Dodo won't harm you," the beggar said, and as he spoke his toothless jaws chewed the words before he uttered them. "Who is your papa, boy?"

"Mr. Bradshaw," Hector said, and he couldn't stop himself from trembling.

"You mean Mazaruni Bradshaw, with the store in Camp Street?"

"Yes, Mr. Dodo."

"Your papa come from some good stock, boy, but he allow badness to ripen and rot inside he. Your grandpa, Busha Bradshaw, was a better man. Not that old Busha didn't like rum and woman, and not that he didn't spend every penny of he wife's money. . . but with all that he wasn't a bad man. He lef' you papa and he yellow-faced sister destitute and your papa had to take to schoolmastering, but the diamond fever burn he up and he go away to the diamond mines and make a fortune. They say he work obeah to find the diamonds that make he rich, that he sell he soul to the Wenpago. . . so they say, and they say further that now he got to drown he memory in rum and find solitude in woman flesh. . . Ever catch your papa working obeah, boy? You ever see he making sacrifice to the Wenpago?"

"No, Mr. Dodo."

The beggar freed Hector's arm. Somehow since he had spoken he had changed from a symbol of terror to a flesh and blood old man. Hector's fear vanished and he examined the beggar curiously. Dodo's head looked like a beach strewn with patches of dirty foam. His face was furrowed and lined and there were such deep hollows in his cheeks you would have thought that the bones of his skull had melted. The layers of rags covering his misshapen body hung about him like feathers.

"Where do you live, Mr. Dodo?" Hector asked, and the old man raised his head above his mound of rags and waved a hand at the sky.

"Under Heaven, young master, under Heaven," he guffawed and continued, "on the roads, the mud roads, the brick roads, the tar roads, the backyards where the dog does bite and snap, the pavements in the town and the grass corner in the country, that's where ole Dodo does live." He pointed a mottled finger, "Tell you father is only the Grace of God why he land up in a big house, why he can afford more women than King Solomon, 'cause all of we could have been road-people."

Dodo hoisted himself up painfully, and just as he was about to hobble away his knobbly akee stick fell from his grasp. Hector picked up the stick and guided the old man's hand to its head.

"I need this stick for dogs and small-boys," Dodo mumbled, "thank you, young master, I hope you grow up to be a better man than Mazaruni Bradshaw." Hector relaxed, pressing his back against the rough tree bark. Dodo took the road that led away from the city, a twisting road that ran close to the sea wall for half a mile and then thrust away across swamps and savannahs. The tide was turning and Hector heard the low murmur of surf and the stirring of wind in the leaves above him. He fell asleep soon after the beggar had gone.

Someone shook him by the shoulder and he woke up. It was a policeman.

"What's your name, boy?"

"What's my name. . ."

"Yes, what's your name?" The policeman brought out a black book and his coarse fingers fumbled with the pages. He found the page he was looking for. He scrutinised Hector to make sure that what the book said was true. "Is your name Hector Bradshaw, boy?"

"Yes, that's my name."

"You better come with me, boy," the policeman said, leading him away. The sea was only twenty yards away from the wall and the waves, pushing up the beach, looked like lizard tongues tipped with foam. The sun was touching the sea and setting the rim of the horizon afire. The wind was cool and damp and it made Hector shiver. The policeman wheeled his bicycle across the stretch of grass and when he reached the road, he seated Hector on the bar and rode off towards Leslie Street. Hector was glad to be going back home. He didn't like the idea of night catching him by the sea wall.

Somebody switched on the front porch light as Hector and the policeman walked up the front steps. His father and his aunt were waiting, standing just outside the doorway.

"I found him by the sea wall," the policeman said.

"Thank you, Officer," Aunt Hanna said in the voice she used when she was entertaining her friends at a tea-party.

"Don't be too hard on him, Miss Bradshaw, he don't look so well." Hector saw his aunt's mouth tighten and he knew that the man was making things worse for him by interfering.

"Go inside with your auntie, Hector!" his father said. Hector didn't move. He felt safer on the front porch with the neighbours looking on.

"You heard me, Hector!"

"But this is a stiff-necked boy, eh," Aunt Hanna said, "after all his gallivanting about the town he comes back home to give us more botheration."

"Have a drink, Officer," Fitz Bradshaw said.

"You stand in the corner until your father's ready for you, boy!" Aunt Hanna led him across the living-room into the dining-room. Martha, the cook was banging about her pots and pans in the kitchen, a gesture of solidarity with Hector in his trouble.

"Martha, will you please make less noise! I'm getting sick and tired of your bangings and thumpings!" Aunt Hanna said.

"Me was only washing up the dinner wares, Mistress!"

"Come here, Hector!" his father said, and he approached him cautiously. "Since when have you become man enough to walk out of this house without permission!" A powerful hand gripped Hector's shirt front and swung him off his feet.

"Daddy, I. . . please, Daddy. . ." Hector hated himself for begging, but for him, the worst part of a whipping was the expectation of it.

"Don't say a word to me! I'm going to make a man of you if I have to whip you every day of the year!" A bullhide whip, biting welts into his shoulders and back, punctuated the words. His father was beating him like a drum to work up his anger. "Don't trifle with me, boy! Don't vex my spirit or I will flail the skin off you! You want to play a man already! Want to take it on yourself to walk out of my house!" Pain tightened his limbs until they felt like dry sticks and stars flared up and darkened inside his head. After a while it didn't matter how many lashes were rained down on him. His whole body felt numb and bloodless. His father pushed him away and he fell on an ocelot rug. Hector went to his bed, and lying between the sheets didn't know if the sudden burning he felt all over was caused by the lashes he had received or whether he was having another bout of fever. He heard the car drive away and knew that Laljee was taking his father to his kept-woman outside the city. Martha and Tojo had told him that the woman's name was Elsa and that she was a big, handsome Negro woman. Why didn't his father bring her to the house to take his mother's place he wondered? He wanted a mother. If he had one he would be able to press his head against her breast and suck the warmth out of her body into his. Martha had allowed him to do this once or twice, and one day he had sat in her lap and she had opened the front of her blouse and allowed him to fondle her breasts. Aunt Hanna had dried up breasts. Hector, peeping through a crack in the bathroom wall, had once seen her naked. Her breasts hung down to her waist and it was as though all the sap had been squeezed out of them.

Hector had caught a chill whilst he had been out by the sea wall and fever and ague sent his mind flying away from him like a short-tailed kite in a high wind. He spent weeks in a trance. He saw faces and heard voices around his bed but recognised no one. He groped his way out of this coma to find Martha bending over him.

"Lord ha' mercy, Master Hector, I thought that Mantop had come for you this time."

"Martha, open the window, I want to see the sun."

"Is the same sun, Master Hector, it en't no brighter nor no darker."

"Martha, bring some water for me, my mouth feels so dry." She fetched him a glass of water and propped him up so that he could drink.

"They sending you away to the Courentyne, Master Hector."

"The Courentyne?"

"Yes, your papa estate in Tarlogie. Is a place that nobody in the family does talk about, neither your papa nor your auntie. The place have a big house on it and an old woman does keep the house."

"An old woman, Martha?"

"Yes, she was working for the family before your papa born and she know all the family secrets."

"What secrets, Martha?"

"Look, Master Hector, you just step away from Death's door. You better rest your weary body and don't ask me too much question."

"Who said I was to go to the Courentyne, Martha?"

"The doctor tell them that they must send you there if they want you to live. . . now don't ask me another question, boy."

*   *   *

Sister stood on the verandah looking at Hector. He did not notice her because of the hanging plants. "This is truly a child of silence," she said to herself; "look how the young boy sitting there quiet as water with no wind on it. It's just like if he was born old, I never saw a child with so much dreaming and quietness in him. Lord, for his mother's sake – she was so good to me – let me bring him up so that he can grow strong and healthy."

"Come and eat your lunch, Hector!" she said, and her voice startled him out of his reverie.

Sitting opposite Hector at the dining-table Sister said,

"Tarlogie don't look like much when you first see it, boy, but just you wait until the sun gets in your blood and the wind start to cool the marrow of you bones, won't be no other place like this for you."

"When can I go for a walk to the foreshore, Sister?"

"The sea sound close by but it's far away, boy. If you climb up a tamarind tree you will see what I mean."

"Tojo can come with me. He was a village boy before he went to Georgetown."

"Take your time, boy. What's all the hurrying for?"

"Tojo and me can go tomorrow. I'm better now, much better."

"Pause for breath, boy, later on I will send Tojo to call old man Doorne, he is the best man to break you in to the ways of the coast."

"Who is this old man Doorne, Sister?"

"He's a hunter-man who was living on the Bradshaw lands since the time of your grandpapa. He's the penkeeper and he does collect land rents for your papa."

"Why did they send me here, Sister?" Hector asked suddenly, and Sister squinted at him and kept chewing a long time before she answered.

"This coast is a healthy place and the doctor said you shouldn't live in the town or fever would kill you."

"But there was more."

"More what?"

"More reasons, Martha told me so."

"What she told you, boy?"

"She just said that there were reasons, then she wouldn't say any more."

"But you can ask plenty questions for a small boy, eh! You better eat your food so that you can put enough muscles 'round your bones to stop the wind from whistling through them."

"You don't want to answer me either, do you?"

"As the Good Book say, boy, 'sifficient unto the day. . .'"

⋆　　⋆　　⋆

Old man Doorne came to the big house when the moon was high. Moonlight in Tarlogie was a quiet time. The village, islanded in swamps, wrapped silence around it. The occasional barking of a dog, the cry of a wild bird or the rumble of cartwheels only heightened the silence. The villagers huddled together on their doorsteps and chatted in undertones late into the night. Palm fronds silvered with dew and moonlight, rustled uneasily and the po-boy trees shivered and sighed like lonesome girls. The blue and silver moon cast shadows that were live crouching things, the ghosts of dead slaves moaning and murmuring.

Doorne walked up the avenue of palms strumming a river chanty on his guitar and singing:

> Gal me lover letter loss
> Gal me lover letter loss
> Gal me lover letter loss
> If you find am me go give you carat stone. . .

"Who is that?" Tojo asked. He and Clysis the maid were sitting halfway down the front steps whilst Sister and Hector sat on the porch.

"That is ole Doorne," Clysis whispered, "he is a rascal-man who does act like he own land and sky when he hardly got anything but the shirt on his back and his guitar."

"Girl, don't try to make your eyes pass big people own. Is so you talking 'bout a man old enough to be your grandfather?"

Doorne emerged from the shadows looking like a man who had just stepped out of a tubful of Indian ink.

"Good night, Sister, good night, young master."

"Doorne, is only now you come? Is long time now I send to call you, man."

"Me working hard on the farm, Sister, and when night-time come me does feel sleepy as mud."

"Good night, Mr. Doorne," Clysis said, and she giggled and flashed the whites of her eyes at him.

"Small-girl, is why Sister don't send you back to you mother to learn some respect."

"That girl got a flyweight brain, Doorne, and if she bother you jus' fetch her a box."

"Me have a heavy hand, Sister, and if me clap it on she, she will dance the marimba."

"Doorne, I was looking out for you 'cause I want you castrate couple pigs for me and I want you to break in the young master. Only today I was saying 'Boy, Doorne is the only man who can take you in hand 'cause he knows this coast like a parson knows the Good Book.'"

"I want you to take me hunting," Hector said.

"And me too," Tojo said.

"You have to creep before you walk, young master, before we start to hunt, me got to show you how to cross the swamp, how to talk bird-language. . . is a lot of thing you got to learn first." The old man sat down with the moonlight on his face. His forehead was broad and curved like a shield, his eyes wide apart and sloe, his nose well fleshed and a moustache drooped around the corners of a mouth that must have known much laughter for it was big and wide and mobile. The muscles of his torso looked like a tangle of lianas.

"How you two sons going, Doorne?"

"Don't ask me 'bout them, Sister, me does curse the day me plant the seed to birth them. Caya lazying away he time as usual and Tengar, to tell you the truth me don't know if he living or dead; since he go 'way to the balata fields me en't so much as hear a word 'bout he. Me have bad luck with me children, Sister, proper bad luck; to think 'bout them is jus' to grey-hair me head more than it grey-hair already."

"Tengar is a big-hearted boy, Doorne, strong as a buffalo and gentle like a humming bird. Is why you so hard on him? I can understand you spirit turning 'gainst Caya but Tengar is a good boy."

"Me try to give them schooling but you think they grateful for it?"

"Is what you expect, Doorne, when the two didn't have no mother?"

"Chu! Mother? Me didn't grow up with no mother. Me papa get call away and the next thing me know was that me mother lef' me with a neighbour and pull out with a stranger-man." Doorne said this without rancour. The memory of his mother's desertion was too distant to inspire strong feelings.

He picked up his guitar, strummed a tune and sang until Hector fell asleep. Sister woke him up and sent him to bed saying that it was bad to sleep with moonlight on his face. Tojo and Clysis retired to their hessian mats in the partitioned ground-floor room and Doorne continued his serenade until slurred and drunken voices drifted in from the road and he and Sister realised that it was midnight and Chinaman's rum-shop was closed.

CHAPTER TWO

IT was Friday night and the drunks were bawling, laughing, cursing at the tops of their voices in Chinaman's rum-shop. Hector sat on the front porch waiting for the moon to rise. Occasionally he heard Chinaman's voice pitched high above the others. Sister was in the kitchen scolding Tojo and Clysis for allowing three of her chickens to go astray. There was a prayer meeting in the schoolhouse and the congregation was singing hymns. The voices carried over the swamps like a dirge. There were lights in the police station. The two Mandoo brothers had been caught stealing Parson Galloway's cattle and Mark-a-book, the sergeant in charge, was questioning them. Tanta Bess' ram-goat, King Saul, was bleating monotonously. She had gone to market in Port Mourant and had not returned in time to feed him. Tojo was telling Sister that he had seen an alligator in the backyard at sundown and he was sure that it had eaten her missing chickens.

"Why you didn't kill the alligator, boy?" Sister asked.

"Was a big she-alligator, Sister, me sure was the same one that eat up Chinaman dog," Tojo said.

"But why you didn't kill it, that's what I want to find out?"

"Me take one look at the alligator and run 'way, Sister."

"I will get Doorne to kill it tomorrow. Boy, like you forget you born right here in the country, you spend couple mornings in Georgetown and now you come back, you don't know a thing 'bout life here, any small-boy in Tarlogie know how to trap alligator."

A convoy of donkey carts and mule drays passed by with storm-lanterns swinging from their axles. The cartmen sat hunched behind their beasts. They were taking produce to the market twenty miles away and were resigned to the all night journey ahead. Jute bags were wrapped around them, protection against the wind and the dew. Boysie careened past with a bus-load of holidaymakers. He had christened his bus TOM KEAN. It was a hideous vermilion monster which was supposed to carry thirty-two passengers but which never made a trip with less than sixty. A lookout sat on the roof of the bus and villagers along the way kept him posted on the whereabouts of lurking policemen. Boysie's surplus passengers were well drilled in the art of vanishing on short notice. The dust-clouds which blew up in *Tom Kean*'s wake caused the cartmen to cough and curse and a few of them took swigs from bottles of bush rum, washing away the dry, dusty taste in their mouths.

Parson Galloway dropped in on his way from the prayer meeting. Clysis had told Hector that the story in the village was that old man Galloway had been courting Sister for forty years and in all this time had never dared ask her to marry him. Parson Galloway was a local preacher and he acted as a standby for the white Minister who only came to the village church on First Sundays. Galloway was a cocoa-brown man, tall and lean with a face as narrow as the head of Tanta Bess' ram-goat. He had a jaunty young man's walk and a wicked look in his sunken eyes and he dressed in a style that belonged to days long past. He wore a white drill suit, a high collar with a large gold stud in it and the collar could easily have accommodated an extra neck.

Preacher Galloway sat down. His body knew every groove and dent in Sister's cane chair. Hector got up from his seat on the front porch and came inside the house. Old man Galloway had exchanged a few words with him, the kind of words an old man reserves for children – meaningless ones coated with a forced bonhomie. The boy was too much on his guard against his elders to swallow this kind of small talk uncritically. He sat in the living-room away from Galloway sizing him up under his eyes. "Why should a stranger-man walk into my father's house like that, acting like if he owned it?" he asked himself. The old man became conscious of the boy's scrutiny and fidgeted with his collar.

"Where is, Miss Etta?" he asked.

"She's inside," Hector said knowing full well that Galloway was hearing Sister's voice from the kitchen just as clearly as he was. A rush of wind brought in the screaming of rain frogs, the sound of surf and the rumble of cartwheels. Hector sat back in his Berbice chair and watched a hardback beetle crawling up the wall opposite him. It reached the ceiling and dive-bombed the light. The hot shade burnt its wings and it fell on the old man's head. He brushed it off unhurriedly and eased his chair back and a couple of beetles struck the shade and fell to the floor soon after. Hector got up and crushed them under his foot. He liked the crunching sound they made and the feel of squashing them.

Sister walked in just then and said, "Boy, if you kill all the hardbacks that come in here you will make a mess of my clean floor."

"Good night, Miss Etta," Galloway said, "I just dropped in to say howdy on my way home." Hector noticed that Sister was wearing her best frock, the white one with the high collar and the frilly laced front. She had powdered her face hastily and it looked as if she had smeared it with flour.

"You always welcome here, Brother Galloway, you don't have to make no excuse to come." She sat down in her rocking chair and began mending one of Hector's shirts. "This is the first time you meeting Hector, eh?" she asked without looking up.

"You forget I know this boy as a baby, Miss Etta. The night his mother birthed him and the night the Good Lord called her away."

"What was my Mama like?" Hector asked, and Sister looked up sharply. Galloway started acting as if his collar was tight.

"Your Mama was a good woman, boy, a pearl of a woman," Sister said, frowning at Galloway. He avoided her eyes and kept turning his long crinkled neck inside the wide circle of his collar.

Why was there always this mystery about his mother, Hector wondered. He had seen the photograph of her which Aunt Hanna kept hidden away in her chest of drawers. Martha had taken it out and shown it to him one day when his aunt was out shopping. He had looked at it for a long time and Martha, who had kept running to the window and scanning the street for his aunt had said:

"Me en't supposed to do this, Master Hector, so don't breathe a word 'bout this to nobody, not even to Miss Ethel."

All he remembered about the picture was that it was yellow with age and at the time he had imagined that his mother had a yellow face and not a brown one like his. He had asked Martha about this afterwards and she had laughed and said, "Your Mama was a fine looking samba woman, she had hair that was black like a marudi wing and she used to carry sheself like she own land and sky." She didn't say anything else although he kept pestering her with questions. Sister, he was sure knew all about his mother but she was a secretive old woman.

He was growing to like Sister more and more. She left him alone in a way Aunt Hanna had never done and at the same time she made him feel that he was wanted for the first time in his life. She was reticent and withdrawn most of the time, but underneath her apparent calm he sensed the almost savage possessiveness she felt towards him.

"I want to find a teacher who can come every day and give the boy lessons when school starts next month," Sister said. Her head was bent over the shirt she was mending.

"I think I know a young man who will do it," Galloway said, "a young man named La Rose who teaches at the Saltan School, he's got a Junior Cambridge Certificate and he studying for Senior now." He announced this proudly because he wanted to impress Sister with the fact that he knew educated people.

"I hear 'bout this young man," Sister said.

"I have to drive some cattle to the Port Mourant market tomorrow so I will tell the young man to come and see you, Miss Etta."

Doorne came around near Hector's bedtime. He and Parson Galloway were not on speaking terms. They had been feuding since they were boys. Galloway always referred to Doorne as a rascal-man whilst the latter claimed that Galloway's preachings and prayings were smoke-puffs behind which he robbed and cheated the simple-minded village folk. The truth was that these two were very alike. They had once been "saga-boys" able to seduce young women up and down the coast, but age had ambushed them and left them stranded like driftwood in a village where time had stopped. Doorne knew that it was Galloway's visiting night but he came just the same. To keep his ancient feud going he had to meet his enemy face to face every now and then. Sister was accustomed to the contrariness of these two old men. She rocked slowly and kept her eyes on her sewing when Doorne entered.

"Good night, Sister. Good night, Master Hector," he said. Hector saw Galloway's neck tighten, and his Adam's apple jump as if he was having difficulty in swallowing.

"Good night, Brother Doorne, thank you for castrating the pigs for me, I don't know what I would do without you in this place," Sister said, and Galloway sat in his chair as if he was gummed to it. Hector could not understand the tension in the room and he looked from one to the other of the men trying to find out what was going on.

"I must go back to my yard, Miss Etta," Galloway said, rising and standing as stiff as an iron bar.

"All right, Brother Galloway, I will see you when the spirit moves you to come this way again."

Galloway nodded to Hector on his way out and if looks could kill, the one he gave Doorne would have wounded him mortally.

"Thank you for the information about the teacher," Sister said sweetly and he muttered under his breath and banged the door shut.

"Why did the parson act like that, Sister?" Hector asked, and she looked at him and smiled but she did not reply.

"I was jus' passing by when me mind tell me to come in 'cause you might want me to do something for you, Sister," Doorne said.

"Tojo tells me that an alligator's eating up my chickens and I want you to see if you can put a stop to it."

"Sound like that reptile got two legs instead of four, Sister. Alligator don't walk all the way to your backyard unless is the rainy season and the village get flood out. Just ask Tojo to step inside here for a minute, Sister, I want to have a word with that boy."

"Tojo!"

"Yes, Sister!" There was the sound of shuffling feet in the

kitchen and Clysis started giggling. Tojo came into the living-room looking like a dog that had been caught eating the neighbour's sheep.

"Tojo," Doorne said, with a purr in his voice, "is not you they tell me, sell three chicken to Paul Slowe?"

"No, Doorne, Tojo's got his bad-ways but he wouldn't do something like that, he wouldn't steal from them who giving him food and shelter," Sister said.

"I didn't steal you chicken, Sister, I swear to Jesus I didn't do it," Tojo said plaintively.

"Boy, you trying to make me out to be a liar," Doorne said.

"Go back to the kitchen, Tojo, I will talk to you later," Sister said and the look she gave him made him wince. He slinked away and Clysis must have said something to him because he cuffed her in the stomach and she started bawling.

"That boy getting out of hand, Sister," Doorne said, "and you got to watch he or he going to bring disgrace on you house. The story I hear tell was that Mr. Tojo sell the three chickens to Slowe, and before the chicken had time to roost in Slowe backyard, the boy thief them back and sell them to Rasaul further up the road."

"But the boy's enterprising, eh," Sister said, making it obvious from her tone that Tojo's enterprise was some kind of satanic gift. "Doorne, I will beg you kindly to take the boy home with you and don't spare the tamarind whip on his back. I'm getting old these days and my hand en't heavy like it used to be."

"I will oblige. . ."

"Sister, Tojo hear what you saying and he run away," Clysis said.

"Run away?"

"Yes, Sister, he scoot down the back steps and make for the yard."

"Don't worry, Sister," Doorne rose from his chair and hitched up his broad cowhide belt, "I will stalk him down, he can't run far and I en't a hunter for nothing." The old man left by the back door. Hector went to the kitchen window and looked out. The ribald shouting at the rum-shop had stopped but Chinaman was cursing and beating his wife, Dookia. He was an ailing wisp of a man whilst Dookia was big and robust. It seemed incredible to

Hector that she should submit so quietly to her husband's blows and rantings night after night.

A dog barked somewhere by the edge of the swamps and Hector knew that it was barking at Tojo. It was bound to give away his position to Doorne. Hector did not want Tojo to be caught and whipped. He didn't think it a crime that the boy should steal three of Sister's chickens. He wanted to go out and help Tojo to escape but the moon had not yet risen and he was afraid of the dark.

Sister was gathering up her sewing and preparing to retire when he returned to the living-room.

"You think Doorne will catch him, Sister?" he asked.

"But is why you got to feel so sorry for that rascal-boy? The boy is a snake in the bosom that succouring he. Is the fear of the Lord he want in his devil-heart. When Doorne bring him back I will make him get down on his bended knees and ask the Lord pardon."

Hector went to his room still admiring Tojo's cunning and enterprise. He lay in bed listening to the surf and the wind moaning through the po-boy trees. He wanted to stay awake until Doorne brought Tojo back but sleep overcame him.

★   ★   ★

Hector was poling a canoe across the swamps, heading for the coconut grove on the reef a hundred yards ahead of him. Tojo squatted in the bow with his legs drawn up under him Indian-style. After the whipping Doorne had given him, sitting down was rather painful. It was sun-high and Sister had insisted that Hector wear a hat, but as soon as he was out of sight he had taken it off. He had bought a sackful of lead pellets from Chinaman and he and Tojo were going to hunt iguanas and birds on the reef with catapults. They had made the catapults the day before, cutting forked branches from a guinep tree and balancing and shaping them to size. Afterwards they had practised their aim on empty tin-cans and bottles which they stuck on top of the fence posts. Far to their right were a few water buffaloes which were grazing in the midst of a cluster of lotus lilies. A flock of white cranes and gaulins were feeding nearby and Hector saw a governor crane step forward to peck ticks off a buffalo's rump.

It was very quiet on the reef, but suddenly the silence was broken by the clamorous chattering of a blue-sakee which had caught a chicken hawk raiding her nest. The small bird attacked the raider frenziedly, flying up towards the sun and swooping down until the hawk thrust its powerful wings into the wind and outdistanced its angry pursuer.

Hector and Tojo sat in the shade of a cromanty tree. A green parrot-snake slithered down a coconut tree opposite them and Tojo picked up a stone and broke the snake's back.

Later on Tojo picked some green coconuts and they drank the milk. They crossed the reef and came to the ricefields. The wind was rolling and tumbling over the tender green stalks. A flock of ricebirds flew out of a bed about fifty yards ahead of them.

They looked like black dust against the flat blue sky. The two boys watched where the flock alighted and followed it. The sun breathed its furnace blasts down on them but the mud and water in the ricebeds were cool. An alligator was sleeping on the dam between the square plots of young rice. They passed close enough to spit on him but he didn't stir.

"Is a man-alligator," Tojo said, "them don't trouble you unless you walk on top of them."

"I thought you told Sister you were afraid of alligators?" Hector said, because the depths of subterfuge in Tojo's heart always baffled him.

"You can't tell everything you know, Master Hector, or people does advantage you." Tojo suddenly remembered how Doorne had chastised him and he looked sideways at his companion and added, "You know, Doorne got a proper heavy hand, that tamarind whip he used on me back was like fire." The disinterested manner in which he said this made it seem as if he was talking about somebody else's experience. Hector looked at him admiringly as he continued, "I prefer a beating with a wild cane, it does look heavy but it don't hurt, but that tamarind whip, it does feel like fire running up and down you back."

"I wouldn't like to feel it," Hector said.

"Was jus' like fire tickling me back," Tojo said. "Look!" He took off his shirt and showed Hector his back. It looked as if he had vines growing under his skin. Hector ran a finger along one of the welts and the boy jumped.

"But he shouldn't beat a small-boy like that," Hector said.

"You en't see nothing yet," Tojo said, slipping his shirt on, "before Miss Martha carry me to you father house, me papa used to come home drunk on Friday night and beat me 'til he draw blood."

"The night after I ran away, my daddy beat me up with a cowhide belt and blood came too," Hector said. He couldn't allow Tojo's papa to get all the credit as a demon.

They didn't bag any iguanas that day but between them they shot a dozen ricebirds. Like true hunters, they roasted the birds over an open fire in the backyard. King Saul, Tanta Bess' ram-goat, stuck his head through the barbed wire fence and looked on stoically. Tojo gave him a piece of old newspaper and he chewed it up as if it were a delicacy.

The sunset sky was striped with black clouds that afternoon and Sister said that it was a sure sign that the whole coast was going to be flooded when the rains came.

★   ★   ★

The teacher whom Parson Galloway had recommended came around one night. Hector was sitting in the living-room trying to read about the eruption of Mount Pêlé in Martinique. It was described in one of the books which had been handed down by his grandfather, a leather-bound one with thick, brittle pages and etched illustrations done in delicate black lines. Sister sat in her rocking chair mending the clothes which he tore so often, she had accused him of having thorns in his skin. There was a knock at the door and Hector answered it.

"I've come to see Miss Smart." The stranger entered, bringing a rush of wind with him. Hector closed the door.

"I am Miss Smart," Sister said, looking up from her sewing.

"Parson Galloway told me to come around, Miss Smart."

"Oh, you must be the teacher, Mr. . . . ."

"La Rose," the young man said, "Jefferson Gladstone La Rose."

"You got a powerful name if nothing else," Sister said dryly.

"I was told you wanted a teacher to instruct Mr. Bradshaw's son, Miss Smart."

"That I want, young man, but before we talk about teaching and instructing, come sit close by me and tell me who you is." The teacher sat in Parson Galloway's low cane chair and Sister never took her eyes off him. "Who is your father, young man?" Sister always saw people in the image of two or three generations of their forebears.

"My father was Bullah La Rose, Miss Smart." The teacher was a tall loose limbed Negro. When he sat down he relaxed so completely you kept expecting his limbs to unhinge themselves and fall away from his body.

"I know you daddy, boy, you come from good stock. Bullah had his ways but he was a good man," Sister said.

The teacher's head fascinated Hector. He wore his hair shaved close to the skull and sitting directly under the light his head had the shine of a mud flat in the sun.

"I would like to take on the job, Miss Smart," he said. After they had bargained about money (Sister agreed to pay him fifteen dollars a month) the teacher left a list of textbooks that Hector would need and departed.

"What you think about him?" Sister asked.

"His head looks like if its got plenty brains inside it," Hector said.

"I like his quietness," Sister said, "I don't like the young people nowadays whose mouth can run like the bowels of a sick nigger who drink salts."

"I didn't hear him say when we were going to start."

"You wasn't listening, boy. He starting the first of September, two weeks from now."

Tojo and Clysis were quarrelling across the partition that separated their downstairs rooms. Sister threatened to come down to them and in the silence that followed, Hector heard Chinaman performing his nightly ritual of cursing and beating his wife.

"I going over to Chinaman tomorrow and warn him for the N'th time that if he don't stop his disgraceful goings on in the midst of decent people, I will put Mark-a-book on him. When your grandfather, Busha Bradshaw, was alive, you think something like that could happen in this village?"

"Was my grandpa a bad man, Sister?"

"He was a raucous red-man with a temper that could flare up and flare out jus' like a match in a high wind. You does remind me of him sometimes, the way your eyes light up when you're glad about something. But you take more after your mother because you're secretive and locked up inside yourself just like she was."

Outside, carts were rumbling by on their way to market and the surf sounded loud and savage. The wind was pressing hard against the house, rattling the jalousies and shaking the doors. The po-boy trees wailed like swamp creatures gone mad.

CHAPTER THREE

HECTOR returned from the foreshore to find Sister with a telegram.

"Your papa's coming this evening," she said.

"Why?" Hector asked. The news made him forget the blue crane he had stalked and shot with his catapult. It was the first time he had bagged such a big bird and he had wanted Sister to share his triumph. "You think he wants to take me back to Georgetown, Sister?"

"Chu, boy! Don't ask stupidness. I can put me head on a block that he wouldn't want to do that. Your papa is one of those people who does find children always getting in his way. If you papa's coming here then must be trouble, and the trouble en't got nothing to do with you."

The few occasions on which Sister mentioned Fitz she always discussed his failings with a malicious candour. Hector did not mind, although he sometimes felt guilty about his indifference to his father's good name. He had only been in Tarlogie a short time but already the memory of Aunt Hanna, Fitz and his sisters had drifted into remote caches of his mind.

"I don't want to go back, Sister," Hector said.

"Leave it to me, boy, you won't never have to go back if you don't want to." She said this with absolute conviction, and as she spoke her old eyes seemed to look inwards. When Sister was certain about something her face could communicate this certainty without her having to say very much. It was a strong black face with the lineaments of age and suffering marked clearly on it. The opaque parchment skin with its deep grooves and its convolutions emphasised the qualities of patience and endurance her slave ancestors had handed down to her.

Fitz Bradshaw and Laljee arrived by car in the late afternoon. Fitz was in a sour mood. After greeting Sister, who promptly left for the kitchen, and Hector brusquely, he flung the front windows open and sat gazing towards the sea. Hector fidgeted in the corner near the passage that led to the dining-room and kitchen, expecting his father to say something to him, dreading it and yet wanting it to be over quickly. His father had never bothered to treat him as an individual. As far as Fitz was concerned he had spawned a cipher and not a son. It was as if they had been drawings on an ancient Egyptian mural with the faces turned away from each other. So now it had been: "How are you, boy? Behaving yourself? Sister tells me that she found a good tutor for you" . . . mechanical questions and statements requiring mechanical answers. Hector waited. The wind blew in through the open windows and shook the bamboo curtains. When he was certain that his father was too preoccupied with his own thoughts he stole into the kitchen.

"He's got some big trouble scraping his insides with worry," Sister said, and for the first time in his life Hector felt sorry for his father. He wanted to return to the living-room and talk to him but he hesitated until his natural shyness reasserted itself.

They ate dinner in silence until Sister called out to Tojo to go and shut the front windows since the wind was blowing in beetles and mosquitoes.

"You seen Doorne recently, Etta?" Fitz asked suddenly.

"He always in and out as usual, comes and goes like a stranger wind. If you want to see him special I will send and call him." Fitz closed his knife and fork and pushed his plate away.

"I want to see him," he said, and he took out a big white handkerchief and wiped the gravy off his moustache. There was something ominous in his voice and Hector wondered what his father had against Doorne.

"Tojo, run and call Doorne, boy!"

Tojo found Doorne sitting on his doorstep and picking his teeth with an accouri thorn.

"The master want you, Mr. Doorne," Tojo said. Doorne spat out a grain of rice before he spoke.

"Which master, boy?"

44

"Mr. Bradshaw."

"I didn't know he was here."

"He and Laljee arrive at sundown and since the boss set foot in the house his face look like a sky threatening rain." Doorne stood up and shook himself.

"Hmm! Them Bradshaws is a moody lot, was the same thing with the old man, one minute his face used to look like a bright morning and the next like a thunder sky. I wonder what's eating him up?"

"I couldn't tell you, Mr. Doorne, the boss en't say more than ten word since he and Laljee drive up." They set out together for the big house. It was dark and the wind was wrestling with the trees. King Saul was bleating for his mistress and Chinaman's hunting dogs were tugging at their chains and barking fiercely. Chinaman rented the dogs out to Doorne and other hunters on the coast, they were trained to hunt jaguars and deer and were fed on meat sprinkled with gunpowder. Doorne recognised the harsh strangled bark of Rover, the leader of the pack and of Sagagirl, the tawny bitch who had lost an eye the last time he had hired the pack. Caya, his eldest son was practising on his tom-tom and the wind carried the drumbeats over and away towards the reefs behind the village. Doorne scraped the mud off his bare feet at the bottom of the back steps and used an old newspaper to wipe them clean.

"The boss upstairs in the front room," Tojo said. Doorne entered with the assurance of one who had known the house since it was first built. He had lived on the Bradshaw lands since he was a boy of nine and could remember when the ruins of the old brick house which Fitz's Dutch ancestors had built had occupied the same site.

"Howdy, skipper," he said blinking in the light and sitting in one of the cane chairs. Laljee entered through the front door like a shadow driven in by the wind. He sat on a rug by Hector's bedroom door, lit his clay pipe and wrapped himself in a cloud of smoke. "Laljee, like that rum you does drink preserving you, pardner, the years beating 'gainst you face but they en't leaving no mark," Doorne said. Hector smiled, but his father gave him a disapproving look.

"How's the estate going?" Fitz asked, turning to Doorne.

"En't no news to tell, boss, 'cept that the dam by Honey Reef got a breach the length of a full grown greenheart tree."

"Why don't you get it fixed?" Fitz asked.

"I wrote you about it twice," Sister said, "but you never send us word to go ahead repairing it."

"If a heavy flood season comes, boss, and that dam en't fix up, won't be nothing left of it. You know how the sugar estate does work, boss? They got a pumping station and when flood threatening they does divert the water to the surrounding lands. We won't stand a chance without that dam, the water will be right up to we doorstep before we know what happening."

Doorne resented Fitz's indifference to his own estate. His father and grandfather had been farmers but Fitz was a city-man who didn't know the difference between a milking cow and a water buffalo.

"Well get it fixed for heaven's sake! I've got enough trouble on my hands as it is," Fitz said, and he emptied his pipe on Sister's polished floor and refilled it with black tobacco. Hector knew that his father had not come to look into the affairs of the estate. He looked at Sister. She was sitting wooden-faced in her rocking chair. Fitz struck a match and puffed loudly.

"Laljee," he said, "go and get a bottle of Russian Bear rum." He fumbled in his pocket and took out a five dollar note.

"I don't want no drinking session in here," Sister said sharply.

"I'll have you know this is my house, Etta."

"Your papa wrote it in his will that I can stay here as long as I live. Better keep you bullying and bossing for them who don't have no rights, Fitz Bradshaw." Fitz laughed uncomfortably.

"You're getting crotchety in your old age, Etta. Since when have you become such a stickler about drinking in the house," he said. He had come to talk to Doorne and knew better than to get involved in a quarrel with the old woman.

"I'm not objecting to a drink or two in the house, all I said was that I didn't want no drinking session here, the rum-shop is the place for that." Hector looked from one to the other, waiting for his father to explode, but Fitz only bit into his pipe stem savagely and looked straight ahead. The boy knew that regardless of his grandfather's will or the hold Sister might have had on his father, he would have shouted her down if something big had not been troubling him.

"Laljee, go and buy the rum," Fitz said, and when the chauffeur had taken the money from him and left, he added, "I'm merely entertaining the men who work for me as I always do, Etta."

"You done impress on me that is your house so what you making excuse for," Sister said, and she got up and walked out of the room.

"Since I was a boy I learnt never to argue with that old Tartar. You just can't win with her," Fitz said and Doorne guffawed and mumbled his agreement.

"How are you getting on, Hector?" Fitz asked. The boy had been dreading this. He had been hoping that whatever his father's business was he would attend to it and leave him alone.

"You don't see how the boy growing muscles, boss?" Doorne said. "He taking to the swamp like he was a countryman. En't goin' be long before I start taking he with me to Black Bush."

Fitz examined his son contemptuously. "The only way he will reach Black Bush is if you carry him on your back, Doorne."

"I won't take no bets on that in couple months time, boss," Doorne said, and Fitz did not pursue the matter.

"Heard any news from your son, Doorne?" he asked. Doorne wondered what his boss was trying to get at because this was not the kind of question he would ask without some motive behind it.

"Which son, boss?" Doorne eased himself deeper in his chair and started to roll a cigarette. Laljee returned with the rum and a few beetles flew in with him before he could close the door. They circled the lamp and flew into the shade.

"I can't stand those blasted insects," Fitz said, "when I was a boy one got into my ear." Laljee brought the bottle and three glasses on a tray.

"Hector, is long past you bedtime, boy!" Sister called out from the kitchen. Hector kissed his father and said good night to Doorne and Laljee. Even Sister made the mistake of treating him like a child sometimes. Couldn't she understand that he wanted to find out what was worrying his father since he was interested in how it would affect him?

He was tempted to stand by the door and listen but he knew that Sister would come in to say good night. He undressed quickly and lay in bed watching the canopy of his mosquito net swaying over him.

Sister came and asked, "You all right, boy?"

"Yes, Sister, I'm all right," he slurred his words to give the impression of being on the verge of sleep.

"I will get you up at foreday-morning so that you can go down to the milking pen with Tojo like you was planning."

"All right, Sister, good night." She lifted up the hem of the net and put her dry hand on his forehead. It was her way of reassuring him that everything would be all right. As soon as she had closed the door behind her he crept out of bed and crouched by the key hole. Doorne was saying:

"He write to tell me that he bringing a woman but he en't say who the woman was, boss."

His father swallowed his drink, leaned forward and said quietly, "I'll tell you who the woman is. It's my woman."

"How come you and Tengar trail get cross up like this, boss, you mean they en't got enough woman in Georgetown to separate all you two?" Doorne asked.

Fitz sat back in his chair. When he was animated his long brown face always looked younger. There were points of anger in his eyes and his heavy lids drooped slightly. He looked at Doorne and found himself resenting the old man's vitality. Doorne was twenty-five years his senior but had somehow managed to bob and weave through the years keeping the sap in his body young. Elsa had made Fitz feel young for a while and she could have sustained this feeling in him if she had not suddenly betrayed him.

★   ★   ★

Fitz remembered the night Laljee had dropped him outside Elsa's cottage in Kitty Village. He had entered and found her sitting by the front window.

"I thought you weren't at home after I didn't see any light," he had said.

"I was sitting here waiting for you. . . I got something that I want to talk to you 'bout."

"Don't tell me you want more money."

"No, is not money I want to talk 'bout."

"If it's something unpleasant I don't want to hear 'bout it. . . not right now."

"What I got to say en't pleasant but I got to say it right now," she said angrily.

"Don't talk to me like that, Elsa, I won't stand for it!"

"You won't have to stand for it after tonight 'cause I leaving you."

"What?"

"I'm leaving you."

"Don't talk balls."

"I will put it like this. I found a man and I'm going 'way with him."

"So you found a man, Elsa?" Fitz's voice was low, purring, the first rush of anger was not against her, but against the stranger who was robbing him of services he had paid for. He had always regarded Elsa as a commodity which could be purchased, used and discarded as he chose.

"Yes, Fitz, I'm cutting loose. Don't act like if I bringing sorrow to you' doorstep 'cause you know in you' heart you can find another woman to take over the back street house and the back street life."

"Who is the sweet-man?"

"That is my affair."

"It must be a white man."

"Is not money I'm after this time, is love."

"You must be reaching the stage of dotage before you grow old, girl."

"Don't try to laugh it off, Fitz, I'm leaving you and I'm going to tell you what I think 'bout you, I always wanted to do it: you're a selfish man. . . a good business man too, you know how to weigh and balance what you going to buy and you don't ever take a pig-in-bag, no, you won't ever do that. I'm a black nobody and you is a big-shot brown-man. You never make me forget me place. When I blow out the light and you plant yourself on top me we was equal but how many times you drive past me like you didn't know me the morning after when I meet you in the town? You would creep up them steps in the dark of night and tell me all you troubles 'bout you' sister and you' children and the business. I had to listen 'cause you pay me to. But did you ever listen to me troubles? Don't get me wrong, you had you' good ways sometimes. You never had glue in you' palm where money was concern. Once I could provide you with the bowl to dip you' wick in, you was always ready to give me frocks and frills. Don't get me wrong, I en't feel that I is no prize-woman 'cause I got me bad ways like everybody else and I never trouble 'bout two-timing you, but if you did treat me like I was a flesh-and-blood woman I would've did stay with you. When you first meet me although I was whoring about I was still a village gal at heart. In them days I did respect you for you' book learning and you' marble-in-the-mouth talk but the months and the years go by and I realise that behind all that was jus' a selfish man. . . ."

"Then why did you hang on so long? I never bound you to me with chains. You had your riggs to cut loose anytime you felt like it. I'm not going to argue with you, Elsa, I'm just going to say that I still want you. Tell me who the man is because quite frankly I don't believe you're giving up the cottage and everything to become a nature-girl. If he's offering more than me, I'll raise my bid. Tell me what you want and you can have it. All right, so I'm selfish, I won't deny that, and I'm getting old, that's harder to admit. It's not that I'm old in years, my old man lived to eighty-two and I'm thirty years away from that. What's happening to me is that my spirit's drying up. It's withering and shrinking up like a forced-ripe fruit in the sun and whatever you might say about how I treat you, you are the one person who makes me feel like I'm still young. I've been studding around and whoring about since I was a boy so I know what I'm saying, believe me."

"I can't be you' saviour, Fitz, you got to find you' own salvation. No matter how much fancy talk you pour out on me now I know you en't never going to treat me like I want you to. Can you marry me, make me you' wife, set me up in you' big house to look after you' children? Answer me that? Can you, Fitz?"

"You know I couldn't do that."

"Well that was what I wanted all along, that's how I could've save you. You make you' money in the diamond mines working like a slave, sweating and cussing and knocking about jus' like any man from the nigger-yards. That was the only time you was ever living, Fitz, and that's why you' spirit drying up now."

"All right, give me hell, girl, piss on me, but stand by me a little longer, tell the man to wait."

"This man is not a waiting man, he blood does flow too urgent, he is a bushman and he 'custom to take what he want, he is a man with small patience and anyhow I want him and I didn't know how much I want him 'til you come here tonight."

"A bushman, eh? You like them wild! Where does he come from?"

"I en't telling you, find out for you'self. And now you better go, Fitz. I going to lef the house in order, only the bed will need fixing 'cause it break down las' night."

"This is my house, I'll leave whenever the spirit moves me not a minute before."

"I only got to stick me head through the window and call out."

"There's always the police."

"You' yellow-face sister will drop dead with the scandal and you' children won't never live it down."

"The house-cat has tiger's claws! Jesus God! So you're threatening me and pushing me around, Elsa?"

"You driving me to it. I never was a cantankerous woman and I never goin' to be one. But I rattle up you' false pride and is you who turn nasty first."

"All right, I'll go, but this won't be the end of it."

It was dark and quiet outside. The new moon and the stars had been blotted out by threatening rainclouds. Laljee guessed what had happened from the look on his master's face and the way in which he sat in the back seat, and not beside him as he usually did. The chauffeur's face was inscrutable as he drove off at high speed.

"You ever got mixed up with a slut, Laljee?" Fitz asked.

"No, boss."

"Jesus! You make me sick with your blasted lockjaw. You knew it was going to happen all along didn't you?"

"Don't know what you talking 'bout, boss." Even when he was his most expansive it would have taken a sorcerer to divine what

Laljee was thinking. Fitz felt like smashing the back of his head in at that moment.

"If I drop dead at your feet one day you wouldn't bat an eye, would you, Laljee?"

"Is what use you want to quarrel with me, boss? Me not goin' to take you on." What his master needed was something to drink and he was taking him to the Tower Hotel which was open all night. He raced down Vlissengen Road. Fitz struck his head against the top of the car when they bounced across a rut. He swore and bellowed at Laljee to slow down, but the East Indian gripped the spokes of the steering wheel and pretended not to hear.

$\star$ $\star$ $\star$

"Then you don't have nothing to worry 'bout, boss, you well rid of the woman."

"Well rid of the woman. . ." Fitz repeated. It took him a few moments to break away from his stream of memories. "Don't tell me about being well rid of her, man, she was bought and paid for, I took her off the waterfront, gave her a house and all the finery she wanted. . . ."

"She must have something special, boss," Doorne said. A devilish grin split his black face and he slapped his leg and rocked back and forth.

"The irony of it is that he's bringing her to live on my land."

"What you want ME to do 'bout it, boss? That is Tengar affair, he's a grown man."

"If that slut so much as sets foot on my property, then the lot of you can go, and if you don't go then you'll have to fight it out with me in the courts."

"I will tell him," Doorne said draining his tumbler and rising. He was laughing once more when he added, "Boss, won't be easy to shift me off you' land, I been living on it since before you father time and I got squatter's rights." Doorne's composure, his refusal to be riled by his master's vindictiveness goaded the latter into blurting out:

"Be-Jesus-Christ, man! You live on my land by my consent and only by my consent. I said it and I'm saying it again if your son brings that blasted woman on my property I'll throw the lot of you out!"

Hector felt embarrassed for his father. He was humiliating himself before Doorne and Laljee. Laljee sat behind his cloud of smoke, listening, observing silently. Hector was sure that Sister had heard it all, too.

"I will see you tomorrow, boss?" Doorne asked from the doorway.

"I'm leaving early."

"I'll send you the estimate for the repairs to the dam."

Hector went back to bed. The wind had died down. His window was open and he could see the silhouette of a tamarind tree against a sky bright with stars. A quack, disturbed in its sleep, was complaining loudly from the swamps across the road. He heard his father moving about the living-room. Laljee was going to sleep on jute bags spread out at the foot of his master's bed. The old East Indian could walk as noiselessly as an ocelot so that even when Hector strained his ears he could not hear him.

Doorne walked back to his hut in the darkness chuckling to himself. He despised Fitz Bradshaw. Despite the man's blustering and vanity he was weak. Doorne judged men by their physical prowess and their cunning. Fitz's father had had these qualities and had been the match of any man on the coast but Fitz was a flaccid-muscled city man.

"He's still a young man," Doorne said to himself, "couldn't be more than forty-eight, and yet he got to buy women. He don't have enough juice in his back to fill up a mopsy with delight. Lord! I can be the man's father and them young gals who does squirm under me don't never have nothing to complain 'bout 'cause they always coming back for more. If Tengar take 'way he woman it serve him right. Better to be a beggar with good sap in you limbs than to have money and position and a sugar-stick with no juice in it."

A piper owl was fluting in the silkcotton tree which towered above Doorne's hut. It was a sign that the rains were coming. He had to fetch his woodskins from Honey Reef; and to add to his stock of provisions, he thought.

★　　★　　★

Hector and Tojo walked down to the cow pen early next morning. The night wind had scraped the sky clean of clouds and the rising sun burnt away the mists quickly. The boys found Doorne milking a black and white heifer, dipping his fingers in dung every now and then to lubricate the tits. The old man was not in a talking mood. He gave the boys cups of warm frothing milk and they drank four pints each.

"When are you going to take me hunting, Doorne?" Hector asked.

"Don't ask me no kind of question his morning, Master Hector, me spirit feel too heavy inside me." Hector and Tojo wandered off to the grove of giant azaleas and cromanty trees beyond the pen. They saw a chicken hawk fighting with a grass snake ahead of them. The snake lashed out with its tail and the hawk hopped away and pounced. The boys crouched behind a cromanty trunk. The hawk was just settling down to its meal when a dragon lizard darted out and caught it by the legs. The hawk tore itself away, pulling frenziedly. It flew upwards, legless with blood dripping from shredded stumps.

"I wonder how it's going to alight," Hector said, and Tojo chased the dragon lizard away and said:

"It will just have to fly and fly 'til it can't fly no more then it will drop down and ants or something will eat it up."

Doorne hallooed for them when he was ready to walk out to the public road with his milk cans. The old man fitted the eight gallon cans, one at each end of an akee stick, hoisted them to his shoulder, balanced them and set out ahead of the boys. He was taking a different route and Hector asked:

"Why are you going this way, Doorne?"

"Because I want to show you something." They skirted the reef until they came to an open savannah. Doorne put down the milk cans and scraped the sweat from his forehead with his thumb.

"You see this savannah here, Master Hector, this is where the slaves stop up the mouth of one of your ancestors with earth."

"What are you talking about, Doorne?"

Doorne laughed and pressed the tips of his fingers together.

"If you pass here on a moonlight night you does hear the dead slaves calling out. Your ancestor was a devil-man and he drive the slaves so hard that they turn 'gainst he. They dig a big pit in the middle of this savannah and camouflage it with twigs and grass. One day they all turn out to work in the canefields as usual 'til a man start to play a quick-time tune on a bamboo flute and all the slaves pick up theyselves and hotfoot it towards the pit. The old boss-man and he overseers set out after them on horses – slaves was property in them days and the old man couldn't stand by and see he property running 'way before he eyes. The slaves run right up to the edge of the pit and when they hear the horse hooves pounding behind them, they open ranks. By this time your ancestor and he overseers was hard behind them, they ride straight through the opening and crash inside the pit and the drummer-men start beating they drums and everybody go mad and start shovelling earth on top of man and horse 'til the whole lot was buried comfortable and quiet." Doorne, looking at Hector, could see the horror and excitement his story was inspiring, and he chuckled and added with a big grin, "Every word I tell you is true, Master Hector, if you come down here on a moonlight night and put you ears to the ground you can hear people groaning worse than a po-boy tree in high wind." Hector glanced around at Tojo. Neither of them spoke but the two boys knew that they would have to return to the savannah and listen for the groaning in the coming moonlight season.

"What happened to the slaves, Doorne?" Hector asked.

"They turn 'round and burn everything that was sympathetic to fire and then they cut out for Black Bush. Your ancestor's wife get killed when the big house burn down, they roast her up in it with the unborn baby she was carrying, but your great grandpa plant plenty seeds in the slave gals belly and is so you come to be here."

"What happened to the slaves, Mr. Doorne?" Tojo asked.

"The news reached New Amsterdam and the Government send militia to hunt them down and hound then down, and them that didn't starve in the bush or join up with the Indians get captured. My great grandpa was one of the ringleaders and they crucify him with a lot of others."

"But why did you have to tell me this story, Doorne?" Hector asked and he watched the old man squinting against the sun.

"I had to tell you because I wanted you to know that you got the blood of the master and the slave in you' veins. You' papa trying to forget it and acting like he is a white man but you mustn't never forget it, boy."

When they came to Doorne's hut the old man crouched down and eased the milk cans off his shoulder. The hut stood on twelve-foot high stilts, and giving it extra resistance against the wind were mora poles planted into the earth and bracing against the outer walls like flying buttresses. Close by the hut was the silkcotton tree which was always shedding blossoms.

Caya, Doorne's son, walked from behind the big tree and greeted them.

"Howdy, Papa Doorne. Howdy, Master Hector, you growing up so fast I can't hardly recognise you from one month to the other. How you getting on smart-man Tojo?" Caya was short and broad shouldered and he had a jovial moon-face the colour of a burnt coffee bean. He was a rascal-man who would go to any lengths to avoid working for a living but he was popular in the village. The Elders deplored his lazy good-for-nothing ways but the majority of Tarlogians felt that if a man was able to live by the sweat of other people's brows then he was only doing what the high-and-mighty folks in the city did, and he should be applauded.

"Tell Sister I got some business to 'tend to and I will come 'round later on," Doorne said, dismissing the two boys.

Hector knew that the old man had sent for his son to discuss Fitz's ultimatum. Caya was a rogue but his advice on dealings with the great ones in the city was valued by all the villagers. He had once seduced a white official's wife and this, in everyone's eyes, qualified him for the role of counsellor. Besides he had plenty of time to think, gaffing and lounging around Chinaman's rum-shop.

Hector and Tojo walked across the burning sand towards the grove of po-boy trees in the back yard.

"Tengar's coming back to the village and he's bringing a city woman with him," Hector said. He felt that he had to share his secret.

"Everybody know that," Tojo said, picking up an empty

coconut shell and hurling it at Tanta Bess' prize sow which had come through the barbed wire fence with a squealing litter trailing behind her.

"You know Tengar, Tojo?"

"If I know Tengar? Chu! You will ask me that? En't nobody on this coast who don't know Tengar 'cause he's a giant of a man."

"How did you hear 'bout him and the woman?"

"You can't hide news under a bushel in this village, Master Hector."

"Boy, is only now you coming back from the cow pen?" Sister regaled Hector from the top of the back steps. "Lord, the boy growing up without manners. You didn't even say goodbye to your papa, boy, and you breakfast get cold."

"I didn't know it was so late, Sister."

"Didn't know it was so late? You don't have eyes in your head to see the sun climbing up high?"

"I'm sorry, Sister."

"Don't worry to tell me 'bout you' sorryness now because I know you lazy away your time on purpose. Anyhow your papa has so much confusion in his mind that he didn't even ask for you. He just fumble and fret over his breakfast and clear out."

Tojo fetched a bucket of water from the vat and Hector washed and wiped his feet before entering the house. He wanted to discuss what had passed between Doorne and his father, what the old man had told him out in the savannah, but something had upset Sister and he saw that he would have to wait.

CHAPTER FOUR

TENGAR and Elsa arrived in Tarlogie at high noon. Boysie dropped them outside Chinaman's rum-shop and roared away in his vermilion bus. Doorne and Caya came out of the shop to greet them.

"So you come at last, Tengar," Caya said, "thought you was going to stay on in the city and try you luck."

"This is me woman," Tengar said, "she name Elsa."

"Howdy, sister-in-law."

"Howdy, Brother Caya, Tengar tell me plenty 'bout you."

"And this is me papa, Elsa." Doorne stood rooted, his mouth hanging open; his lips moved but no words came out. Tengar looked from one to the other. He had, never seen his father at a loss for words before.

"Let we get out of this hot sun!" Elsa said, and the uncalled for irritability of her tone surprised Tengar.

"What happen, sweet-gal?" he asked, wanting his woman to make a good impression on his relatives.

"Let we get out of the sun, me head hurting me!" she said.

Doorne led the way into the shop. "You make plenty money this trip?" he asked gruffly.

"Nothing to shout about. I clear me outlay and make couple dollars, was a lot of brute-work and I en't got much to show for it."

"Come on, let we all have a drink," Caya said. Tengar sensed that his father didn't approve of Elsa nor she of him, but he was not one to attach deep and dark meanings to people's actions. He was sure that they would grow to like each other in time.

"Yes, come on, me throat feel dry as a drought savannah," Caya insisted. Tengar lugged the two wooden boxes with their belongings up the bridge and deposited them in a corner of the shop veranda. Elsa and Caya walked a few paces ahead of him.

"You come from Georgetown?" Caya asked.

"I was living there but I born and grow up in nearby Saltan village."

"I must 'ave did know you when you was a small girl 'cause you face got a familiar look to it."

Tengar paused on the veranda and looked around him. Tarlogie looked small, sleepy, deserted. It was like this every time he went away and returned, the distance between the public road and the courida trees on the foreshore seemed greatly reduced, the huts standing on their tall stilts looked more like nests than human dwellings, the blue arc of sky seemed to have closed in. He looked across the way and saw Tanta Bess' house and the Bradshaw mansion. A brown boy was sitting on the front steps of the big house and he guessed that it was Hector Bradshaw. Old Doorne had written him to say that Sister was looking after the boy. During his months in the bush tapping balata trees he always thought of the village as a big place and the longer he stayed away the more it grew in his imagination. Coming back was a shock. The dream evoked images of neat huts ringed by coconut trees, swamps with lotus lilies in bloom. But the reality was one of broken-down dwellings balanced insecurely on stilts, outhouses with overflowing pits and hogs rooting in the muck, pot bellied children playing in muddy yards, the smell of slime and stagnant water, open stretches which the sun had sucked dry, baked and cracked.

Tengar's journey from the forests to Georgetown and then to his native Tarlogie had been a bewildering one. He had stumbled through so many experiences since he had left the balata fields that he felt a need to rearrange them in his mind. Two days ago he had stepped off the riverboat in Georgetown, but looking back it seemed as though years had passed since then.

★   ★   ★

He had disembarked with the first rush of passengers. The riverboat engine kept pounding for a while before it coughed and clanged to a stop.

The bedlam coming from the market place beyond the stelling

assaulted his ears – voices, the grind of wheels, hoof beats, the incessant tooting of horns. He jostled his way through the crowd until he came to the square opposite the market. He was carrying a heavy balata-coated canvas bag on his shoulder and he flung it down and leaned against a tree. Somehow the feel of the rough bark against his back was reassuring. Dodo, the beggar bore down on him.

"Is good to see you big-Tengar."

"How she going, Dodo? It look like you face beating too hard 'gainst the years, old man." Tengar laughed and tossed a two shilling piece at him and he caught it expertly.

"Things bad, big-Tengar… things bad, big boy…" the old man ruminated between each statement and tears ran out of the corners of his alligator-eyes.

"Things bad all round, pardner, the balata that I gather on this trip take longer than it ever take before, was brute-work and I en't bring back much to show for it." Tengar was glad to meet someone he could talk to. "Tell me something, Dodo," he leaned forward and lowered his voice, "where can I find a good whore house that open night and day?"

Dodo guffawed and tapped his stick on the ground. "You don't have to go to no whore house, big boy, just walk 'bout the market."

"Man, I got so much juice store up in me back, if I don't find a woman quick I will burst."

"Take a walk around the market, big boy, and keep you eyes open. You bound to land something."

Tengar slung his bag over his shoulder once more, tossed Dodo an extra sixpence and headed for the clocktower and the low sheds which stretched down to the river.

He had seen Elsa quarrelling with Jojo in front of a fruit stall. There was a concentrated earnestness about the way they abused each other. It was the kind of row which could suddenly explode in public between two people who had been intimate for a long time. Tengar edged up closer so that he could get a better look at the woman. She was tall, coffee-coloured with a mass of coarse black hair framing her face. Her wide-set brown eyes were shooting off fireworks as she spoke. She had big cheek bones and a small chin, her mouth was wide and well fleshed, her nose small and flat, tilting upwards at the tip and her nostrils were dilating as if she had a bellows inside her head. The controlled fury in her voice sent a thrill through Tengar and he pushed forward until he stood opposite her. She was getting the better of Jojo, whipping him with her tongue. Jojo stood there, a foot taller than she was, broad shouldered with a waist as narrow as a bucks, looking with desperate appeal at the crowd that had gathered around.

"You, Jojo Thompson, you're just a no-good parasite-man, en't no use sucking up to me no more, brother, you been hanging on to me like a tick and now I scraping you off. . . you done shooting you big black mouth off 'bout how a white woman keeping you, go 'long you' way to her. . ."

She kept on goading Jojo and Tengar knew that the only thing left for the man to do was to knock her down. If Jojo had had Elsa at home he would have beaten her like a snake but she had chosen her battle ground well, if he so much as touched her the market police would arrest him.

"Elsa, listen to me, gal, listen. . ."

"I don't want to hear nothing more from you, Jojo, I know every thought that ever lodge inside you' flyweight brain already, man. You listen to me, you en't so much of a man as you think you is, all the white woman will be getting is the leavings, I done scoop up the cream already. . ." It was too much for Jojo. He couldn't stand there and let Elsa attack his manhood. She had said enough to make him become the laughing stock of the waterfront. He sprang at her and she screamed, a deliberate roof-raising scream. Tengar didn't know why he intervened. Perhaps it was because Elsa's eyes had made four with his for a moment and he had detected at once a challenge and an appeal in them. He lunged forward and pulled them apart.

"Why all you want to get yourself in trouble?" he pleaded, grinning stupidly. Jojo's blood was boiling and he wasn't going to allow anybody to prevent him from knocking Elsa's teeth down her throat. He whipped out a knife and went into a wrestler's crouch. Tengar pounced on him so swiftly that not even the people standing nearest him saw him move. He squeezed Jojo's wrist until the knife fell from his hand, and he picked Elsa up with one hand and rushed out of the market, making his way through the crowd as if he was walking through a thicket in the bush. Jojo made a getaway from the police through one of the sidedoors. Outside the market, Tengar hailed a taxi, bundled Elsa in and sat beside her.

"Take we to Bel Air!" he shouted, and the taxi driver stepped on the accelerator and left a hubbub of police whistles and voices in their wake. Tengar kept expecting to hear Elsa object but everything had happened so quickly that she could not find her tongue for a while. Suddenly she straightened her dress and burst out laughing, a hysterical mirthless laughter. Tengar eased away from her and looked on amazed. The laughter stopped and she began to cry.

"I was only trying to save you from trouble," Tengar said, and when she saw the look of bewilderment on his face, she brushed away her tears and said:

"Lord ha' mercy, nothing like this ever happen to me in all me born days." Tengar, reassured, offered her his big sallow hand-kerchief. She took it and blew her nose.

"What's your name, big boy?"

"Tengar."

"Is so you accustom to pick up woman and make off with them?"

"En't never done it before."

He twisted like a big snake which had coiled itself up into a knot.

"Don't let's go to Bel Air, we can go to my house in Kitty."

He didn't look at her. The hunger in his eyes might have frightened her.

"Tell the driver where you living," he said hoarsely.

"Take we to the end of the canal road in Kitty!" she said, leaning forward.

"Why you had to harass the man in public like that?" he asked.

"Tell me 'bout yourself 'cause Mr. Jojo en't never going to hang he hat in my bedroom no more. I give him a long rope and now I don't care if he live or die."

"You was his woman, wasn't you?"

"I wasn't nobody woman, big boy. A big shot brown man set me up and Jojo was me side kick but me spirit weary with both of them."

"I don't know 'bout the brown man but Jojo look all right to me."

"Sometimes quartz does look just like diamond." The taxi stopped and Tengar got out and paid the driver from a fat wad of notes.

"Keep the change," Tengar said. The man grinned all over his face.

"Don't spare the firewood," he said, "if you got a weapon to match your size, pardner, Elsa bound to bawl."

They stood by the roadside and watched the taxi turn around and drive away with the exhaust belching black smoke. The sun was almost directly overhead but a sea breeze took the edge off the heat. The water in the canal which separated the roadway from Elsa's front yard caught the sunlight on the crests of bobbing wavelets and the reeds rustled. The rows of tenements on both sides of the roadway were deserted except for a few old people sunning themselves on their doorsteps and dozing off.

Elsa crossed the narrow bridge and led the way inside her cottage. Tengar noticed the swing of her hips and licked the dry roof of his mouth. The interior of the cottage was cool and dark. Tengar sat on a couch near the front window and Elsa went inside her bedroom to fetch a bottle of rum.

"You feeling hungry?" she called out, "'cause I got some curry and rice in the pot, all I got to do is heat it up."

"I'm not hungry for food," Tengar said. She returned with two half pint tumblers and a bottle of Russian Bear rum.

"Help yourself; big boy," she said, placing the bottle and glasses on a small table beside Tengar. He poured himself a tall drink, gulped it down and smacked his lips.

"This is powerful nectar, gal." He waited for her to pour her drink then he refilled his tumbler. She stood before him enjoying the way he averted his eyes every time she caught him sizing her up. She emptied her glass and knelt close to him.

"You have nice soft skin for such a big rough man," she said, undoing his shirt buttons and caressing his chest. He picked her up and pressed her against him until she cried out.

"Let we go in the bedroom." The bed collapsed under Tengar's weight and they had to put the mattress on the floor. Elsa whimpered like a piper owl in moonlight, a wild, sweet, fluting cry.

"Hush, sweet gal, the neighbours will hear."

"I want them to hear. . . I want them to know that I find a man who can fulfil me at last. . . Lord, Tengar! It sweeter than honey boy!"

They laboured together through sundown and far into the night. The marathon session in bed made Elsa feel as if she had been disembodied and she was floating on air. She pressed close to Tengar and said, "I will follow you anywhere you go, da'ling, anywhere you go."

"Huh?"

"I said I will follow you anywhere you go. . . if you want."

"How you mean, if I want? I'm a lucky man to find a fine woman like you." He was feeling hungry and wanted her to get up and cook him some food but he knew that in the aftermath of lovemaking some women liked to be coddled and petted.

"You think I can satisfy you, Tengar?"

"Sweet-gal, en't no woman ever satisfy me the way you do this day and night. Every time I touch you, you does send me to heaven."

"I'm just a broken down second-hand piece of goods."

He put one hand over her mouth and ran the other up and down the deep groove of her back.

"Don't ever say that, sweet-gal, don't try and run yourself down to me 'cause the world always full of people who ready to mauvaise langue you. From the minute I set eyes on you in the market I say to meself, 'Tengar, that's you woman, pardner, she can hang she petticoat in you bedroom any time.'"

"Tengar, you got more sweet-talk than a running brook, but I like it. All Jojo used to talk 'bout was how other woman was running after he."

"You did love Jojo, Elsa?"

"Who, me? Jojo did love heself so much, he never give nobody a chance to love he. I used to fool meself that he love me sometimes when he start to fuss around me and act like he was Gentle Jesus, but in the end I always find out was because he want something from me. No, Jojo couldn't love nobody but heself and nobody could 'ave love him."

"And how 'bout the big shot brown man who set you up?"

"His name is Fitz Bradshaw and he got a store in Camp Street."

"The same Fitz Bradshaw who own Tarlogie?"

"That same one. How you know 'bout he?"

"I was born in Tarlogie and my papa does manage Fitz Bradshaw's estate there. Lord Jesus! Look how the world small."

"I didn't know you come from Tarlogie."

"You didn't ask me, sweet-gal."

"What your papa name?"

"Doorne. . . Ebenezer Doorne." Elsa sat up and looked at him searchingly. "Don't tell me you know him," Tengar said.

"I hear 'bout him. My mama used to buy milk from him."

"Then you grow up nearby? Lord ha' mercy!"

"I grow up in nearby Saltan Village."

"Is a small world."

"A small world for true."

"Tell me something, how you and Bradshaw part? You part as friend or enemy?"

"To tell you the truth, he en't know that we part yet. I going to break the news when he come tomorrow, and you don't have to feel that you snarling up me life 'cause I would've break with he even if I didn't meet you, Tengar."

"He's a vindictive man and if he know I going with you he will throw me and me fam'ly off he land."

"The coast big and land en't hard to come by."

"But me papa plough he sweat into that Tarlogie land since Bradshaw father was alive."

"I won't tell he nothing 'bout you."

"He will hear just the same."

"You got to make you' choice, big boy."

"I done make me choice already."

Elsa got up and stretched and Tengar lay on his back looking at the rafters. He heard her strike a match and watched a criss-cross of shadows dance on the ceiling. He was conscious of a strong animal smell, partly his own, partly hers, and he felt indolence and satisfaction swathing his limbs, seeping into his pores. Outside, rain frogs were complaining to the stars and the reeds were sighing with the weight of wind and dew on them.

A curlew cried out with a strident insistence until its mate answered. The sea was only half a mile away and he could hear the low, surly murmur of the retreating tide and the occasional hum of a car racing along the coastal road. He turned over on his side and watched Elsa fumbling around the small room. She was naked and her skin gleamed like sling mud in the sun. There was a large dressing table in the corner nearest the door. Hand mirrors, boxes of powder, pressing combs, face creams and the trivia that city women use to beautify themselves were scattered over its top. Tengar was suddenly apprehensive about his ability to support her. She glanced around and caught the look in his eye.

"You don't have to worry 'cause I salt away some of the money that old man Bradshaw give me and I can look after meself. Besides I wouldn't need all these things on the coast. I'm a country gal you know, I en't born with me foot prison up in fancy shoes, I know what it's like to feel mud and water, to hitch up me skirt and work in the ricefields."

"Me mama say the same thing when the old man bring she home to Tarlogie but when the strain start to weigh she down she cut out and hot foot it back to the city."

"Whatever happen I will never do that, Tengar, I will never walk out on you. Cuss me out, beat me, brutalise me and I will still wrap around you like liana."

★　　★　　★

"Come and have a drink!" Caya called out.

"Well bless me eyesight! Tengar, you get bigger and blacker since me see you last, man." Chinaman said. Tengar noticed how the shopkeeper had aged. His swollen testicles hung down like a sack of rice as he shuffled around behind the counter. Dookia stood in the doorway leading to the rooms behind the shop. She was smiling benignly. She was a well-covered, handsome woman, twenty years younger than her husband. Her black eyes were set so deeply behind long lashes that you could never read their expression. Looking at her Tengar wondered all over again how she ever allowed Chinaman to beat and abuse her night after night, for it was obvious that she could crush him like a ripe simitu with her powerful hands.

"I bring a woman with me this time, Dookia. You like she?"

"She eyes look like they don't light on nothing for long, boyah; watch out for she." Dookia glanced swiftly at Elsa.

"Don't worry with she," China said, dismissing his wife and planting a bottle of rum on the counter.

"Bring the good rum, Chinaman," Caya said, "like you forget is me self help you water down this lot." Chinaman replaced the bottle with one from under the counter.

"That's more like it, pardner," Doorne said, pouring himself a drink and holding his glass up to the light.

"Is not that I want to heap bad news on you back just as you come," Caya said, sipping his drink and rolling it vigorously inside his mouth before swallowing, "but things en't right here since day before yesterday."

"What happen?" Elsa asked. She had recovered from her outburst, but kept looking straight ahead, avoiding Doorne's eyes.

"Bradshaw pay we a visit," Doorne said laconically.

"The big chibat say you and you woman not to set foot on he land," Chinaman added, laughing his parakeet laugh.

"I was expecting something like this," Tengar said. He looked at Elsa to see how she had taken the news and saw that her eyes were bright with anger.

"After all we do for that man," Tengar said, "after all the sweat we water he land with, tending he cattle, reaping he crops, guarding the land 'gainst heaven. . ."

"No use groaning, boy, I live on this land for fifty years and en't nothing nor nobody going move me off it." Doorne looked accusingly at Elsa.

"Is not she fault. Bradshaw rich and we poor and if he choose to act niggerish en't nobody to blame for that. If you want to blame somebody then blame me," Tengar said.

"I got a small house out on the reef, you can patch it up and live there," Chinaman said, and when Tengar hesitated Elsa said:

"I en't 'fraid to live in the middle of nowhere. Is better that way, you won't have no neighbour prying and peeping at you."

"You got a point there, gal," Caya said, grinning from ear to ear.

"And what you going to do, Papa?"

"Watch and wait, boy. Let Bradshaw make he move. I can always play a trump to cop he, don't worry."

"Let we drink to Tengar and he woman!" Caya said, looking at Elsa and thinking about the days ahead when his brother would have to be away and somebody would have to keep the home fires burning. Doorne walked out without drinking the toast to his daughter-in-law.

"What wrong with the old vulture?" Tengar asked, and Caya shrugged away the question and poured himself another drink. He had to make the best of it while his brother was still in funds.

"You got a peculiar family," Elsa said, following old man Doorne with her eyes.

"Only trouble does keep we together," Tengar said, laughing until the bottles rattled on the shelves.

"That old man so contrary that the wind does look like a Sunday school teacher alongside he," Caya said.

"Only he and Jesus does know what does go on inside he head. He hard as a lignum vitae tree, wild as a liana, but he's a fighter and when he say he not shifting, then en't nobody in this land to budge he, I can tell you that," Tengar said.

CHAPTER FIVE

THAT evening Hector finished dinner early and was preparing to do his homework. Teacher La Rose, had arrived promptly at eight in the morning. Both Hector and the teacher had known that the kind of relationship they established that morning would set the pattern for years to come. La Rose had been grave to the point of taciturnity. He had never dealt with someone like Hector, the son of a rich brown man from the city, and with the boy's eyes subjecting him to the pitiless scrutiny that only children are capable of, he was conscious of his ill-fitting white drill suit, the awkwardness of his movements and his failure to make what he said sound authoritative. Hector got the better of him because he tried too hard to act schoolmasterish. The boy's show of arrogance, however, wasn't real. The teacher had been thrust upon him when he would have preferred not to have had any schooling at all. His front of brashness was his way of finding out how far he could go with a stranger who had been put in authority over him. La Rose spent the morning and afternoon periods finding out how much his pupil had already learnt. The boy was good at reading and writing but bad at figures. The latter part of the afternoon had been spent doing mental arithmetic and Hector hadn't given a single correct answer. The teacher made him work out the problems in his exercise book and made no comment. Hector was grateful for this. He observed La Rose with a renewed interest, the shaven dome of a head, the big sloe eyes, the wide spread of nostril which convinced the boy that if the teacher tilted his head backwards he could peer deep inside his skull, the opaque navy-blue skin and the hands with their long, thin fingers and pink nails. These hands sticking far out of the jacket sleeves seemed to have a life of their own, to be somehow out of tune with La Rose's bony awkward frame.

Thinking about the teacher after he had wheeled his ancient bicycle down the drive and pedalled away, the thing Hector remembered most vividly was that Sister had bustled in at lunchtime and said:

"Mr. La Rose, I prepared a meal for you," for she had noticed the hollows under his out-thrusting cheekbones.

"I'm sorry, Miss Smart, but I brought my lunch with me. I prefer it that way if you don't mind," he had said.

"Call me, Sister, young man. I don't like nobody who I got to see in me house day in day out calling me Miss Smart." Sister's directness had embarrassed him and he had got up hastily, mumbling something about his lunch being in a saucepan downstairs. He had eaten his lunch under the front porch, sitting on a stool and looking out towards the foreshore. Hector had spied on him through a crack in the floorboards and seen him eating a large portion of brown rice and a few cubes of boiled fish. He was using a tin spoon and ate self-consciously as if a crowd was looking on and laughing at him. Hector had reported to Sister and she nodded and put her hands to her head.

"The poor boy!" she had said, "the poor boy! But he got pride eh? I like a man-chile to grow up with pride like that. Hector, boy, you must watch at that young man and let he example write itself on you' young mind. To be rich and proud en't so hard. Rich man can be proud of he clothes, he house, he can step high and talk big because people afraid to make they ears deaf against he. Rich man can always hold the soul of the poor in pawn, he can spit on the poor with looks and they will fasten they eye on the ground and thank he for kind mercies. Rich man don't have to be proud in his heart because his pride is on his tongue. But the poor man's pride is the pride that does live in a lair in his heart when his foot reaching through his shoe sole to feel the dust of the road and the mud of the swamp, he can still hold his head high as heaven, and when hungriness scraping his belly dry, he still won't bow the head or bend the knee. The poor man's pride has the strength of the wind in it, you can't never see it but it always there, blind as Sampson's eye but powerful enough to tumble the temples of the rich and the Godless. Take good heed of that young man's pride because if he can seed your heart with the pride of the poor, the pride that is blind as Sampson's eye and strong as the strength of the wind, then he will give you more than a whole river of words in the white man books. Them books anyhow is just a lot of scratch and scrawl in black and white, and the words, if you don't sift and sieve them, winnow them like you does winnow paddy, then they does give you indigestion and make confusion in your young heart." When Sister got to preachifying, the words took hold of her and rocked her thin body and her eyes shone like stars over the rim of a whirlpool, and when she came to, she always looked embarrassed and would spend an hour or so grumbling and fretting until she had regained her equanimity.

★   ★   ★

Now Hector, in the midst of homework spotted Tengar and Elsa approaching from the public road and rushed inside to tell Sister. It was Preacher Galloway's courting night and he sat in his cane chair in the living-room screwing his neck from side to side and fidgeting with his high collar. Sister sat opposite him in her rocking chair, acting as though he wasn't there. He cleared his throat repeatedly and made his cane chair creak from time to time. Sister concentrated on her sewing, making the thimble click defiantly against the needle.

"Sister, Tengar and his woman are visiting us!" Hector announced excitedly. She continued her sewing.

"What's wrong with that? You never see a man and woman coming here to visit me before?"

"Sister, you home!" Tengar called out.

"Come on in, Tengar, me was expecting you, boy!"

Hector stood in the corner behind Preacher Galloway's chair. It was an unobtrusive but good vantage point.

"I don't know why you have to wrap yourself up with that man and his family," the preacher grumbled. Sister flashed him a contemptuous look and opened the door. Tengar filled the doorway for an instant before he entered and Hector didn't see the woman behind him until the giant had reached the middle of the room and she had caught up with him and stood beside him.

Hector had never seen such a big man. Tengar looked like the seven foot stump of a mora tree trunk with a head planted on top of it. He was broad and thick limbed and when he carried himself from the door to the centre of the room it looked as if he had propelled his mass through space rather than if he had walked the short distance. Elsa was very much at her ease, and her assurance as she looked around only exaggerated Tengar's gaucheness. He didn't belong inside a room unless it was forty feet square and its ceiling was twenty feet high.

"Howdy, Sister. Howdy, Brother Galloway. Howdy, Master Hector," he said, and when he smiled his teeth were as white as the heart of a coconut palm. Elsa echoed his greeting. Hector's eyes made four with hers and he lowered his, for a woman had never looked at him so boldly before.

"This is me woman Elsa," Tengar said with the pride of a boy showing off his first kill after a hunt. Sister, whose age and standing in the village gave her privileges that the young could not assume without causing offence, examined Elsa from head to toe.

"You choose well, boy, the woman look strong of body and strong of mind, but you mustn't go away and leave her for long because her heart don't lie easy with waiting and her eye can stray with loneliness. But woman who can lie fallow too long en't no kind of woman at all," Sister said, and she fixed Galloway with a look that forced him to gaze at the ceiling. "All you sit down. Tengar you too tall to stand up like a coconut tree over other people."

Hector turned around suddenly and caught Tojo and Clysis feasting their eyes on what was going on from behind the bamboo curtains.

"So this is Mr. Bradshaw son," Tengar said.

"He's a fine boy," Sister said, "got more brains than any Bradshaw I know ever had, and he got better manners too. Hector come and shake hands, boy. Tengar is a better hunter than his papa and since you love hunting so, en't nobody better can take you about the swamp and the forest. But don't get no idea inside your head that you can go gallivanting about the place when your papa paying out good money for your education, you got to wait until the holidays come around. Your papa got his bad ways but he wants to see you grow up to be a professional man." Hector suspected that this lecture was the prelude to Sister's sending him to bed. He shuffled forward and shook Tengar and Elsa by the hand. Preacher Galloway got up to leave and Hector took the opportunity to slip away and join Tojo and Clysis in the kitchen.

"I tell you Tengar was a giant of a man," Tojo said.

"He's a nice man too," Clysis said, "everytime he come from the bush he does give me sixpence."

Sister called out that it was bedtime. Tojo and Clysis hustled away to their rooms and Hector retired to his reluctantly. He was very distant when Sister came in to say good night. He felt that Sister should have allowed him to stay up. After all, he thought, he had taken sides against his father in the conspiracy and he knew what she and Tengar were going to discuss. He was tempted to eavesdrop after she had left him, but he lay in bed and sulked himself to sleep.

CHAPTER SIX

TIME in Tarlogie was a river trapped at an ox-bow and flowing round and round in circles. The seasons of sunshine and rain were too disorderly for them to be forecast on a calendar. The Tarlogians lived within the seasons of each day since light and darkness alone came in regular cycles. The long intractable seasons – the rainy season and the dry season – had brought disaster so often that they were forgotten as soon as they had passed. Tarlogians lived life by the moment. The past and the future belonged to those who had much and expected much. They had little and their expectations were not great.

The population of the village had neither increased nor decreased since slavery was abolished. Many children were born but few survived more than six years. Sickness was accepted in the same way that drought and flood were. Years of hardship had taught the villagers that empty lamentations to heaven were a waste of breath, that silence or laughter were better foils against calamity.

★   ★   ★

At thirteen, Hector was tall for his age and had all the awkwardness of a boy who had grown too quickly. The sun and wind and salt water had given him a dark reddish brown tan. He had put on over a stone during his last summer holiday but he still looked scrawny and rawboned. Apart from the contrast of his man's height and his baby face you would hardly have noticed him in a crowd. He was shy and stiff about the house, even with Sister, whom he loved. Most of his spare time was spent reading in a corner of the veranda or going out on lone expeditions across the swamps.

"He's a quiet one," Sister had complained to Preacher Galloway. "Lord knows there never was a Bradshaw who like books like this boy, and the thoughts that knocking together inside his head, he don't share with nobody, not even me. Yes, he's a quiet one our Hector is, quiet and deep, but you see him there looking like butter can't melt in he mouth, he got the fury of a tiger in his heart. One day Tojo get beside himself and tell him something hurtful, and to tell you the truth if I wasn't there he would 'ave massacre poor Tojo. If he en't got nothing else he got the Bradshaw temper, I can tell you that."

Four years in Tarlogie had defined a number of relationships for Hector. His relationship with Sister, with his teacher, with Tojo and Clysis, with Doorne, Tengar and Elsa. Growing up from childhood into adolescence, he had become conscious of his wealth and privileges. He was master of the village. Sister had never let him forget this. Left to himself he would not have cared, but she was very strict on protocol. A peasant woman who had left the fields and secured an uneasy foothold in a big-house, she had her own status in the village to maintain. In a community perched on the edge of swamps and forests, a place absorbed in the direct struggle of man against nature, it was difficult for anyone to uphold rigid social distinctions. The cycles of drought and flood affected all. But within the limits that these natural disasters imposed, Hector was brought up as the young master of Tarlogie. When he and Sister attended service on Sundays they sat on cushions in the front pew. The rest of the pew remained empty. Even on Harvest Sunday when the aisles were crowded with standing worshippers this rule was never broken.

Sister's prejudices were a part of her strength. Underneath the naked struggle to exist in the village there were insidious currents constantly threatening to overwhelm her. It was easy to give up and live in the mud and the flotsam. Sister had broken away from the undercurrents, and to protect herself from being sucked downwards again, she needed a small, guarded enclosure in which she could live.

The same conditions had forced the Bradshaw clan to dress with elaborate care, to build their house like a feudal castle, to cling fiercely to outmoded customs. The men and women of this clan had done these things by instinct rather than by design, theirs was an unconscious fight to preserve some vestige of human dignity in the face of chaos.

Hector fell in with Sister's ideas. Above everything else he liked to be left alone to read or wander about the swamps and reefs as he pleased. When Sister suggested that he stop "wrapping up too close" with this or that boy or girl in the village he would not object. If treating most of the villagers with a certain aloofness saved him from long sessions of scolding at home, he was quite willing to make the compromise. Moreover, hardly anyone in Tarlogie resented his attitude for it was expected of him that he should act like the master of the village. Had he done otherwise the villagers would have chummed up with him when it suited them and laughed at him behind his back. As things stood he enjoyed a great deal of freedom and in his withdrawn and reserved fashion was happy.

Thanks to Laljee, Fitz Bradshaw had left the Doorne family in peace. Laljee's oriental breadth of vision enabled him to regard his master's interests and his own as one. His livelihood depended on Fitz being in good health and since a regular paramour was as necessary to his master as food and drink, he had cunningly procured one. He knew that Fitz was not a vindictive man by nature, and that he would forget about Elsa if a juicy substitute could be provided. He had therefore ensured his own continued well being by discovering a robust seventeen year old Amerindian girl named Dela and installed her in the Kitty house a fortnight after Elsa had left. Dela had come to the city from a village in the high savannahs. When Laljee approached her, she had agreed to become his master's concubine without any fuss. For months she had been on the loose, drifting from one brothel to the other and being robbed by both her clients and her experienced competitors. The idea of a steady allowance and free accommodation appealed to her. Laljee had presented his master's case with much overstatement, stressing that he was as rich as the Governor, more potent than any Amerindian brave, a stern but benevolent protector, that a mere child like Dela would only destroy herself rivalling the seasoned brothel vultures. What Dela thought of Fitz the first night he presented himself no one will ever know for she had the disciplined inscrutability of her people. She offered up her young succulent limbs and when Fitz was satisfied, asked whether she could send for her brother to keep her company. Fitz agreed. It turned out that the brother was much older than he had expected and he never discovered if the smiling moon-faced brown man was brother or husband. If he was her husband then he was certainly the most discreet spouse Fitz had ever come across. Sometimes when he dropped in unexpectedly he would hear Dela and her "brother" chatting loudly in their Arawak language but by the time he entered the house, there would be no trace of the man. Fitz never even found out what his name was, for Dela was very clever at not understanding a word of English when it suited her.

Once the matter was settled, Laljee asked for an increase in salary and Fitz gave him an extra three dollars a month.

★   ★   ★

Elsa had shed her veneer of city habits like a lizard changing its skin. She had reverted to being a peasant woman in a matter of weeks – working in the ricefields, fetching firewood from the foreshore, helping Tengar to build a new hut on Chinaman's land at Maiden's Head, carting ground provisions to the Port Mourant market. The change made her more attractive, more vital. She became plumper, stronger and the sun gave her skin a dark sheen.

Hector visited them often in the new hut Tengar had built on his way to and from the beach. When he was twelve, Sister had allowed him to hunt with his grandfather's double-barrelled Stevens, a beautiful sixteen-bore shotgun with a hand-carved oaken stock and long blue-steel barrels. Tengar and Doorne had trained him to use it with Sister looking on.

"You en't going to be no kind of hunter 'til you can hold that gun to you shoulder with one hand and fire it," Tengar had said the first time Hector had handled it. But the recoil had knocked him flat on his back. Doorne had then taken him in hand. The old man had bought a thick length of rope, tied it to a branch at the top of a tamarind tree and suspended it down to the ground.

"When you can mount to the top of that tree, hand over hand on the rope, not using you foot at all, then you will begin to be strong enough to handle that gun, Master Hector," Doorne had said.

Tojo was able to climb up the rope with ease. Hector was a weakling compared to most of the country boys of his age. He had to subject mind and muscles to months of training and discipline before he could perform feats that others did easily, but once he succeeded he outshone even the older boys.

Sister hovered around like a mother condor guarding a sickly chick. The boy was hardly ever conscious of her solicitude for she left him alone as much as possible, but she never allowed anyone to crush his hypersensitive spirit. She was always warning Doorne and Tojo not to laugh too much at his failures. There were long spells when he sulked and brooded and touched her heart with the hurt and hopelessness in his eyes. She got him out of these melancholy moods by acting as if she was unaware of his self-pity. When she felt that he had indulged too much in this, the pastime he enjoyed most, she would suddenly appeal to his vanity and pride – praise him for something he had done. It worked wonderfully. He would sulk for a while longer and suddenly his mood would change. His big brown eyes would flash with laughter and he would boast about his hunting exploits. Most of his stories were a mixture of fact and fiction. He garnered them from his own imagination, the books he had read and the tales Doorne and Tengar had told him.

After five months of training Hector was able to climb up the rope. He had gone to the beach every afternoon when his lessons were over and staggered back across the swamps with a log on his shoulder. The beach was deserted in the late afternoon and he was able to run and swim, cut down courida trees and do handstands before he set out for home. The day he ran to Doorne shouting how he had mounted up the rope, the old man had asked:

"How many time you do it?"

"Once!" he shouted. "Right up to the top. You can come and see for yourself."

"One time en't enough, Master Hector. You got to do it at least six times, I en't only thinking 'bout you handling the gun, what I got in mind is the day when we got to go to Black Bush hunting."

"I'm ready to go now, Doorne, you just try me out."

"You en't quite ready yet, Master Hector, is twelve mile of swamp 'twix here and Black Bush, the worse-est swamp God ever make, and once you get midway en't no use bawling to heaven 'cause all that's there is swamp and sun and the blue horizon."

It had taken Hector a year to climb up the rope six times. Now he was ready for the trip to Black Bush and Doorne said that he would take him there during his summer holidays.

★　　★　　★

The villagers could tell the time by La Rose's comings and goings. He was even more reliable than Boysie's bus. He arrived at the big house at eight in the mornings and left at four p.m. After four years the teacher was wearing the same grey felt hat, stained above the band with patches of oil and sweat, the same ill-fitting white drill suit with his bony wrists sticking far out of the sleeves, riding the same ancient bicycle with its twenty-six inch frame, big cracked leather saddle and fat tyres, bringing his lunch in a saucepan and eating it under the front porch, delivering his lectures in a laboured, precisely inflected voice and never permitting Hector to break out of the teacher-student relationship he had established on the first day.

La Rose was very good at teaching mathematics, history, scripture and geography but he had no feeling for literature and languages. During the four years, in addition to instructing Hector, he had taken and passed the Cambridge School Certificate and the Second Class Teacher's examination, and he was planning that by the time Hector matriculated, he would have passed his First Class and be eligible for a schoolmaster's job.

One morning they were discussing Keats's 'Ode to a Grecian Urn' during an English literature lesson. La Rose was looking at his pupil across the big square table at which they worked. He leaned back in his chair and sucked in his cheeks before he spoke. Hector knew that that was a sign that he didn't approve of his comments on Keats.

"You said here, Hector, that the words sound like poetry but you can't imagine why a man should write a poem about an urn. Now tell me, what's an urn?" He leaned forward and puffed his cheeks out.

"It's something like the water jars our women carry on their heads, Mr. La Rose."

"Good. And is the poem about an urn?"

"About two figures on the urn, a man and a woman who never grow old. How can they grow old anyhow if they're just paintings on the urn?"

"This is one of the masterpieces of English poetry and if you're asked about it in an examination that's what you're supposed to say."

"Why, Mr. La Rose? Why is it a masterpiece? Just because a stranger-man says so in a book? Sister says that sometimes when people write poetry they have moon-madness."

"It's a masterpiece because the metre is right, the rhyme is right. The whole thing from beginning to end..." La Rose ran out of words. This was the first time that Hector had questioned one of his statements openly. He was the teacher and he was supposed to relay to his pupil what was written in the text. The text had said that the 'Ode to a Grecian Urn' was a masterpiece. The man who had compiled the *Collected Modern Poems* was a white professor steeped in all the mysteries of English Literature. Hector might be a rich man's son but he wasn't white. How could he ever question the dictum of a white professor? If he encouraged the boy in this kind of rebellion he would never get through his examination. 'The 'Ode to a Grecian Urn' *is* a masterpiece Hector, there's no question about it."

"But why, Mr. La Rose?"

"Why don't parallel straight lines ever meet? Tell me that?"

"You still haven't answered me, Mr. La Rose. You still haven't told me why it's a masterpiece. I don't believe it is. I think it's just a silly old poem."

La Rose pushed his chair back, got up and walked to the window. A donkey cart was bumping along the public road with clay pots full of water and behind it women were carrying earthenware jars on their heads. La Rose massaged the top of his head with his fingers, turned around suddenly and rejoined Hector.

"We'll be doing the History of the British Empire next period," he said curtly, and Hector knew that he had won a victory. The teacher could explain all of Euclid's theorems to him but he didn't know why the 'Ode to a Grecian Urn' was a masterpiece.

Tengar's new hut had taken two months to build. He could not stand upright in the old one without knocking his head on the rafters and disturbing the marabuntas that were nesting there. He had cut all the timber he needed from the forest near Honey Reef on the eastern boundary of Fitz Bradshaw's land. When the logs had been squared and cut to size, he had hired Chinaman's team of oxen and hauled them across the swamp to Maiden's Head, a barren, sandy reef. He and Elsa had planted courida trees to fence their yard in and to act as windbreakers. The swamp water around Maiden's Head was salty, viscous and stagnant and it had satu-rated the sand and clay of the reef making it impossible for anything to grow there but clumps of tough buffalo grass and couridas. It was a good spot for a hunter like Tengar to occupy for flocks of cranes, gaulins, ducklas, pikers and curlews were always grazing close by.

Hector had helped him to transport his building materials. In the afternoons, after his lessons were finished, he hurried down to the koker opposite the police station where his canoe was moored and poled swiftly up the straight canal until he came to the forest. He would then listen in the silence for the sharp explosions of Tengar's axe and sing out:

"Hal-o-o-o-!" and Tengar would answer without breaking the rhythm of his strokes. He always found the giant naked to the waist, his torso glistening with sweat, his axe blade flashing. The wonder he had felt watching Tengar's muscles coil and uncoil like lianas with springs in them, never left him.

"Tengar, you think one day I will grow muscles like you?" he asked.

"I en't see why not, Master Hector, when I was you age I was same way scrawny. Lord! You could 'ave pour a pint of water in the hollows at the bottom of me neck and not notice it. . . and besides they tell me you' grandpa was a Sampson of a man when he was young."

"But I eat plenty and do a lot of exercising and still I don't see any difference."

"You got to wait 'til Nature good and ready to paste the muscles on to you' frame, Master Hector." This made Hector believe that he would suddenly wake up one morning and find muscles bulging all over him.

"I wish it would happen soon."

"Take it slow, Young Master, you thin and supple, so why you want to go and carry 'round a lot of weight with you? Anyhow, you getting book learning and you don't need muscle to read the white man books. Folks like me need muscle-power to stay alive but you don't never need to have it."

When the halter was fastened on the buffalo's necks and the logs tied together and roped on to the halter, Hector would haul his canoe over the embankment separating the canal from the swamps. Towing his canoe behind him through mud and water that reached up to his knees, he and Tengar took turns to crack long whips over the heads of the straining beasts. Once a boa constrictor disturbed in its nest of bisi-bisi reeds had coiled around the belly of one of the buffaloes. The animal had plunged forward frantically bellowing with fear and pain. Tengar had whipped out his cutlass and sent the boa's head flying with a neat flick of his wrist. The tension in the coils snapped and the snake fell back into the water threshing about fitfully.

"We got to look out for the mate," Tengar had said, "these snake does walk about in pairs." Two days later the mate made a pass at him when he was crossing the swamp and he killed it.

Hector had learnt from Doorne and Tengar that only the small poisonous snakes like the labaria were really dangerous. The big ones gave off a strong putrid odour that you could smell twenty or thirty yards away and you could kill them by breaking their backs with a stick or pouncing swiftly and chopping their heads off. With the medium sized ones you could seize them just below the head and snap their spines like dry twigs.

One morning Hector was poling his canoe close to the right bank of the canal when a huge boa tumbled out of an overhanging coconut tree and fell at his feet. The violent writhings of the snake overturned the canoe and a blow from the powerful tail almost knocked him unconscious. He had clung to the canoe expecting to feel the snake's coils tightening around him. His cutlass was at the bottom of the canal and he could not defend himself, but the boa was as frightened as he was and it streaked across the twenty feet of water and disappeared.

★   ★   ★

Doorne would have nothing to do with his daughter-in-law. Tengar had made several efforts to bring them together. He could not understand the old man's attitude and one day he asked Elsa:

"Why you think the old man got it in for you, gal? He never set foot on this reef since that day you meet he in the rum-shop. That old man heart is a close place with all kind of thing lock up in it that only he and Jesus know 'bout."

"Don't ask me, ask him."

"Just as I touch on the subject he does get lockjaw. I know him long and I know he got peculiar ways, he does carry grudgefulness in he blood but I never see he bear grudge 'gainst nobody the way he bearing it for you."

"I know he nursing grudge 'gainst me but I en't losing no sleep over it."

Tengar had never understood his father. The old man was too secretive, too quick to bear malice. Tengar's mother had walked out when he was seven years old but he remembered her clearly – a tall, black woman with big ripe breasts and the shoulders and arms of a woodcutter. She had had a way of throwing back her head and laughing so that he could see all of her even white teeth and a part of the pink roof of her mouth. She had been born in a Georgetown slum and although she had the body of a peasant woman, hers were the quick, nervous movements peculiar to the city. She had appeared to be robust but she could not stand heavy manual work. He and Caya had often worked with her in the ricefields and by high-noon she would be complaining about the weight of the sun on her back, and when they returned home in the evenings she would strip to the waist and stretch out on the mud floor, and he and his brother would pour coconut oil on her chest, stomach and back and massage the aches out of her weary body with their bare feet.

Tengar remembered the night she had left Tarlogie. His father had been out sporting in Kiltearn Village and had come in drunk. Without any warning she had jumped on him and sunk her teeth

83

into his shoulder. His father had forced her jaws open and pushed her away, and for a long time he stood petrified, watching the blood trickle down his arm. Tengar had rushed out of the hut to call the neighbours.

He returned with a crowd of excited men and women who from the story he had babbled out, had come to stop Doorne from murdering his mother. When they burst into the hut, Doorne had left and his mother was tying up her belongings in a cotton sheet. She was crying and her lamentations were more heart-rending than the songs at a wake.

"Lord Jesus, look down on a poor black mother! 'Cause even You when You was on the cross didn't have to bear the strain I bear with this man! And don't vex with me, Lord, if me leave me two boys to the mercy of this devil-man! 'Cause me body weary and me spirit aching me and what going out of this door is the shadow of what come in. I love me pickny-children, Lord, but I can't take them with me 'cause the sky will be the only roof over me head! And as for that black devil-man all me can say 'bout he is Lord have mercy on he, 'til he learn to have mercy on heself and them around he, them closer to he than the hair on he head and the water in he eye!"

Tengar remembered every word, every move – his mother's eyes red as if swamp flies had stung them, her lips swollen and her hands moving jerkily as they tied the knot on her bundle. The neighbours had tried to dissuade her from going.

"Stay overnight, Sister Vivian! Don't go like this in haste. By the time morning come you will feel different and the sorrow in you' belly will ease." But she would not change her mind and would not be comforted. She had snatched Tengar to her and pressed him against her bosom until he cried out.

"Don't grow up to curse you' old mother, chile! Don't grow up to heap blame on my grave for walking out on all you!" She had left and Tengar had watched a candle sputtering in a corner of the hut and cried himself to sleep. When he woke up next morning, he knew that his whole life had changed. In the months that followed, Doorne had come and gone leaving him to fend for himself and for Caya, who, though older than he was, was a cry-baby of a boy. Caya would sit in the hut and whine and snivel from hunger whilst he went out and begged for food or sold his labour. He had a wild beast's cunning and an instinct for survival which he had inherited from slave ancestors who had scrounged around for morsels and kept their race alive on crumbs that dogs would have spurned. He had not understood his father at the time his mother walked out and, if anything, he understood him less now.

To some it might have seemed extraordinary that Tengar and Caya had grown to manhood at all. But their story was the story of half the youths on the coast. Usually it was the father and not the mother who abandoned the family. The women generally had the strength, the resilience, the enduring sense of calm to hold their families together and to will their sickly, starving children to live. The womb of every mother on the coast was an archive which housed the memory of a black race, a memory snatched from dark and lost centuries.

Tengar had grown up feeling no malice towards father or mother. Each had acted according to the rules imposed by an implacable nature, an environment ruled by a cruel sun that crawled up and down a hard blue sky, staining the bitter earth with blobs of shadow, lengthening the shadows at sunset and reappearing at day-clean to begin its secret game once more. Tengar did not know of any other people who lived under the crawling sun by any other set of rules and so he laid no blame at his parents' doorstep. Blame is borne out of comparison – one man's actions judged against another's. Tengar accepted what had happened as fate. For him fate was a blind beggar staring at a pitiless sun.

* * *

Hector poled his canoe towards the foreshore late one afternoon. Sister had grumbled that he would be late for dinner. He had insisted on having his way because Tengar had promised to join him. It was springtide. The sea would be right up to the roots of the courida trees that bordered on the beach and from the cover of the trees they could take flying shots at crookbills and geese as they flew low over the bursting surf. Strong gusts of wind were buffeting him as he poled across the open swamp and he had to crouch low.

A purple afterglow rimmed the dark silhouette of courida trees that curved around the horizon ahead of him. There was something ghostly and exciting about the late afternoons in Tarlogie. The wind felt moist, oleous and the surf sounded like a fanfare echoing inside a cave. The darkening sky was always filled with flocks of herons, ducks and cranes, boosted on the wind and scattering like black and solid spray.

As Hector's canoe steered through growths of weeds and lotus lilies, solitary birds rose up in noisy flight. Far to his left pale lightnings flickered through breaks in the dark clouds. He saw Tengar standing underneath his hut as he approached Maiden's Head and he called out to him,

"Hallo Tengar, isn't much light for shooting, man!"

"The moon should be out by the time we get to the beach!"

Hector drove his canoe hard up on the sand and sprang out. He took the Stevens out of its oilskin bag and buckled his cartridge belt around his waist. Tengar liked going hunting with Hector. Ely cartridges cost tenpence apiece and the boy always had a generous supply which he didn't mind sharing. He could afford only two to three cartridges a day whilst Hector used a dozen when the lust to kill took hold of him.

If Elsa was at home, there was no sign of her. The hut was in darkness.

"Where's your woman, Tengar?"

"She gone to the shop."

"What's it like to live with a woman, Tengar?" Tengar laughed his rich, booming laugh and said:

"You really turning into a big man these days, Master Hector. That's a proper difficult question you ask me. All I can tell you is that living with a mopsy is like walking 'cross a swamp full of alligators, you might get through with couple bite; you might even get through without nothing happening at all; on the other hand you might end up piecemeal in some alligator stomach."

"What I don't understand is why men have to live with women at all."

"Don't worry, Master Hector, the day will soon come when you will understand that and more. You come from a breed of man who if they hear the swish-swishing of a woman skirt in they sleep, they will jump up and make a grab. We better make it for the beach bird-speed or won't be nothing to shoot time we get there."

They set out at a fast pace. Doorne had taught Hector to walk through the swamps and after years of training he could do so adeptly, his toe pointing downwards so as not to splash up water when his foot broke the surface, his body bent forward so as to give himself extra thrust, his legs slightly apart so that his feet would not get stuck together in the mud.

The moon edged its way above the clouds, a huge yellow moon which brightened as it rose higher. Half a mile from the beach the sea sounded very close. The surf was booming like massed cannon and they could hear the waves scraping up and down the sloping arc of sand and pebbles. The last stretch of swamp was a black, saline ooze which decaying tree trunks and pot holes made treacherous. At every step clouds of mosquitoes attacked them, buzzing angrily, covering every inch of exposed skin. They swished branches in front of their faces to prevent the insects from flying up their nostrils. Tengar moved into the lead since the sling-mud in some of the pot-holes could suck the uninitiated down in a few minutes. Hector never took this route when he was on his own. Every now and then Tengar, with a hand over his mouth, called out to him to veer to the right or to the left. Tengar's voice and the noise of their footsteps frightened sleeping birds in the trees that towered over them and occasionally they heard a startled puling or the raucous cry of a quack. They quickened their pace when they caught a glimpse of golden sand in the bright glare of the moon. With the swamp and the trees behind them, Hector stood on the wet sand and it was good to feel the moonlight in his eyes and the cleansing wind brushing the mosquitoes from off his body. He waited for a rush of oncoming surf and ran towards it whooping.

"You still got you cartridge belt on!" Tengar shouted. Hector turned back and hung the belt on a low branch just above the guns. "Lawd, Master Hector, you wild eh! You and the sea same way wild."

"I'll race you, Tengar!"

"Come on then!" Tengar was as fast as an ocelot on his feet

and he left Hector ten yards behind him. The muddy salt water washed away the dry, musty smell the mosquitoes had left on their bodies. Hector was a good swimmer and he kept abreast of Tengar who used brute-strength to thump his way through the waves. They swam close to the shore. It was the queriman season and the sea was infested with sharks. When they were tired they returned to the shadows under the trees. Hector was glad that Tengar had come with him. Big-Tengar, on occasions like this, could share his boyish games, his laughter, his exuberant small-talk. In spirit, they were boys together enjoying their freedom from women. There was an endearing quality of gentleness about Tengar, a simplicity which only those with superhuman strength seem to possess. Tengar knew that some day his master's son would grow apart from him. Book learning and a consciousness of social difference would create a widening chasm between them. Sometimes the thought saddened him. Elsa was always harping on this theme, saying that "them kind of folks does only wrap up with you when it suit them, then they does cast you aside and turn up they nose when they meet you in the street." Tengar defended Hector by saying: "Look how he love Sister, she is an ordinary village woman and yet the boy love she more than if she was a queen."

"Just wait 'til he grow up and start to smell he sweat," she had said, "wait 'til he got to show Sister to he high-and-mighty friends, will be a different story then."

The two crouched in the shadows, loaded and cocked their guns. A pair of sea geese was approaching from the west.

"They flying too high," Tengar said and Hector watched the birds' wide wings flashing under the moon. Tengar made a honking noise out of the corner of his mouth. The geese went into a dive and levelled off.

"Take the inside one," Tengar said, "follow it with you barrel and aim a foot in front." Hector aimed and held his breath. They fired in quick succession and the birds plummeted down. One hit the sand and lay still but the other started flapping its wings and hopping towards the sea. Tengar was after it like a streak of arrow. He caught it as it hit the water and wrung its neck. Hector retrieved the other bird and waited for Tengar.

"Is thirty pound of meat we got here," Tengar said; "they got a powerful rankness 'bout them, but if you season them good there en't nothing sweeter in a curry."

"Wait 'til Sister sees this, she's going to put her hands on her head and bawl! It's the biggest bird I ever shot, and it was a flying shot too! Just wait 'til she sees it!"

"You think you can make it back through the swamp, Master Hector?"

"You will ask that? Come on, Tengar, let's go!"

In his eagerness to show off his bag to Sister, Tojo and Clysis, Hector forgot about the mosquitoes and the sling mud. He slipped and stumbled and almost fell down several times. He reached Maiden's Head panting, spattered with mud but jubilant. When he arrived home, Sister scolded him for trailing mud and water across her clean living-room floor but Tojo and Clysis regarded the goose admiringly and he was pleased.

"Boy, is what I going do with you?" Sister said. "You growing up like a regular savage. Just because you kill an old bird you come home acting like you do something great. You better buckle down to your book work, that is more important."

CHAPTER SEVEN

ON the first Sunday of every month, Reverend Grimes, the white minister from New Amsterdam came to Tarlogie to preach in the Congregational Church. This occasioned much activity amongst the Godly in the days immediately before he arrived. Preacher Galloway was conspicuous in the hum of preparation, doing very little himself, but somehow giving the impression that but for him, Tarlogie would disgrace itself in the eyes of the white parson. On Saturday he directed the washing and scrubbing of the church floor, the polishing of the pews and the arrangement of the flowers around the base of the pulpit and along the mahogany rails of the altar.

The churchgoers in Tarlogie were a class apart. They were drawn mainly from those who could afford to buy shoes and who could endure the pinch of shoe leather for three hours on Sundays. Tarlogians had broad feet. Their toes had grown strong and spread wide in order to grip the muddy earth and shoe manufacturers in England had not been advised on their special needs by the agents in the city. To be able to buy and to wear a pair of shoes was a mark of social distinction in the village. During the week everyone walked around barefooted, even Hector, the master of the village, for shoes were an unnecessary encumbrance in the swamps. But on Sundays and festive days, the shoe made the man.

Tengar was a regular churchgoer, whilst Elsa was not. He had tried a number of inducements to get her to accompany him at first but she would regale him with stories about the parsons she had met in the Georgetown brothels and the innocent girls they had befuddled and seduced in their parishes, until he retreated with his hands pressed to his ears. Sunday, for her, was a boring day which made her restless and sent her mind harking back to her free-and-easy life in the city. A part of her resented her man leaving her alone while he enjoyed an experience she had refused to share. She would have liked to tear apart and destroy the need in Tengar for hymn singing, praying to a white man's God and making a fetish out of a book that white strangers had written to confuse black people. Her religion was centred around her body and its appetites. She had no other.

In order to work himself up into the right mood, Tengar started out his Sundays singing hymns in a powerful bass voice. This annoyed Elsa so much that she would gather up her washing, take it to the far end of Maiden's Head and leave him to prepare his own breakfast. In the wet season when the thought of ruining his "dry goods" (his serge suit and black shoes) in the rain was too much for him, he would stay at home and Elsa would taunt and jeer whilst underneath it all she would be pleased to have her man at home with her for the whole day.

The first Sunday in June was hot and windless. Tengar woke up early to start his preparations for the ten o'clock service. Elsa flounced out of the hut with her washing. He breakfasted on mangoes, a large papaya and a loaf of dry bread which he washed down with two quarts of milk. He sat on his doorstep for a while, scratching his bare stomach, chewing a blacksage stem and occasionally breaking into song. Tengar could relax for hours with his mind in a state of pleasant vacuousness. He had spent much of his adult life alone in the forests and had cultivated the habit of shedding the burden of thought and yet feeling good within himself. After a while he looked at the sun and stood up. It was time to get dressed. He called out to Elsa when he was ready to leave for church, wanting her to admire him in his Sunday best, but she ignored him deliberately. He had tied the laces of his shoes together and slung them over his shoulder. He would put them on once he had poled his coreal out to the public road. His serge suit looked as if it had been poured like hot latex over the bulging muscles of his chest, shoulders, back and buttocks and he dared not button up the jacket.

★   ★   ★

91

Hector did not like going to church. On weekdays Sister allowed him to wear swimming trunks when he was going hunting and for his classes with La Rose he wore a cotton shirt, shorts, long socks and shoes. But on Sundays he had to wear a felt hat, a serge suit, a shirt with a starched collar and a tie. He always felt like a dressed up dummy and was conscious of being on show. He had tried many ruses to escape this ordeal, pretending to be ill, claiming that he had to study, suddenly announcing to Sister at table that he did not believe in God and calling down her wrath on his head for weeks, but the old lady was wily and adamant. She had let him off once or twice but never on first Sundays.

He had never managed to establish contact with the white minister. The man meshed him around with platitudes as soon as he opened his mouth to say anything to him. The only reason why he respected the Reverend Grimes was that once, after hearing him preach about hell fires burning up the wicked, he had had nightmares for months.

The Godless ones in the village, like Caya, claimed that old Grimes liked to knock back the bottle, that it wasn't the sun alone that rouged his face. Caya had said that the Reverend kept a bottle of rum hidden away in a corner of the pulpit, and when he knelt down to pray he would take a swig to oil his throat for the sermon.

The walk from Hector's house to the church was about half a mile and before he had covered the distance he could feel the perspiration flowing from under his arms, running down the groove of his back and causing his shirt to stick to his skin. He walked slowly beside Sister. She seldom went out but when she did decide to, she spent hours over her toilet, preening herself like a young girl before her speckled mirror, patting her frock into place, combing, brushing and plaiting her hair, powdering her face and manicuring her fingernails. The powder she used had a musty aromatic smell and was meant to be used on fairer complexions so that when she daubed it on it looked as if flour had been sprinkled on her opaque, black skin. White was her Sunday colour and she wore a tight pleated bodice with a lace collar, a long billowing skirt and black boots that reached just below her knees. On her head was perched a rimless, shallow hat made of organdie and artificial roses and this unique piece of head-wear looked like a pile of crushed tiger-beard orchids. She walked with short, firm steps, holding a Japanese parasol firmly above her head and carrying herself with the poise of a young woman with a pail on her head.

The villagers without shoes, men and women, sat on their doorsteps dallying away the hours and swapping gossip. Now and then they shouted at their naked children playing in the yards amidst pigs, sheep, goats and chickens. They interrupted their gossiping to call out greetings to Sister and Hector.

"Howdy, Sister!"

"Howdy, Master Hector! You growing up into a fine young man, just like you' grandpa!"

Sister acknowledged the greetings with stiff nods, never turning her head to the right or the left.

Other Godless ones lay in hammocks slung across bottom house beams or the low branches of trees in their yards, rocking gently while they tapped out rhythms on drums, strummed guitars or struck up tunes on their harmonicas. No one worked in the ricefields or on the provision farms on Sunday except the East Indians who fished and farmed as usual.

As Sister and her ward walked to church, the conversations rippled up and down the village:

"Dookia's cow break down the fence around Preacher Galloway garden and eat up all he young cassava. . . they say the preacher taking she to court for it. . . ." The mid-morning sun burnt fiercely over Tarlogie and the many tramping, shuffling feet on their way to service left puffs of dust in their wake. The church bell rang with a sharp clangour, mingling its peal with the rhythms of drums, concertinas, guitars and tongues clacking:

"You see Tengar pass by? Lord! He's a nice man, eh? . . . Me don't trust that Elsa though, she is a tricky woman if there ever was one. . . She got he like a fish in a duckla belly. . . You hear what happen to the white overseer at Port Mourant? No, tell me, gal. . . Well the story come to me like this: He make heself fast and take up with a coolie-man daughter, had the girl with she leg up in the air in the canefield. And what you think happen? The coolie-man catch them an' he run and call all he folks together and they march the white-man all the way down to the public road, naked like the day he born, and all the way from the back dam, they beat drum behind the white-man and make he dance, prodding he with cutlass everytime he want to stop. . . Lord! Must 'ave been a sight to see, eh?. . . They say the new Governor is a man who like the bottle; Freddie sister's cousin chauffeuring for he and he tell say that the Governor always more drunk than sober. . . Well, chile, is not so the great ones stay, then is the 'powers and the principalities' that the Good Book talk 'bout, but what is we to do, we the poor black ones? The day borned the Governor and his kind and midnight borned we."

The avenue of eyes hemming Hector in with their bemused, friendly scrutiny made him feel more uncomfortable than the heat did. If he had been alone he would have run all the way to the church.

⋆　　⋆　　⋆

Caya spent Sundays on the veranda of Chinaman's rum-shop, practising on his drums, eating, drinking and gaffing. He was the best drummer-man in the village and this entitled him to preside over the many fetes that were held. The more respectable Tarlogians would have told you that the Harvest Festival was the most important event of the year but this was not true, for the wind-dance was what the villagers looked forward to most. This was an illegal ritual dance which had come down from the slave days. It was generally condemned and universally attended. People like Sister and Preacher Galloway were savage in their denunciation of this pagan dance and described it as "going back to Africa". The time for the wind-dance was approaching and Caya, the "high priest" of this fête was storing up stocks of bush rum and getting his hand in with his drums. No one really knew how Caya was able to live as well as he did without working. In a village where secrets were harder to hold on to than money, he managed to guard his. It was whispered that he and his father had a rum still in the forest near Honey Reef, that he bought off Mark-a-book and his subordinates at the police station with regular supplies of illicit bush rum, that he and Chinaman worked hand in glove, but there was never any evidence to support the whispers. Caya lazed away most of his days on the rum-shop bridge and at nights he retreated to his hut on the edge of the swamps.

His hut was avoided by all, because his neighbour was Batista, the obeah-man and he had spread word that Batista had drawn a ring of fire around his dwelling and to come too close was to call down disaster. Those in trouble and seeking advice could consult him during his drinking hours but once he had retired for the night, only his women friends (of whom he had many) were permitted to slip across Batista's obeah ring.

When Caya had called out his greeting to Hector and Sister, Hector had waved to him but Sister had kept her head straight. She did not approve of Caya. He was a no-good drunkard, a corrupter of the young, a sweet-skinned rascal who was content to lazy away his time from can-see to can't-see time day after day.

A group of gaffers gathered around Caya as soon as he positioned himself for his Sunday activities. He squatted down with a drum between his legs and began to finger the tight goatskin.

Tojo and Clysis followed Sister at a respectful distance. Tojo flashed Caya a grin but did not dare call out to him. Caya tapped out a message on his drum and Tojo nodded.

Reverend Grimes was late and by the time he arrived Preacher Galloway had started the service and was reading the First Lesson from the Book of Psalms: "Purge me with hyssop and I shall be clean, wash me and I shall be whiter than snow. . ." Bull Mackenzie, a teacher from the neighbouring village of Kiltearn, was making a great drama out of playing the harmonium during the hymn-singing. It was more entertaining to look at his antics than to listen to the music. He swayed, tossed back his head, see-sawed on the pedals and ran his fingers up and down the keys with plenty of flourishes. Old man Doorne said that Bull Mackenzie played the harmonium according to the Bible so that his right hand did not know what his left hand was doing.

Preacher Galloway was disappointed when he saw Reverend Grimes arrive because he had been hoping for years to preach on a First Sunday. He descended from the altar and took up his seat on the pew behind Sister's with a martyred dignity. Reverend Grimes looked old and tired and Hector noticed that the crow's feet at the corners of his eyes had multiplied and crinkled deeper since he last saw him. He was wearing a black three-piece suit, and apart from the cock's comb flush on his face and his inflamed eye balls, did not seem to mind the heat. It was as though the sun had already dried up all the sweat in him. The parson climbed up to the pulpit which had been carved out of a solid block of leopard wood, said a short, silent prayer and continued the service. The tall, narrow windows that ran the length of both sides of the church were open wide and the wind blew in, bringing the smell of swamp water with it. The parson chose as his text: "Yea, though I walk through the valley of the shadow of death, I will fear no evil. . ." Hector, struggling to keep awake, heard snatches of the sermon, and Sister nudged him repeatedly.

The parson's voice was clear, pompous, practised in the science of droning out sermons:

"It is over a century since my forebears brought your ancestors up from slavery into the fold of Christ, brought them from the dark place, the valley of the shadow, away from the iniquities of false gods and animistic cults towards the eternal light. . ." Sister murmured a quiet "Ahmen", and nudged Hector.

"Our Father's House has many mansions but some are empty, waiting for the pagan souls that dwell in this village. I am told," the parson paused to let his eyes search the row upon row of dark faces before him, "I am told that something called the wind-dance is still practised in Tarlogie, and I must tell you that this is an evil thing, a harking back to the valley of the shadow which your ancestors left a century ago. . . ."

Caya was beating out a fast one-three rhythm on his drum and its echoes drifted in to mock the parson. Caya found more solace in a drumbeat than he did in church bells and the holy words that rolled off the parson's tongue. The wind-dance was a link with Africa. His ancestors had been hauled out of this continent and scattered over a hemisphere. They had arrived naked and empty-handed, bringing nothing with them but their memories. But wherever a man wanders he will find the neighbour-wind, the companion-wind, the messenger-wind howling its welcome, fanning awake the still leaves, lying down and rolling on the grass and the reeds. Neighbour-wind can live next door to a man who is afraid of the strangeness of an alien land. Companion-wind can strum familiar tunes on the harp-strings of trees. Messenger-wind can carry a cry of anguish across continents and seas. The

96

wind was a symbol of absolute freedom, it was invisible, amorphous, imbued with titanic energies; no stockades could contain it nor could whips and chains humble it. For the descendants of the slaves the meaning and the message of the wind-dance had not changed.

Reverend Grimes mopped his brow and leaned forward with his elbows on the open Bible in front of him:

"The valley of the shadow is in the heart of each and every one of us, brethren, it is where you cradle your pagan longings, but Jesus in his omnipotence sees and knows. . . you must uproot this evil. . . Now!"

★   ★   ★

A small boy came to the big house on Sunday night to say that La Rose was ill and he would not be able to come on the following day.

"Who are you, boy?" Sister asked.

"I am the teacher's brother, Mistress," the thin black boy said, keeping his eyes on his bare feet.

"What happen to your big brother?"

"He take sick all of a sudden, Mistress, and when me mama send for Doc Saunders, the Doc say that he must lie in bed couple days."

"Hector!"

"Yes, Sister."

"You and Tojo must take some fruit and things for the teacher tomorrow morning bright and early."

"All right, Sister," Hector said, thinking that it would be interesting to see his teacher in bed. During the years he had known La Rose he had never thought about him as someone whose visits could be affected by illness. The bony, gangling man had come and gone so regularly day after day that the boy could not conceive of anything but holidays disrupting his routine. He had passed by La Rose's house in Satan Village several times but had never visited him. La Rose was neither friendly nor unfriendly. Their relationship was a neutral one confined to studies. La Rose was being paid by his father to instruct him until he matriculated and the teacher was doing just that.

The small boy, having delivered his message, seemed anxious to go but Sister continued questioning him.

"Is how many of all you in that family, boy?"

"Me big brother and seven of us, Mistress."

"Your mama and papa alive?"

"Me papa dead, Mistress."

"How long since you' papa dead, boy?"

"Six year less three months, Mistress."

"Lord pity your poor ole mama! She got a heavy load to carry with all them mouths to feed. All right, boy, run along now. . .and tell you big brother that Master Hector will be coming 'round to see him tomorrow." Sister settled down in her rocking chair and began mending a pair of Hector's shorts. "I never see a young boy wear out clothes like you, Hector. They got too many poor people on this coast for you to go about ripping up and tearing up everything you wear," she said. She could see him through the bamboo curtains. He was sitting at the dining table reading. "You doing your homework?"

"Yes, Sister." He was reading a Buffalo Bill novelette. La Rose's illness meant that he could postpone doing his set assignments.

"In another two years you will have to pass your matriculation, you will just have to because your aunt won't never let me hear the end of it if you don't. She sitting back there in Georgetown waiting to prove that living in the country behind God's back, with an ignorant black woman as your guardian, was the ruination of your education. She going to push you' two sisters 'til they suffer from brain indigestion to show that she more civilised than me. I does feel that woman maliciousness in me bones so don't let me down, Hector," Sister said. She was in a talking mood and Hector knew that the only way to stop her so that he could continue his reading was to put her on the defensive.

"Why do you think I'll let you down, Sister?"

"I'm not saying that you' going to, boy, because the teacher say that although you lil' bit slow, you got a good brain in your head."

"You think Mr. La Rose will be better soon, Sister?"

"En't no reason why he shouldn't be, he come from good enough stock to stand lil' sickness. Used to know his father in the old days, folks used to call him 'Dutch Axe'."

"Dutch Axe? That's a funny name."

"Dutch axe is a kind of axe that have two blades, so that it can cut both ways."

Hector and Tojo visited La Rose on the following morning. He lived in a cottage which stood about forty yards away from the roadside canal. From the narrow bridge across the canal Hector saw the inverted V of a thatched roof above tree tops. The trees, mango, guinep, cock's comb, cromanty and locust, were stunted. Beyond these were tall coconut palms with drooping fronds. As the two boys approached the cottage a tawny mongrel rushed at them, barking and baring yellow fangs. Tojo put down his basket of fruit and vegetables, snatched up a grapefruit and flung it at the dog. Tojo's aim was practised. For him, pelting dogs or using his catapult on them was a sport. The grapefruit caught the dog on the snout and broke and the juice blinded him. He ran away howling with his tail between his legs. La Rose's mother came out on the front porch smiling.

"I sorry 'bout that dog, Master Bradshaw, but it does act crazy sometimes," she said. She was moon faced, capacious, and her countenance, black and shiny, radiated good humour. "All you come in and watch out for the steps 'cause couple treaders missing. I was always telling me son, Jefferson, to bring you round but he's a peculiar one that son of mine, like to keep himself to himself too much."

La Rose was sitting up in bed with a white handkerchief tied around his forehead.

"Good morning, Mr. La Rose," Hector said, and Tojo chimed in:

"Sister send some things for you, Teacher. . . ."

"And she said that she hopes you'll be better soon," Hector added.

"Sit down, Master Bradshaw," Mrs. La Rose said, drawing a chair close to the wooden bed. There was a strong smell of bay rum and cooked food in the room. Hector felt that he should make conversation but he had never spoken to La Rose outside of classes and he was at a loss for words. Tojo had gone into the kitchen with the basket and he could hear him chatting with one of the teacher's sisters. Mrs. La Rose brought Hector a glass of goat's milk.

"Drink this, Master Bradshaw, 'cause you have a long walk in the hot sun ahead of you," she said, and Hector wondered how this amiable woman could have such a dour son.

La Rose's eyes looked jaundiced and his lips were parched and cracked. He licked them before he spoke.

"Have you done your homework, Hector ?" he asked.

"Chu, Jefferson! Don't talk 'bout homework, the young master come to pay a visit and it en't the right time for talking 'bout things like that."

A naked, bawling child burst into the room and Ma La Rose picked him up and comforted him against her bosom. Hector drank the milk and toyed with the empty glass.

"I was asking you about your homework," La Rose said when the child stopped crying.

"I haven't finished it yet, Mr. La Rose."

"I'll be up and about in a couple of days so you had better have it ready."

"Jefferson La Rose, you en't going be neither up nor about in no coupla days so long as I running this house. Only last night you was next to death's door with you' head hurting and you' stomach pumping out everything that try to settle in it. Rest you weary body, boy, and don't talk no stupidness 'bout upping and abouting, besides the Doc say you must stay in bed for at least a week," Ma La Rose said. She was fond of her eldest son and afraid of his preoccupation with the white man's books. She felt that the books had infected him with a madness that was separating him from his family and the land. In spite of this, however, she was proud of Jefferson. He never had to muddy his hands with field work and the villagers, who regarded learning as a form of magic, treated him with reverence. La Rose's attitude towards his mother was one of remoteness. His experience of sharing the thoughts and ideas of strangers across the seas who had written books was one he could not share with her. At first he had tried to tell his mother about the things he read, about his dreams, his ambitions; she had listened patiently but nothing had registered. She could not relate abstract ideas to the reality of long days of labour, and nights when her body, bruised by the sun, was sluggish and crying out for sleep. His book-knowledge had forced him to live astride two worlds – the world of swamps and forests and wide skies, and the world of the straight lines, the written word, the Faustian conflict. He had tried to link the two but his mind had exhausted itself in the struggle, leaving him with a tenuous foothold in each of the two worlds. Some day he would have to tear himself away from one or the other. He knew this in his heart but he evaded the moment of decision, acquiring more and more diplomas in the meantime.

Looking at his teacher in his rough bed with a frayed spread covering his legs, Hector suddenly felt a kinship with him. He wanted to reach out and touch La Rose's hand and he would have done it if Ma La Rose had not been there.

"I will have the homework ready, Mr. La Rose," he said, getting up to leave.

"I'm glad you came," La Rose said, "and thank Miss Smart for the things she sent." Teacher and pupil looked at each other for a long time until the former added in a matter-of-fact voice, "Try and read up on your geography of Europe, we'll be starting on that as soon as I resume my teaching."

When, by the end of the week, La Rose had not turned up Hector paid him another visit. He found him lying in bed with the same white handkerchief tied around his forehead. His mother kept a bowl of aloes sap at his bedside and every now and then she dipped the handkerchief into it and re-tied it. La Rose's eyes had grown larger in his wan face and they had a wild look in them that bordered on terror.

"Leave Hector and me alone, Mama, I want to talk," he said in a firm voice.

"Don't talk too much, boy, you know how the fever does rack you' body when night-time comes. You better save up you lil' strength," Ma La Rose said, bending momentarily over her son before she turned to Hector. "Lord, Master Bradshaw, me son too sick! The Doc say he had hookworm so long that it weaken he and bring on the fever. I praying to Jesus night and day to make he strong again 'cause he is the apple of me womb, the joy of me ageing heart. In all the years since I birth this boy he never say a rude word to me, and after Mantop come for he papa, he alone been supporting this fam'ly – sending he brothers and sisters to school and lighting up the shadows in his old mother's heart." She walked away sniffing and wiping her eyes with her apron.

There was a detachment about her sorrow. She was like an actress, demanding an audience's sympathy, and once she had extracted it, using it to explore fresh pastures of anguish.

Hector sat down and watched the light from the window behind him making deep hollows under La Rose's cheekbones and turning his face the colour of moss.

"I was hoping you would come around, Hector." With a great effort La Rose turned on his side and faced his pupil, "You did your homework?"

"Yes, Mr. La Rose."

"Good. You know what I've noticed about you in these four years since I've been teaching you?" Hector was confused by the intimacy that was creeping into their relationship and when he did not answer his teacher continued, "You're not bright, and you'll never be bright. . . you're a plodder, with a big, slow mind. . . your mind's like the stomach of an anaconda snake, it can swallow up plenty and then it takes a while for you to digest the meal. You're wondering no doubt why I'm telling you all this, well, I'll tell you, boy: it's because I'm a failure. Jefferson Gladstone La Rose is a tree bark without any trunk to encase. I'll tell you why I'm such a failure. I set my sights too high, wanted to do too much. If I live, and I know I'm going to, at least for a couple morning's longer, I'll keep passing more and more examinations, all the time knowing that I'm a failure. Somewhere back in my small-boy days something got stamped to death inside me, and what it was I myself don't quite know – all I can tell you is that thing that's dead in me is alive in you, and you won't be a failure if you keep it alive. You think I'm mad, eh!" He shot the statement at Hector and the boy squirmed because he was thinking just that. His teacher's burning look and the way he licked his dry lips every now and then terrified him. "The fever has deadened some senses and heightened others but I'm sane. I'm twelve years older than you and by the time you live through another twelve years I may be dead. I know it, because I don't want to live. I can't go on living

102

with the sense of being a failure. This sickness is my friend, it will come and take me away anytime I call on it. I'm going to tell you some of my own life story so you can understand what I mean. You won't understand it now but one day you will. I started out to school when I was ten, couldn't do it before because my father didn't believe in schooling. He took me to work with him on the farm. He didn't register my birth so no school inspector could come around and check up. He ruptured himself and had to spend his days around the house. My Mama took over and she sent me to school. I was bright and I did four years work in twelve months, used to light a bonfire behind the house to study at night because we couldn't afford to buy oil for the lantern. By the time I was thirteen I had passed the pupil teacher's exam and got a job teaching. All during those years I trained myself to eat little and to study hard and something inside me turned all dried up and dead. I never had a girl, never went to a fête. In the early days when I started I used to love reading. Every book, good or bad, used to fill me up with wonderment and gladness, but soon everything turned to ashes – the words were ashes, the pages felt like ashes – dust and ashes, Jesus!" He lay back again and Hector had to lean forward to catch what followed. "My mind was a wheel that started turning round and round and I can't stop it, boy, I can't stop it I tell you! I've hammered out the habit of learning like a parrot and that's all I've been doing these last ten years. You know what I mean, Hector?"

"No, Mr. La Rose, I don't know, sir."

"Hmmm! I realised all this that day when you asked me why Keats' 'Ode to a Grecian Urn' was a masterpiece. I didn't know why it was a masterpiece but somehow you knew why. You're not half as clever as I am and yet you can get something out of the books you read that I can't. I used to tell myself that it was because your father's got enough money to buy time for you, time to read and think and dream, but that's only partly true. . . a man's got to be born that way. Mind you I'm not running myself down. I had to starve and study or eat and leave my mind like a savannah in a drought and I choose to starve and study. Perhaps you'll starve someday, you never can tell, boy, but starving when you're a small-boy and doing it when you're grown up is different. The cramp in your belly doesn't feel the same. If your belly's known the warm, fat feel of food all through your youth and suddenly it's all dry and empty, then you might even like it. When you're too young an empty belly kills all the joy in you before you even learn what feeling joy is like. . . ."

"Lord, Jefferson! You been talking a hundred to the dozen, boy, give you broken down body a rest now, eh." Ma La Rose had re-entered the room.

"All right, Mama, all right, I will have lock jaw from now until the day I get out of this bed."

"Master Bradshaw, I will have to ask you to go now, sir, me son's condition's too serious for him to do more talking."

La Rose closed his eyes and his head looked like a black skull against his pillow. Hector got up quickly. The smell of sickness in the small room and his teacher's voice drumming inside his head made him want to rush out into the sunlight.

"Don't worry, Hector! I'll be up in no time and you'll matriculate in the next eighteen months. I'll see to that. I'll teach you all that the white man wants you to write down so that you can get your piece of paper," the teacher said, and Ma La Rose dipped the handkerchief in the aloes and re-tied it.

Hector walked home along the dusty, red road, waving mechanically to the villagers who shouted greetings.

Two weeks later La Rose turned up looking gaunt and dehydrated. He treated Hector as if nothing had happened, continuing to be his detached dry, matter-of-fact self.

"I'd like you to have lunch with me, Mr. La Rose," Hector said a few days before his summer vacation started. It had taken a great effort for him to blurt out this invitation. La Rose gathered his books and papers together and said, "My mother's a good cook and she's jealous about my ever eating out." The tone of his voice made it sound as if Hector had insulted him and he walked away without another word. Hector always found it difficult to strike up friendships the way Tojo and Tengar could do with such assurance and naturalness, and La Rose's rebuff left him feeling miserable and inadequate.

CHAPTER EIGHT

THE promise of rain in early June, which the clouds, the sunsets and the rings around the moon had dangled over Tarlogie, was not fulfilled by the end of the month. Hector's summer holidays started with clear days and the sun drying up the swamps until it became impossible to pole a canoe between the reefs. Doorne decided to keep his promise and to take Hector to Black Bush. He also invited Tengar and they spent three days preparing for the trip.

"Boy, you so excited you gone off your food," Sister said on the morning of the third day. "Well I declare! I never see anyone preparing to punish they body with so much gladness. It's only big, crusty men like Doorne or Tengar who can walk to Black Bush, and you are just a strip of a boy. Why you don't wait, Hector?"

"I can manage, Sister, I know it," Hector said, feeling a momentary twinge of doubt creeping into his heart. Sister knew how much it meant to him. He would be miserable for the whole of his holiday if she didn't allow him to go. In any event, Doorne and Tengar would look after him and see that he did not kill himself.

"You sure you don't want Tojo to come along and carry you' gun for you, boy? When your grandpa used to go hunting he always carry a small-boy with him."

"It wouldn't be the same if Tojo carried my gun, Sister."

"All right, you know best what you doing, boy, but try and don't do too much 'cause you still so young."

"I'm fourteen, Sister, and that's old enough. I read about boys younger than me doing all kinds of brave things."

"The white man does tell a pack of lies in they books so don't you go believing all you read about!" Hector saw a chance to reinforce his argument.

"But the Bible doesn't tell lies."

"That's the word of the Lord, boy."

"But white men wrote it."

"Even white men got to tell the truth when the Lord instructing them to, if they didn't the Almighty would 'ave struck them down."

The hunters were only going to be away for two days but Sister prepared enough food to last Hector for a week – unleavened bread and bits of jerked pork in it, strips of tasso, cassava bread, baked breadfruit and bottles of curdled milk.

Tengar, Doorne and Hector started out from Tarlogie before sunrise. The hot sun caught them a few miles past Honey Reef. The old man and his son were carrying wareshis and Hector his gun, and a small balata pouch. The sky was intensely blue. The occasional cirrus cloud heightened the hard, starched texture of its blueness. The plop-plop of their feet and the intermittent rise and fall of their voices sounded unreal in the wide silences. Far to their right, negrocups, tall as men, were feeding amidst the lotus lilies and laughing-girl weeds. The negrocups raised their heads to gaze at the intruders before resuming their pecking and strutting. A flock of ducks and herons, grazing in a cluster of bisi-bisi reed ahead of them, rose up in clamorous flight. The negrocups held their ground, twisting their long necks nervously and preening their wings for flight. Far in front of them, beyond the dark green strip of Boundary Reef, the horizon was a circle of mirages where the swamp melted away, calcined by the sun before it merged with the sky.

The three stopped at Boundary Reef. Stepping out of the cool mud and water on to the hot sand caused Hector's feet to burn and he walked towards the shade of the trees like a cat on hot ashes.

"Take a good rest, Master Hector," Doorne said, "this last stretch to Black Bush more bad than all the rest." The boy stood with his back against a tree trunk. He knew that if he sat down he wouldn't be able to get up again. He felt as if flames were licking around the inside of his head. Tengar passed him a water bottle and said:

"Wash you' mouth out and gargle you' throat, then spit it out. Don't swallow 'cause it will make you feel more tired and wind you when you start out again." Hector saw the concern on his friend's face and tried to smile but all he managed was a tight grimace.

"Can't stop too long," Doorne said, "the shadow longing out and we don't want night to catch we on this swamp." They pushed forward, Doorne in the lead and Hector bringing up the rear. The boy walked with his head down. He knew that if he kept measuring the distance to Black Bush he would panic for already every forward step had become for him an act of will.

"You see it, Master Hector? You see it?" Tengar asked, and the boy looked up and saw clumps of golden plumed bisi-bisi and wild cane growing out of clear water half a mile from Black Bush.

Black Bush was a rain forest extending inland and rising towards high savannahs and mountains, the whole landscape like a petrified green ocean stretching for over a thousand miles to the foothills of the Andes. A narrow plain led into Black Bush and the sun had withered the grass and sage on it leaving it parched and bare. When the three hunters crossed the reed beds they saw a wall of forest, clusters of cocorite palms, tall trees strangled by tapestries of vines and creepers and massed growths of bamboo.

"Is how much further we got to go, Doorne?" Hector shouted in a cracked voice. His face was grey and his lips covered with a thin film of dry saliva. Doorne turned around, looked at him angrily but did not reply. Hector was past the stage of caring what anyone thought. He couldn't go any further and stood swaying, trying to keep himself from falling. "Is how much further we got to go? Jesus! The sun's blazing inside my head. I didn't know I'd have to stand this kind of punishment or I would 'ave stayed home. Why did I have to leave my comfortable house to come on this beast-walk!"

"Come on, Master Hector, I'll give you a hand, man," Tengar said.

"Leave him alone!" Doorne bellowed. Some of his anger stemmed from the boys' reminding him of his own fatigue. "I done tell you this swamp wasn't no place for no rice-pap mother's boy. Was you who say you wanted to come, kept after me day in day out, 'Doorne carry me with you to Black Bush' you did keep saying. Well, I bring you now, so act like a man. It don't matter now that your papa is a big chibat, that you' head full up with book-story. You wanted to show that you was a man, well, be-Jesus-Christ, show it 'cause not a soul en't going to help you reach that dry land ahead of we."

"Keep you foot wide apart to fight the mud, Master Hector, give you'self leeway. . . bite you' teeth hard and jus' keep going, we en't got far to go," Tengar said and the gentle cajoling in his voice was more effective than Doorne's bellowing.

"I think I can make it, Tengar, but it's hard, boy, it's hard." Tengar slowed down to make him catch up. Hector staggered forward splashing water as he went. Doorne broke into a melancholy chant, celebrating another victory over the swamps, and Tengar joined in with a voice resonant with the ancient sorrow of his race. The sound of their chanting caused flocks of birds to rise out of the forest and sprinkle the sky like dust. Hector pitched forward and lay face down with his feet still in the water. Tengar attempted to help him but the old man said:

"Leave him alone to catch his breath. I must give it to the boy, he got a strong mind, although he cry out lit' bit and me had to talk to he lil' rough, he still bear the strain to the end. Take a swig of this, Master Hector." Doorne turned him over on his back and held a flask to his lips. Hector swallowed a mouthful of the rum and it burnt its way down, choking him. "Feel better?"

"Yes, Doorne." He closed his eyes and turned over on his stomach once more. Doorne and Tengar sat beside him with their backs to the sun.

"We going to camp right here," the old man said. "After we rest lil' bit we can start building a hut."

"I will cut down some bamboo and Master Hector can help we build," Tengar said.

They began erecting the hut towards sunset. A land breeze brought the smell of eucalyptus and locust gum, and the squawk-ing and puling of birds. Doorne poured water on the dry earth and when it had soaked in Tengar drove uprights into the mud and tied cross beams to them with bush rope. Hector plaited cocorite palm leaves together and helped with the thatching. When the hut was finished they sat close to the camp fire and piled green branches and leaves over the flames so that the smoke could drive away the mosquitoes. Night fell quickly and stars and fireflies appeared. The land breeze and the sea wind met and contested the empty spaces above the swamp and forest. There was a hissing as the green branches burned. Hector watched the flames brighten Doorne's and Tengar's faces into godheads against a wall of darkness. The swamp was silent but the forest was full of noises – the roar of red howlers, the insistent exchanges of who-you birds, the clarion trill of trumpeter birds and the distracted moaning of the night wind in the trees.

The dew-soaked wind made Hector shiver and it was a pleasant feeling, for the memory of sweltering in the open swamp was still vivid. They ate tasso and cassava bread and drank curdled milk.

"This tasso's harder than a car tyre," Hector said.

"Hard as a tapir rump," Tengar said, "and it taste like ashes." Doorne looked up and grinned. "Tasso's good for the teeth, en't nothing like it."

"We got to make a big fire when we done eating," Tengar said, "'cause jaguar does have a way of coming down to the waterside to drink."

"En't got to worry 'cause we en't got no dog with we. Them big cat got a sweet tooth for dog meat but they not too fond of human flesh. . . to tell you the truth me don't blame them. Take a tough old stick like me, jaguar know better than to try eating me up. All the puss would get out of it would be a bellyache."

"What are we going to hunt tomorrow, Doorne?"

"Bush hog, Master Hector."

"I never saw a bush hog alive. Once you told me that when you hear the hogs stamping down a trail they shake the earth."

"Don't worry, Master Hector, you will find out for you'self at day-clean, God willing."

"One day up the Mazaruni," Tengar said, "me catch a whole pack of hog swimming 'cross the river. I row me canoe right in the middle of them and start using me cutlass and all of a sudden the quiet water turn white and alive 'cause the cannibal fish scent the blood. I bag four hog and the fish kill ten. Was a sight to see I telling you!"

Doorne spat out a piece of tasso and belched contentedly.

"Today was a day of days for you, eh, Master Hector!" Doorne liked to gloat over the weaknesses of the young and he wasn't going to miss the chance to taunt his master's son. "That walk 'cross the swamp make a man out of you, boy! For the first time you learn the lesson that sun and swamp don't pick favourite, that sun and swamp neutral, them two don't care if you is a king or a beggar boy. It is a good lesson for a young man like you to learn. . ."

"Papa, the boy try hard. Is why you got to rake up what past?" Tengar said.

The old man ignored his son and continued, "Like me was saying, is a good lesson for you to learn. Out in this swamp with the sun like fire all over you, you only better than another man if you got more strength and stamina than he. Take note of that lesson, Master Hector, 'cause you wouldn't learn it if you did read all the white man books."

"He en't do so bad," Tengar said; "me see big man cry in that swamp already when the punishment get too much for them."

Hector retired to his hammock with a heavy spirit. He had wanted to defend himself against Doorne's sarcasm but he had not dared to. The old man would only have poured more brine into an open wound and won out in the end. He was grateful to Tengar for defending him. Somehow, in whatever one did, Tengar could find something worthy of praise.

Day was breaking when Hector woke up next morning. He jumped out of his hammock and held his face up to the dew. Tengar had gone off into the forest and Doorne was tending the fire. Hector approached the old man.

"Morning, Doorne."

"Aye, aye, Master Hector, you sleep the sleep of the just las' night. You was snoring and moaning like a bushmaster snake." They heard the sound of a shot and the old man said, "Listen!" After a few minutes there was another report. "I bet you is a pair of bush turkey Tengar bag. When you shoot one the mate does fly away and then it does come back to see what happen." Doorne was boiling some grey, speckled eggs in a pot.

"They look like alligator's eggs," Hector said.

"Is land-turtle eggs, boy, en't nothing like this to put strength in your back."

Tengar found them eating breakfast. He was pleased with his bag and held up the turkeys for Hector to admire.

"You should 'ave taken me with you, Tengar."

"Don't fret yourself, Master Hector, you goin' have plenty game to try you' aim out on today. Is dry weather and the game don't rove too far from the swamp."

"Let we get ready to go," Doorne said wiping his mouth with his forearm. They had used water lily leaves as dishes and they threw them into the fire when they finished eating. The old man and his son harnessed on their wareshis. Black Bush was alive with birds, and leaves streaming in the morning wind. The sun was a pale steel disc behind the mists that hung over the swamp and the weeds and lotus leaves were studded with brightening dew drops.

They walked into the twilight of Black Bush, moving silently across a carpet of dead leaves. Doorne led the way, alert and bending slightly forward to balance the weight of his wareshi. His eyes took in everything.

Life in the forest was geared either to stillness or lightning movement – the stillness of a tall tree or the speed of a snake striking. The forest is a womb in which life is lived in an eternal, dark gestation, only the undulating belly of treetops is exposed. Hector sensed a change coming over him. He had to attune himself to the secret rhythms of an interior world. He felt a peculiar tension possessing his limbs, sharpening his senses. He was conscious of the slightest sound or movement – his breath, his footsteps, the stirring of a branch, the distant cry of a bush rabbit, a leaf falling. While he walked under them, the trees breathed their stillness and their strength into him. Sunlight and wind had not reached down to the forest floor for a long time and the air was heavy with the smell of decay. Hector lost all sense of time, distance, direction. If Doorne and Tengar had abandoned him he would not have known where to turn.

At last Doorne picked up the trail of a flock of bush hogs. He knelt down and examined the hoof prints whilst Tengar ran back and forth crouching low and sniffing.

"They been passing here couple days well," Doorne whispered. Tengar rejoined them holding a section of a snake's backbone.

"They kill a big snake here, once you reach a bush hog trail you don't have to worry 'bout snake, them hog is snake kinna."

"This is a jaguar footprint," Doorne said, stirring the sand with his toes, "is a big puss, and he following the flock for a meal." He examined the trees along the trail. "Let we climb up that one." He led the way to a tree with low branches. The old man unharnessed his wareshi and when he was firmly astride a branch, Tengar passed it to him. Hector and Tengar cut down a dozen saplings, trimmed them and handed them to Doorne, who tied them across two branches making a rough platform. Tengar joined Doorne and Hector followed him. The three sat close together on the platform. They had a clear view for twenty yards on either side of them. The tree rose two hundred feet above them and at the base its trunk was six feet across. The branches directly overhead were decorated with lianas and rainbow orchids. Opposite them was a smaller tree of the same species and a termite nest bulged like a huge goitre halfway up its trunk. Hector had hunted in the open swamps long enough to have learnt the discipline of remaining motionless. They sat scanning the trail for a long time.

"I hearing something," Doorne said. Hector listened but heard nothing until he followed Doorne's and Tengar's eyes and saw a jaguar approaching. The tension inside him was so great that he felt he had to break it or his whole being would disintegrate. The jaguar barely touched the ground as he walked, his movements were oiled, effortless, his green eyes bright as sunlight on a mirror. The rumble of bush hogs coming down the trail broke the silence. The big cat sprang on to a branch directly above him and flattened himself against it.

"He got a hunting pardner."

"Goin' be hell to play."

"You think he will catch our smell?"

The three hunters had to say something to quiet their nerves. The leader of the bush hogs, then his flock came into view. They moved in a phalanx, the sows and their litters flanked by boars and a few stragglers scouting in the rear. The leader, his bristles sticking out like thorns, his eyes smoky as a snake's, his narrow flanks sloping back from an ungainly head was ten yards away from the hunters when the jaguar arched and sprang. He landed on the back of a straggler. His fangs tore the vertebrae loose where it joined on to the skull. The hog squealed once and was silent. Holding the hog firmly between his jaws the big cat regained his position on the branch easily. The herd turned around and milled about on the ground directly below their enemy. The branch broke under the extra weight and the jaguar fell into the midst of the flock. Certain of his strength and cunning he crouched down to spring free but the restless, grunting pack were on him and he spun round and round, shaking off the attackers which were snapping at his legs and belly and climbing one on top the other to reach his throat. He tore his way through with fangs and claws and fury, maddened by the scent of blood and the pain of his wounds. Blades of grass on the trail, where they were not trampled down, were turned into red stilettos. The hogs that could not reach their enemy turned on their own wounded and killed them. The jaguar fought for room to manoeuvre in, snarling and growling his hoarse anger. Four times it seemed as if the big cat had cleared enough space to break away but each time the hogs surged in again. The spot on which the jaguar fought became the centre of a whirlpool fed with energies from a stream of enraged hogs.

"He done kill twenty of them!"

"Twenty-one!"

"Twenty-two!"

"He can't hold out!"

The jaguar went down twice under a flurry of bristles and dripping tusks. He came up again striking out in a frenzy of ebbing strength. He snarled a hoarse, gurgling snarl and rolled over, still working his jaws up and down. The hogs tore his belly open and played tug-o'-war with his entrails. Finally all that was left were pieces of bloodstained skin and a savagely grimacing skull. The hogs kept milling round and round. Their leader was dead.

The fight sickened, and at the same time, fascinated Hector. His sympathies were all with the jaguar and up to the end he

wanted him to escape. He found himself shouting encourage-
ment, and when the jaguar was defeated fury took hold of him.
He sprang down from the platform and rushed at the hogs.

"Come back!"

"You mad, boy!"

The main body of the hogs was already in retreat. But the rest
turned on him. He went down on one knee and began firing and
reloading with a cold precision. He kept this up until he had no
more cartridges, and then he whipped out his cutlass. He didn't
know when Tengar and the old man joined him. Tengar picked
him up and ran back to the tree whilst Doorne kept the hogs at
bay. Tengar hoisted him on to the platform. "Stay there, boy!"

Tengar ran back to help his father, just as the hogs were
rushing him. He arrived in time to chop them down with his
cutlass. He bent down low and cut off their forelegs as if they were
twigs and once they were down slashed through their backbones.
The rest of the herd scattered.

The old man and his son were in a sour mood and for a while
they didn't talk to Hector. He sat where Tengar had planted him.
He knew that he had acted stupidly. He also knew that the two
were angry not so much because he had risked his life but because
he had endangered their livelihood. If anything had happened to
him they would have had to face Sister and his father and no
amount of explanation would have absolved them from blame.
He watched them cutting up, cleaning and salting the carcasses
and packing a maximum load into their wareshis. Hector was
unrepentant. "A lot of things might have happened to me," he
thought, "but nothing has happened so why should they keep on
acting like I murdered somebody. It was my own sweet self that
I risked. I didn't even know what I was doing at the time. The
feeling just took hold of me and before I knew it I was on the
ground firing into the herd. I felt I was doing something brave at
first but now I'm not so sure. At least I have something to boast
to Sister and Tojo and Clysis about!"

"You ready, Master Hector?" Doorne asked sulkily.

"Yes, I'm ready." He climbed down and followed the two men
up the trail. He had thought of cutting out the jaguar's teeth to
keep as trophies but he knew that this would only put the old man

in a worse mood. Trails of blood led off in all directions and they walked close together, on the look out for any wounded hog that might attack them.

"I wonder what's going to happen to all the dead hogs we had to leave," Hector said, addressing himself to Tengar for he knew that the son, unlike the father could not bear malice for long.

"What goin' happen to them?" Tengar repeated his question and laughed. "In coupla days time the macushi ants en't goin' lef' nothing but white bones pick clean; them ants can eat up a thirty foot anaconda snake in a night."

"But is why you had to do the most god-almighty foolish thing me ever see anybody do?" Doorne exploded. Hector had been expecting a dressing down.

"This old man can never keep his big mouth shut," he said to himself, "he's got to rake up and dig up what's done and finished with and make a big ballad about it, as if he's sure I'm on the verge of doing something like it again."

"With all due respect to you ancestors, Master Hector," Doorne continued, "me think that you inherit some of the Bradshaw mad blood in your veins. You could've get yourself kill and to tell you the truth that wouldn't have been so bad because if you push your head in tiger mouth you deserve to get bite. . . but what is more you nearly get me and me son kill too. Is who tell you you is any hero? All you is, is a maugre, skin-and-bone pickny with a lot of book story spinning confusion inside you' young head . . . that is all that you is, and be-Jesus-Christ if you do something like that when I take you out hunting again I will take off me broad belt and whip you all the way home. Ebenezer Doorne en't the kind of man to play tomfoolery with."

"You don't see the boy sorry, Papa? Is why you got to stretch story long like liana after it finish and done with?"

"Chu! You make me sick, Tengar. You is me son but sometime you does sicken me. Is why you always got to be sucking up to the young master? You don't know that once he grow up he goin' start acting like if dog is better than the likes of we?"

"I can judge folks for meself, Papa, and me don't need no prophecy from you to help me out. Besides me don't suck up to nobody. I got me health and me strength, the Good Lord give me them and is them me have to depend on. You was always one to lash people with you' tongue, to empty the bitterness in you' heart over other people head but you never did stop to cast the mote out of you' own eye."

"Chu! Words. . . words. . . that is all the young people got today, just like if they grow up eating birdseed. You wait and see, Tengar, jus' you wait and see, boy!"

Tengar was carrying a hundred and eighty pounds of pork in his wareshi and Doorne ninety pounds. They made the journey back in slow stages and arrived home near midnight. Hector was so tired that he fell asleep in a Berbice chair while Sister was preparing a hot drink for him. The old lady undressed him, sponged him down with alcohol and put on his pyjamas. She woke up Tojo and between them they carried him to his bed. Hector slept for twenty-four hours, the longest and most satisfying sleep he had ever enjoyed.

CHAPTER NINE

HECTOR spent a week in Georgetown towards the end of his summer holidays. His father had sent Laljee to fetch him. Sister had acted as if she was pleased that he was going but when he had embraced her on the front porch before setting out, he had felt her hands tremble on his shoulders and knew that she was afraid and unhappy.

"I will miss you, sweet girl," he said, "you are my one-eye and my right hand."

"Chu boy! You got more sweet talk than a shango priest," she had said, turning away from him to hide the gladness in her old eyes.

He had looked forward to visiting the city but once he was in the big house in Leslie Street, the strangeness of the place made him long to return to Tarlogie. Age had heaped a mountain of bitterness on Aunt Hanna's spirit, turned her into a desiccated condor bird with feeble claws and loud croakings. She needed young people around her so that she could prey upon them. Her febrile spirit sucked in a vicarious life from them day by day.

Ethel and Cynthia had ripe women's bodies, full breasts and round hips and their every movement was instinct with seduction. They regarded Hector with bright, cruel eyes, taunting and teasing him with their presences, their smell, their reckless innocence. He protected himself by treating them with a harsh disdain. By the second day after his arrival he had already learnt how to injure their vanity and to incite them into throwing tantrums. Whenever they were around he felt impelled to attack them either with words or with blows. The girls were as strong as ocelots but as soon as he touched one of them they would run and complain to his father or to Aunt Hanna. Inevitably, he would end up having to listen to a lecture on chivalry and how Tarlogie had turned him into a savage.

Martha understood the situation and spoke up for Hector.

"What you expect, mistress?" she interrupted one day when Aunt Hanna was scolding him, "Master Hector is a man-chile and he got to defend heself against he two wildcat sisters who only harassing he whole day. Is the girls you must talk to."

"You keep out of this, Martha. What right have you got to come dipping your tongue into my private affairs?"

"What right me got, mistress? I will inform you what right me got. I been with this fam'ly since these pickny children was too young to wipe the snot from they nose, that is what right me got." Aunt Hanna had never been a match for the cook and as the former had grown more querulous and dried up, the latter had become fatter, more of a matriarch. Aunt Hanna was mistress of the house but it was Martha who ruled it. Fitz, seldom at home, was as usual preoccupied with his business, his rum drinking friends, his Indian woman in Kitty Village. Laljee was his shadow-man, a neutral figure, an observer rather than an active partici-pant. What he thought of, or if he thought at all, no one ever knew. Hector discovered that spending most of his time in the kitchen with Martha was the best way of escaping any involvements with his sisters. They respected and disliked the cook because she understood them too well.

Fitz was suffering from middle-aged vanity. He had started wearing elegantly cut suits, grooming himself and spending hours massaging his face. He had dieted and exercised away his paunch and had in the process developed a bad heart. In spite of all this, however, his face and neck still betrayed his age. Deep furrows grooved his face from the outer edge of his wide nostrils to his jaw and lines webbed the corners of his eyes. His complex-ion was bile-yellow as if he lived on juices extracted from grass and the sun never seemed to change this.

Dela had survived. She and her brother still occupied Fitz's cottage and everyone who knew her was certain that she would remain there to the end of her days. She had not changed. Fitz did not understand her and never would and this was a part of her insurance against his ever casting her out. He got a perverse delight out of knowing that he had bought Dela but could never own her. She was a child of silence. She belonged to a race of waiting people. No one knew the purpose of their waiting. Perhaps it was the destruction of all other races but their own. It had taken them ten thousand years to trek down from the Behring Straits and they seemed willing to wait another ten millennia for the fulfilment of their private dreams. They were a forest people. The forest was a good place in which to wait. And although Dela had left the forest to come to the city it was as if she had brought invisible jungles with her and planted them all around her cottage in Kitty.

Once Fitz had offered to marry her. He did not quite know why because he could not admit his motives to himself. He had wanted to get closer to the wellsprings of Dela's strength and marriage was a clumsy device through which he thought he could have achieved this. Dela had smiled and made the longest speech she ever made to him.

"Why marriage, Fitz? Dela already Fitz woman."

He had grown accustomed to talking to her and having her answer him in monosyllables. Once it had suddenly struck him that talking to her was like pounding his fists against a granite boulder and he had laughed and crushed her in his arms. When he was satisfied she had wrapped herself around him like an anaconda and clicked her tongue and cooed to him until he fell asleep.

Fitz liked the way his son was growing up. He was losing his adolescent awkwardness and developing a slow gracefulness of movement. But Hector's reserve was as invisible as Dela's. The exchanges between father and son were polite and guarded as though they were strangers, both wanting to draw closer and both incapable of communicating.

Fitz stayed at home to talk to his son the night before the boy returned to Tarlogie. Ethel and Cynthia had gone to a party.

Hector had refused to accompany them. Part of him had wanted to go out of curiosity, but he hated meeting strangers. He was a country boy and had none of the social graces that his father paid so dearly for his sisters to learn at the Queen's High School. In any case going out with his sisters would only give them the chance to laugh at him. The only kind of relationship he had had with girls of his own age in Tarlogie had been a master-servant one and it had never stirred up any uneasiness in him, but when his sister's friends had visited the house, their bold looks and their sophisticated manners had made him feel like a bush rabbit in the presence of a snake.

Fitz sat in his Berbice chair on the veranda puffing away at his discoloured clay pipe and filling the air with the smell of Brazilian tobacco.

"I've been getting regular reports from your teacher, boy," he shifted his pipe to the corner of his mouth and sat back in his chair. "He seems to think that you've got a good mind. . . thinks I should send you to a university to read for a profession after you matriculate. How do you feel about it? Made up your mind what you'd like to study yet?"

"I'd like to go to a university, Daddy, but I don't know what I want to study for."

"Hmmm. . . don't know what you'd like to study eh! Well take my word for it, boy, all that's open to you is medicine, law or the ministry, and then there's teaching but there isn't any future in that. Anyhow you've still got time to decide." Hector wanted to be a hunter or a gold or diamond miner but he knew better than to admit to this. Aunt Hanna would immediately start pressing his father to remove him from Sister's care. She would prefer to see him dead rather than have him follow such good-for-nothing callings. "You like it in Tarlogie, Hector?"

"I like it all right," Hector wondered what the old man was leading up to.

"I often keep wondering if it wasn't a mistake letting you grow up there." Hector knew that it had not been a mistake but he could not say so. "Anyhow it's too late to bother about that now. You think you'd like to stay with us for a while, boy?"

"I don't know." He wanted to return to Tarlogie. He had too much freedom there to abandon it for life in the small enclosure of Aunt Hanna's prejudices. Fitz laughed and refilled his pipe.

"We're strangers, boy, you and me, out-and-out strangers. You never open up and speak to me like I was your father. You know I am your father, don't you?"

"Yes, Daddy."

"I know you're going to grow up feeling I'm your father in name only. Well I'm not sorry. Your aunt always telling me how insensitive I am, and you know something? That's my strength. Know anything about the family history? Did the old woman ever tell you about it?"

"Only a coupla things about Grandpa. She said he was a good man."

"A good man! Don't make me laugh!" Fitz leaned forward balancing his pipe in his palm, and Hector could smell the rum fumes on his breath. "He was a peculiar man, old Busha Bradshaw was, but as for being a good man I wouldn't hold any brief for him. He was more sensitive than I am and he had big vices and big virtues. He was a drinking, whoring, kindly savage son-of-a-bitch. Living in the same house with him like I had to do, I found that the man had so many sides I never knew which one he'd show me from one day to the other. My mother died when I was six and he never married again. I was the one child of the marriage but he must have had a dozen illegitimate ones by a dozen different women. . . Yes, old Busha Bradshaw could never sit still once a skirt swished past him. . ." For the first time Fitz was talking to his boy as if he was an adult.

Hector watched the light deepening the lines on his father's face. The boy's five years on the wild coast had broken the love-hate tensions that had once made him search this visage apprehensively for every change of expression. Sitting there on the veranda he could look his father in the eye and feel easy in himself. It was as though the half-drunken old man opposite him had become an effigy of the irascible, loudmouthed father who had whipped him so savagely the night after he had tried to run away.

"The Bradshaws and the Hingensens have been intermarrying for two generations," Fitz went on, "Busha Bradshaw married a Hingensen girl and I married one of the daughters of her cousin. I'm sure that old man Busha married my mother so that he could lay his hands on Tarlogie, and once he got control of the estate he all but ruined it. If I hadn't given up schoolmastering and gone to the diamond mines I'd still be saddled with old Busha's debts. . ."

"What's happened to the Hingensens, Daddy?"

"Only two of them are left, Joe and Eric and they're both in the U.S. Eric's a lawyer and Joe's a preacher. . ."

"Why doesn't anybody ever want to tell me about my mother. . . I mean why don't you talk about her. . ." Fitz got up suddenly, crossed the veranda and leaned against the carved railings with his head lost in the foliage of the hanging plants. Hector remained seated. The cane chair was uncomfortable but he felt rooted to it. His father had been trying to make friends with him, to put their relationship on an adult footing and he had spoilt everything. Hector remembered the night he had asked Sister the same question and the way she had reacted. He also remembered Martha's evasiveness the morning she had taken his mother's picture out of Aunt Hanna's chest of drawers and he had questioned her.

Why is there all this mystery surrounding my mother's name, he asked himself; and he knew then that he would have to clear it up. Since no one in the family would help him he would start questioning outsiders.

"Laljee!" his father called out.

"Aye, aye, boss!"

"Get the car out!"

"Me thought you was staying home tonight, boss."

"Get the car out you god-damned coolie son-of-a-bitch or I'll have you out on your arse before you can say 'Jesus wept!'"

"All right, boss, all right, stop frying up you fat." Accepting these outbursts with equanimity was all part of the job for Laljee. He was saving up enough money to invest in a salt-goods shop and until he had done so he could go on bowing the head and bending the knee. He had an oriental patience and subtlety which made him more than a match for his boss. He could always strike back by planting the odd scorpion in Fitz's shoes or taking his money off him when he was drunk. Fitz muttered "Good night!" and left.

Hector found Martha in her ground floor room, sitting under a naked electric light and mending a petticoat.

"Sit down, Master Hector. Me hear you' papa bawling out poor Laljee just now. Is a long time since me hear he shouting so, like howler baboon. The trouble is that you papa does drink too much and when the rum start scraping against he liver it does turn he into a devil."

"I'm going back tomorrow, Martha."

"I know, boy, and me old heart heavy with the thinking about it. Me can't tell you how much it please me eyes to see you growing up into a proper samba man. Lawd! You going to be taller than you' papa and proper handsome too. Many is the night me sit down here and say to Vivian: 'Gal, that Master Hector goin' be the best Bradshaw that ever was because he jus' eating up the book-knowledge and the Lord bless he with a wise heart on top of that.'" Martha was always outlandish with her praise, and although Hector would be deprecating, it filled him with a glowing feeling and he loved her for it with an egotistical adolescent love.

"Martha, if I ask you something will you promise to answer truly?" The question put her on her guard and her eyes shone like a doctor-bird's in her fat face.

"That depend, Master Hector. You know one thing that life teach me is that 'promise made is promise to be paid' so that when you take the plunge and make the promise you must know what you promising."

"Martha, why is it that nobody won't tell me about my mother? Why everytime I ask 'bout her its like throwing a brick into a flock of birds and I'm left alone feeling stupid."

"Is that's why you' papa was bellowing so just now?"

"Yes."

"Well take a tip from an old lady who love you as much as anybody will love you in all the mornings the Good Lord give you life to see; don't never ask you' papa that question, and what is more don't never ask nobody because the person who answer that question for you, boy, will be your worse-est enemy."

"But why, Martha? Why? Was my mama such a bad woman?"

"Your mama was the goodest woman that ever plant she foot on this land, boy. Since you was a lil' baby who didn't know that the sky had a name I used to pray that you grow up to be like you mama."

"So you're not going to answer my question either, Martha?"

"No, Master Hector. No, and I pray God nobody don't never answer it. Look, boy, you' young and you got the whole of you' life before you. In couple years time you will be going 'way 'cross the big water to study for a profession. Take me stupid advice, set you' heart on that and as for what past, all me can advise you is to 'llow sleeping dog to sleep."

Hector slept restlessly that night and by morning he had worked out a plan. He was going to walk around the Stabroek Market to see if he could find Dodo, the beggar. Tengar had told him that Dodo was usually under the big tree in front of the market until near high noon when the old man would set out on his rounds. He had picked on Dodo because he remembered the morning the old beggar had spoken to him on the beach he had sounded as if he knew a lot about the Bradshaw family.

"I'd like to go shopping in Water Street before I leave," he announced at breakfast.

"Laljee can take you after he takes your father to work," Aunt Hanna said.

"It wouldn't be the same, Aunt Hanna, I want to go by myself. I haven't been anywhere by myself since I came."

"All right but be careful and come straight back home now."

"I'll come straight back, Aunt Hanna, I promise."

Ethel and Cynthia giggled and whispered something about his getting lost. He glared at them and forced himself to finish his omelette. Martha knew that he liked omelettes and she had prepared one specially for him and it would upset her if he left any of it on his plate.

"Take a taxi home," Aunt Hanna said when he was ready to go, "you've got to leave at midday and it wouldn't be a bad idea if you came home and had a rest before you set out on that long journey, boy."

It was ten o'clock when he reached the market square and the crowds reminded him of the bush hogs milling around the jaguar. He had forgotten what a city crowd looked like. Streams of people jammed the square like logs on a river after the cutting season. The massed bodies moved as if they were floating on cross-tides. It was a colourful bedlam of people and vehicles. Human voices were contesting the right to make more noise than wheels, engines, claxoning horns and hoofbeats and the voices were winning out, and as if to celebrate this victory of man versus the machine there was plenty of loudmouthed laughter and shouting. The sweating black and brown faces in the crowd broke into easy grins and tongues clacked like castanets in tireless hands. It was a gay, motley, vari-coloured crowd dressed in all the hues and shades of random orchids in a rain forest. Hector found Dodo dozing under the big tree.

"Morning, Dodo."

"Have pity on the poor, young master, and the Lord will bless you and make you days bountiful." The beggar rattled off his set piece without recognising Hector.

"Dodo, here is two shillings but I want to talk to you." The old man reached out greedy talons, seized the coin and felt the edges.

"Who is you, young master? What you' name?"

"My name is Bradshaw, I'm Mazaruni Bradshaw's son."

"Bradshaw? Bradshaw? Yes, you' papa sell he soul to the Wenpago spirit and make a pile of money out of diamonds. Is what I can tell you young master? You got more money with you, another shilling maybe?"

"Yes, here!"

"Money is oil to the tongue, the wheel on which the world does turn."

"You know anything about my mother, Dodo?" The beggar closed his eyes and moved his jaws like a cow chewing its cud.

"You' papa, Mazaruni Bradshaw, who did sell he soul to the Wenpago for a sackful of diamond, marry a Hingensen gal and she bear him two pickny. . ."

"But there are three of us, two sisters and me!"

"Young master, why you want to look back? The past is a big darkness where many does stumble and fall and some don't never get up when they fall down. Leave old Dodo alone, he is a ole beggarman living under heaven and hanging on to life by the thread of a spider web; if the wind blow hard or the rain fall heavy or the sun burn too hot the thread can break and me will have to take up me begging in the forest of the long night. Don't bother 'bout the past, young master 'cause it's a mighty darkness with plenty wild creature in it to ambush you."

"Why did you say my mother bore my father two children, Dodo?"

"Don't worry 'bout the past, young master, is a mighty darkness. . . a man who sell he soul to the Wenpago got a thorn in he heart, a web round he spirit, a stone weighting down he soul. . . ." The old man's speech trailed off into an incoherent mumbling and Hector left him.

CHAPTER TEN

IT was moonlight in Tarlogie. The surf was quiet and the wind barely ruffled the surface of clear patches of water in the swamp. A moonstruck dog was howling in one of Chinaman's kennels and Caya was knocking up a one-three rhythm on his shango drum, preparing for the wind-dance. Most of the villagers were sitting on their rickety doorsteps gaffing in broken cadences. Cartmen on their way to the Port Mourant market shouted greetings as they rumbled by on the public road.

Moonlight was a season of enchantment. It turned the world of green and parched brown into a gun-metal blue. Black faces tinted by moonlight became navy blue, the yellow-green saffron, the green ricefields, the shadowed groves on the reefs, the weeds and the lilies were all glazed with azure. Palm fronds wet with dew gleamed and rustled in cold spasms. A piper owl, the sweetest of all singing birds, fluted its song high up in a po-boy tree.

Hector sat on the front porch recapturing the feel of the village after his stay in Georgetown. Sister sat close by him in her rocking chair, and she said:

"The piper owl's an old higue bird."

"How can an old higue bird sing so sweetly, Sister?"

"The voices of the damned always does sound sweet, boy. Why you think that bird does always sing sad songs? I will tell you why, it's because the souls of dead planters does live inside them."

"Was my grandpa a planter, Sister?"

"When I say planter, I mean them old, bad Dutch planters. Those that used to bury their gold in old sea chests, and then kill a slave so that his spirit could stand watch over the gold. Them old planters was greedy men, men with stony hearts where pity never

127

had a place to lay its head. On nights like this when the wind is high you can hear the slaves crying out over the swamp and the piper owl does sing songs over them to mock them."

"Doorne showed me a spot in the savannah and he said that if you put your ear to the ground on that spot you will hear dead people groaning."

"This village got plenty sorrow pile up on top of it, boy."

"But my grandpa was a planter just like the old Dutch planters."

"It wasn't the same I tell you boy, because your grandpa had the blood of master and slave in he veins and the slave blood was mixed with Indian blood. He was a santantone man with eyes like blue ice, coarse Indian hair and a face that was brown as the spots on leopard wood. And it was always like he had three contrary voices shouting discord inside he belly all the time."

Tengar approached from the top of the drive. He was strumming a guitar and singing a chanty:

> Timberman, work weary me
> Sun going down and me eye can't see
> Timberman, me want to go home
> Timberman, work wearying me
> Sun going down and boat a-come
> Timberman, me want to go home. . .

"'Night, Tengar!"

"'Night, Sister! 'Night, Master Hector! All you enjoying the moonlight."

"How you do, boy?"

"So-so, Sister, me mind just give me to come and visit you. I tell Elsa to come along but the field work weary her today and she catching some sleep."

"When you coming to castrate the pigs for me?"

"Day after tomorrow, Sister. I got to harvest some ground provisions tomorrow so I'll be at the farm from fore-day-morning to can't-see-time."

"Tengar, I got something to talk over with you, boy." Sister got up from her rocking chair and dipped her head into the moonlight. Her hair gleamed like silk-cotton and her dark creased face was burnished. Tengar unslung his guitar and walked halfway up the front steps.

"I dream 'bout you last night, boy."

Hector saw Tengar's face tighten into a mask and the palm fronds, as if they understood his sudden anxiety, shivered. Sister's dreams had hung over Tarlogie for half a century, and were forecasts of disaster. The villagers would doubt the existence of God before they doubted one of her dreams.

"Good or bad, Sister?" Tengar asked the question already knowing the answer.

"Tengar, the dream was heavy, boy. I saw you walking through a forest, a forest where it was cool and dark like the inside of the stone church in Georgetown, and somehow the darkness bandage up you' eye and you lost your way. The monkeys was laughing over you, the marudi was cackling and you start to stumble about like a drunken man, when all of a sudden it was like if the bandage fall away from you' eye and you see a flower growing out of a tree trunk. It was the kind of flower that eye never see before, and light was shining out of it. You run up and pick the flower and you drink in the scent of it but when you turn to walk away the flower turn into a serpent and this serpent had all the colours of a rainbow boa and it bite you on the wrist and strike at you' chest, and you cry out with the pain. . . it was at this point of the dream that me wake up. . . Tengar!"

"Yes, Sister."

"This is a heavy dream, boy, you got to watch youself."

"Yes, Sister?"

"You worse-est enemy living closer to you than the smell of your sweat. Take my foolish advice and watch the woman you living with. Is not that she is a bad woman, but she got a roving eye and you with all you' simpleness and you' big-heartedness can't read deception in a woman face."

"I have trust in me Elsa, Sister. She en't going to two-time me."

"All right, boy, but when you got to carry you' cross to your own Calvary I hope you can do it without ripping your heart to pieces."

Tengar walked away slowly. Voices from the rum-shop were shouting above the hymn-singing in the church where Preacher

Galloway was holding his weekly prayer meeting. Tanta Bess' ram-goat was bleating peevishly.

"Shut up you mouth, King Saul, before I come down there and shut it up for you!" Tanta Bess called out. The moonlight had come through her open window and awakened her and having shut the window she was trying to sleep again. She had to set out for the market before sunrise. Caya had warmed to the rhythm of his master drum and was beating out variations as if he was presiding over a shango ceremony and creating new rhythms for invisible dancers.

★   ★   ★

September was the month of birds in Tarlogie. Migratory cur-lews, herons, ducks and geese flew down from the north in great flocks. The birds timed their coming with the rice-cutting season and the farmers dotted the ricefields with scarecrows to frighten away the intruders. Those who could afford guns and ammuni-tion slaughtered the birds whilst others invited sportsmen from the towns to do so for them. There were laws against this untrammelled slaughter but Mark-a-book and his subordinates at the police station received daily gifts of wild fowl and seldom enforced the statutes laid down by the great ones in the city. The police were men from the coast and they knew how much damage a flock of ducks or geese could do to a ricefield. Their sympathies were with the villagers. Occasionally Mark-a-book would arrest a farmer for shooting birds out of season but this was done with the farmer's consent. The sergeant would explain that he had to keep his superiors happy and arrests were made according to a rota system. Before the culprit arrived at the station one of his relatives would be there to bail him out. One evening Sister sent Hector to the station to pay Doorne's bail, and on the way home the old man had complained that he had been arrested out of turn.

"I going to stop supplying that niggerman with bush rum," Doorne grumbled, "is who he think he is at all! Was Roopnaraine's turn this time and he just swoop down on me when I wasn't even prepared." The old man regarded this as a betrayal and the next day had sent a message demanding an apology. Sister, who according

130

to Doorne, respected both the law and the shadow of the law, had invited the two men to the big house for drinks and over a bottle of Chinaman's best, Mark-a-book explained that Roopnaraine had been away selling cattle, and since Doorne was such a good friend he had assumed that he would understand. Harmony was re-established and Doorne presented the sergeant with a demijohn of white rum and advised him to cure some fruit in it for Christmas.

Hector had bagged two ducklas near Honey Reef one afternoon and was on his way home when he met Elsa returning from the ricefields. It had rained earlier on, and her dress was wet and pasted against her body. Hector felt uncomfortable looking at her. He noticed the big nipples of her breasts, the arch of her loins and the way her belly trembled when she laughed. She had grown plump but her flesh was still firm and she had retained the habit of wearing brassières to prevent her watermelon breasts from sagging.

"Eh, eh, Master Hector, like I lucky today, I got company to walk me home."

Elsa's eyes looking at the lean of his brown body made Hector feel as if a hot dry wind had blown over him.

"I was out hunting," he said.

"I glad for the company, Master Hector. You know when sundown come I does begin to feel like me whole body turning heavy with weariness. . ." She chatted all the way and he kept wondering why he had been so disturbed during the first moments of their meeting.

*   *   *

Since his return from Georgetown he had been having wet dreams. He had tried to hide the evidence from Sister by putting his pyjamas at the bottom of the dirty clothes basket but he had seen her examining a pair one morning.

"Do you think I should go and see a doctor, Sister?" he had asked.

"En't nothing to see no doctor 'bout, boy, this is a natural thing that does happen to all young men when they growing up," she had said, and the casualness with which she had spoken had dispersed the fears of his suffering from a terrible disease.

"But why does it happen, Sister?"

"Boy, me don't know all the ins and outs of it, all me can tell you that it does happen to all the young men when they healthy. You must talk to Doorne or Tengar; they will tell you about the workings of a man body when it start ripening out."

He had questioned Doorne and the old man had said:

"When you got too much juice in your back it does have to find a way out and so Nature does make it come out in you sleep. That is the juice that does seed a woman. Couple more years of eating all the rich food you does eat and taking all that exercise and you will have to find a woman."

"Find a woman?"

"Yes, you will have to start using the weapon the Good Lord equip you with to use. Don't worry, Master Hector, if you don't find the woman then the woman will find you. Only trouble is, you got to watch how you plant you' seed because pleasure does bring pain."

Doorne's lecture had only added to the boy's confusion. He understood some of what the old man had implied but he did not like girls and was sure that he would live the rest of his life having little to do with them.

*   *   *

Hector was late for dinner that night. He knew Sister would be annoyed. He found the old lady in her rocking chair on the porch.

"Boy is where you been so late? I bet you never used to miss your meals when you was staying with your aunt."

"I shot two ducklas, Sister, big ones too."

"Chu! That is all I does hear from you: 'I shot this and I shot that.' You don't get tired shooting things, boy?" Her chair grated against the floor as she rocked. It was dark and the wind was shaking the windows and jalousies. "You better go and eat right away, boy, so that Clysis and Tojo can go to bed early; when you come in late like this you does upset the working of my whole household."

He was accustomed to Sister's complaints but somehow he knew that she always shared his triumphs no matter how trifling they were. He remembered how interested she had been when he had described his experience of the hunt to her. She had sat holding on to the arms of her rocking chair and when he had told about how he jumped off the platform and faced the wild hogs her long witches' fingers had tightened their hold and she had reproved him:

"But look how death was calling you, boy! I know when it happened because I was fussing about in the kitchen and all of a sudden was like if somebody press a cold iron against my spine and I say to Clysis and Tojo: 'I feel in my bones that something evil ambushing my one-boy' but just then a donkey bray and I knew that was a sign that the evil spirits couldn't touch the life in your young and wild heart. But it was a brave thing you do, boy, a proper brave thing, only you must never do it again, you hear me, because if anything should happen to you it will anchor me grey hair to the grave."

★   ★   ★

"Glory be, Master Hector! Is what good wind blow you this way at this time of afternoon?" Elsa said. She was sitting on the floor of her hut peeling a yam over a basin. She finished peeling the yam before looking up. "I saw you crossing the swamp but I couldn't believe me eyes 'cause is still sun-high and I know you does be having lessons at this time."

"Teacher La Rose left early today and Sister sent me with a message to Tengar; she wants him to mend the fence around her kitchen garden. Roopnaraine's pigs broke it down."

"You just miss him, Master Hector, only lil' while ago he set out for the foreshore with his gun. He gone to cut firewood and I know he en't coming back in a hurry." Elsa looked the boy up and down. He was only wearing his trunks. He felt excitement rising inside him and looked about stupidly. Elsa bent over the basin and he saw the curved ripeness of her breasts, the deep darkness that cleaved them apart. She was conscious of the spell she had cast over him and played with him like a jaguar with a bush rabbit.

"Why you don't sit down, Master Hector, and cool off youself before you go back?" He obeyed her, moving in a trance. He did not feel the hardness of the upturned box under him as he sat down. His saliva was like paste in his mouth. He wanted to rush out of the hut but sat petrified, wanted to say something, but was tongue-tied. Elsa went outside to fetch some coconut milk for him and he looked around the hut like a wild creature caught in a snare, resorting to cunning after the first frenzied attempt to escape had failed. There was a heavy smell of baked cow dung, stale food, human bodies and swamp water in the hut and he felt faint. She returned and stood close to him and her animal perfume at once repelled and excited him.

"Drink this, Master Hector!" She handed him an enamel cup full of coconut milk and jelly. He took it from her and drank slowly, moistening his dry lips, soaking his tongue and wetting his dry throat. As soon as he emptied the cup his throat felt parched again.

"Thank you, Elsa." His voice sounded disembodied and hollow. She looked down at him noticing his feverish eyes, the ripe pomegranate flush of his cheeks and the way his body seemed to be straining against a leash of fear and terror.

The wind was ruffling the thatch and pressing against the walls of the hut. A flock of parrots flew screaming across the blue and burning sky. A dull report echoed from the foreshore and there was a hullabalooo of shrill, plaintive, squalling birds. Elsa put her hand on Hector's shoulder and her fingers felt like leeches on his soft skin. He trembled and she moved her fingers up his neck and pressed his head against her belly. She was wearing a dress with nothing under it and her rubbery skin was alive, reaching out to enfold him. He jerked his head away and his breath came out like an explosion. He jumped up and would have run away but she embraced him and threw herself on to the floor pulling him down on top of her. Her warm, glowing black flesh consumed him, drowning his virginal desire in a tumult. He fumbled and writhed. Reaching into her was like dipping into wild honey. There was something compelling in the rhythms of her body as if she had drummers inside her heart ordering these rhythms. She laughed and groaned and murmured sweet obscenities and Hector exulted in the power he felt in making her do these things. His body harnessed itself to the rhythms in hers. He marvelled at his male strength and knew that he would never be the same person again.

Before he went home, he plunged into the roadside canal and swam about until he was certain that he had washed away the smell of Elsa's body. He felt no guilt about what he had done but he swore to himself that he would avoid Elsa for the rest of his stay in Tarlogie. He was gay and full of bigmouth laughing that night and Sister was caught up in the infection of his good humour. He was almost sure that she suspected nothing and he felt pleased about his calculated deception. But in the midst of his mirth Hector wondered if Sister really did suspect nothing. After all the old woman had a sorceress' gift of being able to ferret secrets out of people's hearts. Only a few nights before she had warned Tengar about Elsa's impending unfaithfulness and he had been present. He tried to detect from her eyes, her voice, her gestures if she was nursing any suspicions but if she was, there were no outward signs to go by.

★   ★   ★

When Hector left, Elsa washed herself, took out the jute bag to be aired and burnt Indian incense inside the hut. Tengar came back from the foreshore and found her preparing dinner.

"You shoot anything?" she asked.

"Only four crook-bills, gal." He noticed that she looked more attractive than she had done for a long time. "Don't worry 'bout the dinner now, I feel like some frolicking, sweet mopsy."

"The food will spoil."

"Is better the food spoil than the blood keep rushing up to me head and suffocating me, sweet gal." He ran his thumb down the deep groove of her spine and she tittered. He lifted her up and set her down on the floor very gently.

★   ★   ★

"Gawd Almighty! I fed up with this place," Elsa said. She was standing in the doorway with her arms akimbo, her legs wide apart, her whole body exuding discontent.

"What happen to you, sweet gal? You was all right this morning and now you acting like if a mountain of trouble sitting on top you' head." Tengar was sitting on the floor in a corner of the hut enjoying his siesta. He couldn't understand his woman. What was itching her all of a sudden? he asked himself. She been having these up-and-down moods couple weeks well, one minute she face will look like a morning sky and the next minute it start looking like thunder, all set up and heavy and ready to pelt down with quarrelling.

"I fed up with this place. . . this village. . . with all the mud and the tumbledown houses in it. . . the mud and the slime and everybody just sitting down and waiting for Jesus knows what! Gawd Almighty! Sometimes I does wish I had wings to take off and fly out of it all. . ."

"But sweet mopsy, is only the other day you been telling me how you like it. . ."

"Like it? Me?" she gave an ugly laugh. "How you mean I tell you I did like it? The place is one big stink, you can't turn, you can't go nowhere without mud gripping you' foot. All these years I been living with you we en't go nowhere. You want a beast of burden, not a woman. Because you is a big, crufty, niggerman with the strength of an ox and a mind big and empty like midday sky you think me is the same. Well let me inform you, Mr. Tengar: me, Elsa Rodney, is a woman who the Good Lord bless with more than enough to get the pick of men. Even Jojo for all he good-for nothingness was a man who all the women used to covet. . . I want to get out of this place! I want to go where a samba woman like me can live, you hear me? Live ! Not just to spend me juicy days like a lump of mud, sweating out me substance in Tarlogie sun. Is where you ever take me since we come here? You just answer me that?"

Tengar looked at Elsa with dismay. It was just like her to pick a quarrel with him when his mind was half-asleep, to snipe at him with words when he wasn't in the mood for following up all the illogical resentments behind her attack. Sometimes Elsa had to ease up the pressure of things inside her when she herself did not understand them. And since he was around he had to allow himself to be picked on and almost crucified by her tongue. It was as if she resented him for not knowing what went on inside her better than she did herself. Her attacks sprung from no recognisable core of discontent, the source of her outbursts was often impossible to find.

"I will take you to the pictures in Port Mourant, honey, we can go off for a whole day and you can buy the frock you been planning to buy from the Syrian at the same time. I know I been working you hard, honey, and I know we en't been going nowhere, but I'm a poor hustling man, I'm poor and black and ignorant and all I got is me strength."

"I'm getting old, Tengar, and I can't see meself staring old age in the face shut away in this village. I want more out of life than this village got to give me, man. I don't want to live the high-and-mighty life of no princess, but I want to feel safe and me way of feeling safe is not shutting meself away but living life like it supposed to be lived."

"How life suppose to live, sweet gal? Tell me?"

"Why you asking me to tell you? You en't live long enough to find out for yourself yet?"

Tengar remembered Sister's dream and suddenly it was as if huge bat wings were flapping inside his head.

"If you planning to two-time me, Elsa, then we better part now, gal, because when angryness and vexation burst inside me en't no telling what I will do. The love I have for you is a big love, gal, and the root of this love spread so wide and sink so deep that to pull them out would mean that you have to root up me life with it."

"Is who talking about two-timing you ? Chu! You can talk some funny kind of talk sometimes, eh!"

CHAPTER ELEVEN

HECTOR sat up late working out the geometry and algebra problems La Rose had set him. He heard the drunken voices fading out after Chinaman closed his rum-shop. An oskudoo owl was hooting from the churchyard and he knew that this was a bad omen. Doorne had told him so. The old man had said that these birds were messengers of death. The wind was moaning like a man during a bad dream. The owl's regular plangent notes were clear during lulls in the wind. Chinaman was cursing Dookia. Hector opened the front door and stepped out on the porch to get some air.

The shopkeeper's slurred, drunken voice sounded very near:

"You nasty whore-dog! Is why me have to put up with you when you' womb barren. . . barren like savannah during drought. . . is twenty year you feather you' nest under me roof. . . twenty year and you en't bear one pickny in all this time. . . me going to throw you out and get a young gal who belly can swell up when you plant seeds inside her. . ."

Dookia interrupted him with a flood of abuse.

"So is *me* womb barren, eh? All you listen to this bruck-down coolie man! Listen to he! Let me tell you something man, is not me who is barren, is you, you en't got no seed to plant and you never did have none. . ." Hector listened, cupping his ears to catch her words for it was the first time he had ever heard Dookia defend herself. "Don't raise you' hand to me tonight, husband! Don't try it! I will carry you to the cross if you so much as touch me tonight because you vex me spirit. You curse me in front of all you' friends tonight, and you never do that before. Why you had to curse me about me barrenness before all you' drunken friends? You take matters too far, husband. You hurt me grievously, husband, you leave me belly all empty and aching with the sorrowfulness of it. . . ."

"Woman, is so you talking to me, eh! I going to scatter licks like fire on you this night!" Chinaman screamed, and there was the sound of scuffling and of blows.

Chinaman's hunting dogs started up a hoarse, uneven chorus of barking and a pair of spurwings somewhere in the swamp chattered shrilly. Hector, looking on from his front porch, saw Chinaman stumble out of the shop with a lantern in his hand. He weaved and swayed across the shop bridge and when he reached the roadside grass, tripped and fell. Dookia burst out of the shop after him and he staggered up still gripping the lantern. Chinaman's shirt tail was flying in the wind and impeded by his swollen testicles he was moving too slowly to escape his wife. Dookia caught up with him. She was carrying a cutlass. She swung it and the hand holding the lantern fell away. Chinaman bellowed like a wounded red howler. The lantern hit something hard and broke, scattering flames that illuminated the two figures.

Dookia chopped her husband down and kept swinging the cutlass.

"Is why you had to make me do this?" she chanted over and over again. Hector shouted for Sister and the old lady ran out in her nightgown.

"What is happening, boy?"

"Dookia killing Chinaman."

"Oh me God! Lord have mercy!" She ran up the drive in her bare feet and Hector followed her. He stopped outside the front gate but Sister walked up to Dookia. Dookia was standing over her husband's body. She didn't even seem to notice when Sister took the cutlass away from her.

"Me had to do it, neighbour," Dookia said, "me had to do it after the man shame me before all he drunken friends."

Sister led her away. They walked past Hector on their way to the police station. Dookia was sobbing and in between sobs was saying, "Is me give him life to live and is me take he life away. . . is me feed him and give him clean clothes to wear. . . is who else but me would 'ave bear with he drunken ways and he sickness? . . . tell me that, neighbour. . . tell me that. . . is who else would 'ave stomach all that?"

Hector wanted to go and look at the body. He alone had witnessed the killing and he felt that somehow he had participated in it, that he and Dookia were accomplices, but he was afraid and he went back to the house and woke up Tojo. Tojo had a strong stomach and the sight of blood never worried him.

"What happen, Master Hector, you sound like if something frighten you?" He sat on the edge of his bed dangling his bowed legs and kneading the sleep out of his eyes with his knuckles.

"Dookia killed Chinaman with a cutlass and Sister's gone with her to the police station! Nobody knows about it yet. . . the body's lying near the shop bridge." Tojo didn't seem surprised.

"It must be late," he said jumping down and putting on his shirt and shorts, "it must be proper late."

"It's half-past one."

"You wake me out of a sweet sleep, Master Hector."

"I want us to go and look at the body. By the time Sister and Dookia reach the station the whole world will be up and about."

"It properly dark outside," Tojo said, striking a match and lighting his lantern, "and the wind's got a lot of sorrow in its belly and an owl's calling from the churchyard; I hope the coolie man don't haunt we. You must turn you' back to the east before you look at him, Master Hector."

They walked down the drive in silence, and Tojo was swinging the lantern as if he wanted to shoo the darkness away. Hector kept looking sideways at his companion. He could not believe that Tojo could be so nonchalant about an exciting event like a murder. But Tojo was so much a part of the village it was as if he understood the secret rhythms of life and death, as if long ago he had sensed that underneath the surface calm there were unplumbed caches of violence. Before they reached the top of the drive excited voices were already singing out the news. Lights flared up in the huts on both sides of the public road and when Tojo and Hector arrived at the shop bridge a crowd had gathered as noiselessly as moths in the darkness.

"Lord, but look how she chop him up, eh!" a woman said, and others added:

"Still water does run proper deep. All these years the woman

140

been going 'bout like if butter can't melt in she mouth and now look what she do to poor Chinaman!"

"Look how the blood still wet on the grass!"

A few people lit wicker torches and from the fringes of the crowd Hector saw the dead man's brains staining the ground like broken egg yolks.

"We better fetch weself back home before Sister get back from the station," Tojo said, and Hector was glad to go.

When Sister returned the two boys were sitting on the front porch.

"Tojo, if you don't march back to bed this minute I will pepper your skin with a tamarind whip, boy!" she said.

"I woke him up, Sister," Hector said.

"You didn't have no right to do that. You mean there en't enough trouble already without all you heaping more on top me head!" She sent Hector inside for her shawl and when he brought it she said, "I want a word with you, boy, I don't want you to breathe a word about what you see. You en't getting mix up in no court story, you hear me. I done tell Mark-a-book that Dookia call out to me and when I wake up and go to she, she tell me what a horrible thing she do and ask me to walk with she to the station."

"What will they do to her, Sister ?"

"Only Jesus in Heaven know that, boy."

"Will they kill her, Sister. . . I mean. . . Doorne says that they hang you if you murder somebody. . . but then if they kill you the man who does it will have to be killed too. I don't understand all this mixed up business."

"If you kill, then the law comes in and law is a mighty thing, boy, a powerful thing and the white man does control it – there's one law for the white man and one for the black and it's the great ones in the city who does decide that."

"Who is the law, Sister?"

"Poor folk like we don't know that, boy. The law is like the power of darkness and when the shadow of this law fall across you only Jesus in Heaven can save you."

"I don't think they should kill Dookia."

"Don't fret your young spirit with them things, boy, all you got to do is take my advice, keep your mouth shut tight and act like you en't never see nothing nor hear nothing."

"Dookia is a nice kind woman, she's always giving me roti and sweets and lending me her canoe."

"You too young to know what lock up in the tight places of people's heart, boy. Is plenty things you got to learn about the trials of this life."

*   *   *

Caya visited Dookia before the police van took her away to prison in New Amsterdam. There was much speculation in Tarlogie about what passed between them. Some people said that Dookia didn't want to defend herself in the coming trial, that she was going to let them hang her without saying a word, others claimed that Caya had offered to get Rodriguez, the obeah-man to put a spell on the judge, that Caya wanted Dookia to be freed so that he could marry her and take over the shop.

"Caya is a sly-mongoose of a man," Tanta Bess had said to a group of women who had visited her to discuss the murder, "he more tricky than a tree-full of monkeys." She dropped her voice to a whisper, "to tell you the truth it won't too much surprise me if Caya did spur on Dookia to do away with she husband. Caya take after he father, nobody don't know how the both of them does live and yet they living better than me and you."

Dookia had left Caya in charge of the rum-shop and the drummerman spent his days in the corner of the shop veranda that overlooked the kennels. He didn't reopen the shop. That would have called down too much suspicion on him. A police sergeant-major had come from New Amsterdam, and with a superior breathing down his neck, Mark-a-book had to act right, to go about the village as if he was in a strait jacket, treating friends and enemies impartially and making it clear that whilst his boss was around all hands had to avoid not only evil but also the appearance of evildoing.

The rice cutting season came around and Tarlogie was quiet, deserted through the daytime. The villagers left for the fields at fore-day morning and returned to their huts long after sundown. They set out singing, laughing, discussing Dookia's chances, and they returned in silence, their limbs sluggish with fatigue, their eyes feeling like stones in sleepy sockets.

Flocks of black and yellow ricebirds and robins raided the rice beds and the threshing floors and the children who were too young to work spent their time shouting them away. Scarecrows, made in the form of crosses topped with the bleached skulls of animals and draped with old clothes which flapped in the wind, frightened both the winged raiders and the children.

*   *   *

Caya lingered in the cool of the veranda until the afternoon sun lost its sting, then he set out for the foreshore in Chinaman's coreal. He was on his way to gather firewood. Nobody in the village had time for woodcutting during the harvest and the logs and faggots he collected could be sold for high prices. He disliked farming, it was brute-work which brought in only marginal gains.

"Is why black people does always try to make a living the hard way?" he had asked Tengar one day, "You does ever see the white folks and the brown folks sweating theyself dry in the hot sun? From a logical point of view, pardner, them who don't brutalise theyself with hard work does eat the cake while the nigger-people does only scrape up the crumbs. I got sweet-skin, man, so me got to live by me brains."

It was ebb tide when he reached the foreshore and the beach was covered with driftwood. The rivers around Tarlogie burst their banks in the rainy season, uprooted trees and disgorged them into the sea, and the water scattered them along the coast, leaving them stranded on the beach with roots and branches twisting like limbs in pain.

On the few occasions that Caya did work, he set about it with a concentrated efficiency. As soon as he reached the beach he began selecting the trees which were not water soaked, cutting branches into ten-foot lengths and piling them on to a rough sleigh. Since none of the trees were hard-woods he could work quickly. It was illegal to collect driftwood without permission from the police but this did not worry Caya. There was too much mud and water, too many sandflies and mosquitoes between the police station and the foreshore and the upholders of law and order were a precious-skinned lot. In any case Caya had the keys to the rum-shop and a few bottles of "Russian Bear" were enough of a bribe to establish his rights to all the timber the Guiana rivers could vomit out into the sea.

Caya piled the coreal high with wood, tied a rope to its prow and hauled it across the swamp. He unloaded at Maiden's Head and made his way home in the darkness. He would do business at day-clean before the villagers set out for the ricefields. He called out to Tengar and Elsa, chatted with them for a while and then headed for his hut. When he arrived home he lit his lantern, heated up the curried rice and peas left over from lunchtime and sat in a corner of the square hut scratching his belly and belching from time to time as he ate. He stood up and stretched when his enamel plate was empty and the yellow lantern light sprawled his shadow all over the room. A stool, a baked mud fireplace, a bundle of hessian bags and four drums were all his furnishings. He picked up a drum and sat on the stool.

Dark clouds had been gathering at sundown but a rising wind was sweeping them away, leaving smoky scarves to drift across the face of the new moon and the stars.

Caya held the drum between his knees and fondled the tight goatskin. He tuned up and began beating a monotonous one-three tempo until suddenly he broke into a chant:

"Who can beat drum better than drum heself? Who can talk sweeter than drum own voice? Who can make music like drum own music? Drum, drum, drum is a woman who don't never lef' you – drum is a sweet mopsy who does coil up inside you' heart – drum is a wind you can't stop from blowing, drum is a echo always echoing – echo drum! Echo you' loud echoing, send message over the sea, over the swamp, over the forest – drum is a messenger wild with he message – drum is a prophet with a belly full of prophesying. If you got a drum you don't need no woman – is who make music but drum heself – music borned in the belly of a drum – make the sweetest music, drum, make the music so all can hear, make it so that foot can dance and belly-skin can shiver – drum, drum, you make me laugh you make me cry, you make Caya feel like he want to die – drum can set you free, yes, set you free, put wings on you' foot and rum in you' blood – now

144

listen to what a drum can do, you hearing? All you hearing? This is a blind beggar tap-tapping down a city street – this is a river singing a samba-man song – this is a red howler roaring – this is a who-you bird calling – and this, pardner, this is a wild-wind talking – you hear it? You hear it ? – Talk like wind does talk Mr. Drum – holler like a moonstruck madman, Mr. Drum – you can hear the dizzy, dizzy bird-flock flying – You can hear a two foot high baby crying – cry drum cry! Was a time when only drum had tongue and the drum had a tongue like a fast running river – and man didn't have a word on he tongue, not a word on he tongue 'cause Mr. Drum had all the talking – talk, drum, talk!"

In the midst of his chanting Caya stood up and moved round and round his hut with the eyes in his round Buddha's face bright as dew. Slowly at first and then faster and faster he shuffled his feet and moved his body rhythmically.

The drumbeats and the chanting transformed him into a bard, a Shango high priest incanting before a jungle altar, a witch doctor in the courts of the Boshongo kings, an oracle in the temple of the sun.

Some of the villagers heard the drumbeats and the chanting and they spread the word that the prelude to the wind-dance was over. This meant that Caya was certain that the night of the full moon would be a night of clear skies. Caya had made contact with the Shango gods and they had smiled on the village.

★　　★　　★

"You going to the wind-dance, Master Hector?" Tojo asked. The two boys had been hunting wood doves on Honey Reef and were resting under a cromanty tree.

"Are you going?" Hector knew that Tojo wasn't the best person for keeping a secret and he was being cautious.

"Me got to go, Master Hector, me is Caya's right-hand man. I does beat the kettle drum whilst he working out on the big tam-boom."

"I didn't know you could beat a drum."

"I can beat drum like fire, skipper, en't nothing me can't do better than that."

"I would like to go. I never saw a wind-dance, but the trouble is: How can I get past Sister, she will make no end of botheration if she finds out."

"It don't start 'til near midnight so go to bed early and do like you sleeping and when Sister settle down, then creep out softly-softly. That's what me planning to do. The thing is that we got to be smart and act natural and don't even go near Caya while he round and about."

"You ever went to a wind-dance, Tojo?"

"You will ask me that, Master Hector? Me learn to dance before me could walk and me mama take me to me first wind-dance when me was three year old."

"But who goes to the wind-dance?"

"Everybody, Master Hector, everybody."

"You mean even the churchgoers? Parson Grimes warned them not to go."

"Them same folks who does warm up the church pews on Sunday does dance shango 'til the moon tumble down and the sun jump up. Is only Preacher Galloway and Sister does stay away and me won't be surprised if them two didn't go to shango dance when they was younger." Tojo had much more down to earth views about people and events in the village than Hector.

"I would like to see what a wind-dance is like," Hector said, "And Caya said that I can come to this one."

"You're lucky, Master Hector, 'cause Caya don't allow outsiders to watch on."

"I'm not an outsider, my father owns the village."

"Your papa own the land, Master Hector, but not the folks living on it. Is who will work the land if all the people pick up theyself and clear out?" Tojo had heard old man Doorne ask this question a few weeks before and he was sure of his argument. "Land without people to work, is like having money and nothing to buy with it."

"My daddy can always find people to work his land, he said so."

"Grown up people does talk a lot of big mouth talk sometimes, Master Hector, you mustn't believe everything they tell you."

"My daddy doesn't tell lies."

"En't nobody who don't tell lie, Master Hector; my papa used to lie faster than a horse can trot, and them story old man Doorne

146

does tell, you think they is all true? Besides Caya tell me that lying makes the world go round."

"I read about a man named George Washington and he never told a lie."

"What kind of man this George what's-his-name was, a high and mighty man or a poor man? And was he a black man?"

"He was a white man and he was a powerful man. . ."

"Well that's what I mean to say because the high and mighty white man don't have to tell lie, they can pay the poor folks to tell lie for them. If me was a rich man you think me would have to tell any lie? Chu! Me would hire the stupid black people to do it for me, and once me pay them couple cents they would tell more lie than there is sand on the foreshore."

"They had poor men who never told lies, I read about them."

Tojo gave his young master an incredulous, pitying look.

"Master Hector, me head lil' hard and me en't got as much learning as you but me can tell you this, the white folks who does write down book-story is the biggest and baddest liars of all." Tojo's wisdom impressed Hector enormously but he wasn't going to lose face and give way to the houseboy's formidable logic.

"Some of the folks who write books might tell one or two lies but not all of them. In any case since you can't even read how can you tell?"

Tojo and Hector were both nearly sixteen but they were as different as an Eskimo is from a Zulu tribesman. The fact that they had grown up in the same household had made the difference more defined, more absolute. Tojo knew what he wanted from life – a speck of land under the sun, a wife, long cool evenings when he could make bacchanal and fête away the hours. He had no other ambitions. Hector, on the other hand had so much to look forward to that he did not know what he wanted. Tojo was a merry rascal-boy with the face and body of a gnome, a big-mouth laughing boy with a thick skin, and the ability to bounce like a rubber ball out of any trouble that befell him. He was midnight black and a brilliant smile could split his face quicker than a cutlass could open a green coconut. He spent most of his days being a buffoon because this was an effective way of deceiving those above him but underneath the buffoonery he was growing up wily and cunning. Because he had many weaknesses, he had an instinct for the failings of others and could exploit them to advantage. He lived in a sub-world, in which his ancestors had existed since they had been brought from Africa as slaves. They were a plastic race, a resilient people and they had survived by living secret lives among themselves, acting a servile role while they corrupted, absorbed and destroyed their masters; disciplining themselves and their children to a point of implacable docility all the time knowing that time was on their side. Occasionally they had erupted out of their sub-world when their discipline had cracked. Their frightened masters had then mashed them under hobbled heels and the survivors had retreated to their stockades of waiting once more. Feeling the bite of their master's fury had been their way of testing his declining strength and every time they tried to emerge they had realised that in order to keep them in a ditch their masters had to sit on top of them in it.

Tojo was content with his heritage of waiting, but Hector had the blood both of master and slave in his veins and the problems of both to solve. Before him lay the choice of allegiance, the question of loyalty, the need to discover who he was and what he was. Some day Tojo and his midnight people would break out and he would have to take sides. His years in Tarlogie had been idyllic until Elsa had pushed him away from the interlude of his adolescence towards the complexities of manhood.

Hector wanted to go to the wind-dance partly out of curiosity. Sister and the Reverend Grimes had denounced it too strongly for him not to want to find out for himself whether it was as evil and as demonic as they claimed it was. More powerful than this however, was an unconscious impulse to discover how deep his roots in Tarlogie were planted, to see which was more valid for him – the abstract heaven and hell about which the white minister preached or Caya's shango bacchanal with its drumming and dancing harking back to the African forests of long twilight.

For the villagers there was no problem, no conflict of beliefs. They had embraced the Christian faith which guilty masters had forced upon them, with enthusiasm, for by claiming a common God they could remind their overlords of their responsibility for the continued survival of their brothers and sisters in Christ. But they wore their Christianity like the clothes they put on to go to church on Sundays only, for the rest of the week the shango gods Damballah, Legba, Moko were theirs.

CHAPTER TWELVE

THE shango gods kept their promise to Caya. The full moon shone out of a navy blue heaven and made the night instinct with magic. The wind, light as silkcotton blossoms, barely whispered through the trees. In the glare of the moonlight, with silver palm fronds curving over them, the village huts on their tall stilts looked like watchtowers in an enchanted garden. There were clear stretches of water in the swamps where buffaloes had trampled down the rushes, the weeds and the lotus lilies, and these were striped with incandescent bars of white-gold when they caught the moon's reflection. A piper owl was singing in the giant silkcotton trees near to Doorne's hut and its high, fluted melodies could be heard all over Tarlogie. Chinaman's hunting dogs were howling as if they had seen a jumbie, and the villagers, preparing for the wind-dance, whispered to one another that the shopkeeper's ghost was roaming about his yard because his spirit could find no peace in the forest of the long night until Dookia joined him.

Hector heard the clock in the living-room strike half-past eleven and he crept out of bed. He could hear Sister wheezing in her four poster in the room opposite the dining-room. He climbed out of the window on to a length of rope which he had tied to the greenheart sill. He slid down the rope and found Tojo waiting in the shadow of the tamarind tree. They walked away from the house quickly, silently. Tojo spoke for the first time when they reached the stretch of swamp behind Doorne's hut.

"We will reach just in time if we hustle." There was a light in the hut and Hector said:

"Like the old man isn't going."

"Don't worry, he will be there, he does help Caya sing the ballad before the dancing start."

"I hope he doesn't tell Sister he saw me."

"He won't tell she nothing 'cause he won't want her to know he was there either."

"You think so, Tojo?"

"I know so. Is long time now me was dealing with that old man."

"What does it feel like, Tojo, when you're beating the drum and watching the people dance?"

"You does feel like you got a hot wind blowing inside you' bones, and the drum and the people and you does get mash together in the same feeling. It does feel like if you' sleeping with you' eye wide open . . . you know everything that happening and you' blood does run like cold fire through you' body. . . part of you does be awake and part does be sleeping. . . if me try to tell you what it feel like whole night you still won't understand, Master Hector, because is a thing you got to see and feel for yourself."

They moved across the swamp quickly and when they were passing by the spot where Hector's ancestor, Hingensen and his overseers had been buried by the slaves they listened for the sound of moaning.

"You hear anything, Tojo?"

"I don't hear a thing, Master Hector, except for that she-alligator in the bisi-bisi reeds calling for she young ones. I done tell you that grown up folks does tell big lies. Look how old man Doorne full we up with that ballad 'bout how if we come here on moonlight night we will hear Hingensen and he overseers calling out."

"I can hear the wind passing through the bisi-bisi softly-softly. . . and you know that sounds a bit like people crying. Perhaps Doorne wasn't telling a lie after all."

They heard Caya tuning up on his master-drum and Tojo said: "We got to hurry."

"Who made Caya a Shango priest, Tojo?"

"There was a priest in the village before me and you was born and when Mantop come for he, his spirit walk all over the village and one night this spirit-thing creep inside Caya when he was sleeping and from that minute Caya did know that he had to take

151

over the priest's work. Is so it does work out, nobody don't know who will succeed a dead priest 'til the spirit creep inside you, and once you born in Tarlogie don't matter where you go or where you try to hide the spirit does search you out and make you know, and once you get the message en't nothing you can do 'bout it but take over."

"But supposing you don't want to take over? What will happen then?"

"Mantop will come and tear the living heart out of you' chest-box."

"I never heard about that happening either in this village or anywhere else. If the spirit came for me I wouldn't go."

"It en't never happen that the man who the shango spirit call didn't answer the call."

"You think Elsa will be there?" Hector had wanted to ask this question all along but he had to get it in unobtrusively so as not to arouse suspicion.

"Tengar bound to be there but as for Elsa, he tell she that she's not to come 'cause he don't want he woman to mix up in shango fête. Some women does go mad when the drumming take hold of them and en't no telling what they will do."

"I didn't know that Tengar could tell Elsa what he wants her to do, I thought it was always the other way round."

"Tengar quiet and easy-going but when he stamp he foot down then Elsa does know it en't no use arguing."

They found Caya sitting in the centre of a semicircular altar when they reached Honey Reef. The altar had been built around the trunk of the cromanty tree and the moonlight had cast the tree's shadow away from it. Caya sat on a stool with his master-drum, the tambo-top gripped between his thighs. He was hold-ing himself still, erect, his shoulders thrown back. He was looking over the heads of the crowd of villagers gathered at a respectful distance in front of the altar. People were talking to one another in a muted desultory fashion. Basdeo, an Indian boy of Tojo's age, was kneeling before a tung-tung drum on Caya's left. Three steps led down from the platform to the hard sandy floor of the reef. There was a chechere, a sacred broom on one step and below it was a machete with a blade as bright as quicksilver. Tojo left Hector near the front of the crowd, circled the altar, climbed up from behind and took his place on Caya's right. A few of the villagers greeted Hector uneasily but when the boy's eyes made four with Doorne's, the old man nodded and looked away. Fruit bats were flying in and out of the branches of the cromanty tree over Caya. One flew so close to Caya that its wings must have fanned his face but Caya did not move, he just kept looking in front of him towards the blue velvet sky. He raised his arms above his head suddenly, holding his drumstick in his right hand, and torch bearers standing in a ring around the crowd lit their torches and held them up. Tojo and Basdeo opened up with a slow one-three beat and Caya, the Shango priest punctuated the rhythm with sharp, resounding notes on his master-drum. During the long intervals between Caya's drumbeats Hector was conscious of the burden of silence which had settled on the crowd. He edged forward until he was standing between two torchbearers and looking around he noticed Tanta Bess' sick daughter, wrapped in blankets and lying on the sand far to the left of the crowd. King Saul, the ram-goat was standing over her looking bored and disdainful and holding up his half-moon beard so that it caught the light. Doorne moved forward and stood between the crowd and the altar and at the same time two torchbearers broke away from the ring and stood facing the audience, one on either side of the altar.

Doorne started chanting in a voice as high-pitched and sweet as a piper owl's:

> Babba tea matele
> Babba tea matele
> Babba tea matele

He repeated the words and varied the tune until Caya broke in with his baritone chant:

> Legb-a-a-a Papa Legb-a-a-a
> turn you' ears and listen to me
> spirit of the wind
> strong as night
> soft as night
> wrap we round
> bandage we eye

take 'way the shadow
that no evil thing can ambush we days
Legba, occuru-Legba
talk to Moko
sweet-talk, Amanja
warble like Tinamou to Osein
make Ele like blind bat
and burn up he kinnah 'gainst the sun
Legba-a-a, Legba-a-a!

Caya, still keeping his drum locked between his thighs, danced slowly round the altar, then handing his drum over to Tojo he put on a long white robe and jumped down from the altar. Tojo and Basdeo began beating out a slow, ceremonial rhythm. Caya picked up the sacred broom and pointed to Tanta Bess' sick girl. Two men brought her to the foot of the altar and she lay inert, only her big white eyes shining like an ocelot's. Caya danced round and round her sweeping the moonlit air, swishing the coconut broom until it sounded like a man panting for breath. Sweat broke out all over Caya's face and when he passed close to Hector the boy could smell the clean raw odour of his body. The crowd joined Doorne in the chanting. Caya stood over the sick girl, pointed at her once more, and raised his arm slowly. She sat up, looking dazed. The chanting grew louder and the girl rose to her feet and walked towards the ram-goat. She picked up the rope which was tied around the ram-goat's neck and King Saul followed her meekly when she led him to the altar steps. A man brought a block of wood which was grooved to fit the ram-goat's neck. Caya replaced the sacred broom and picked up the machete. The girl and the ram-goat were standing on either side of the block. Caya did a sword dance, leaping, twirling the machete, cutting the air. Once or twice the machete passed inches away from Hector's face. The drummer boys hotted up the rhythm. Caya approached the ram-goat with a gliding movement until he stood facing the worshippers, the sacrificial block directly behind him, his arms outstretched and his shoulders twitching. He turned around, pressed the ram-goat's head on to the block and resumed his original stance. The girl untied the rope from around the ram-goat's neck. Caya danced backwards. He stood a foot away from the block, his back to it. The ram-goat had not moved. No one was holding it down but its neck still lay across the block. Caya spun around and with a single backhand stroke chopped the ram-goat's head off. Someone had passed a gourd to the girl and she caught King Saul's head in it and moved away so that Doorne could catch the spouting blood in a large brass bowl. When the flow of blood was reduced to a drip Doorne passed the bowl to Caya who drank some of the warm blood and passed it back. Doorne drank and passed the bowl around.

Caya wiped the machete on his robe and returned it to its place on the step, and then he took up his position on the altar once more. Tanta Bess' daughter had not walked for a whole year and now she was dancing as if she had wind in her feet. Caya pointed at her for the third time. She bowed down before him and when he signalled her to stand erect an ague took hold of her. Her limbs began to jerk as if they had individual, separate lives in them. The paroxysm continued until she passed out and a man carried her away and laid her in the shade of the cromanty tree.

The drums changed their rhythm and the villagers began to shuffle and dance to a slow monotonous beat. Hector felt the drumbeats twisting inside his head and he didn't know when he had joined the dancers or how long he moved round and round with the crowd of worshippers. He only felt a dizzy heat suffusing his body and his limbs turning to liquid. He was released from all that was his life in Georgetown and in the big house in Tarlogie. The disciplines imposed by his father and aunt, by Sister and his teacher fell away. The savage singing of shango drums had exorcised them.

Caya gauged the mood of the dancers, giving them time to warm up and at the same time not tiring them. They needed their energies for the finale. He quickened the tempo of the master-drum slightly and the drummerboys, taking the cue, beat out a fast and varied accompaniment. The dancers milled around with bodies vibrating effortlessly. The more vigorous dancers moved nearer the altar and the torchbearers made way for them. Caya circled the altar. The drum, imprisoned between his legs, had become a part of him. He waved both arms above his head and the dancers fanned out. Two men lit a fire and piled locust wood on to it. The flames leaped upwards and burnt the overhanging branches of the cromanty tree.

Tanta Bess' daughter had recovered and was standing to the right of the altar shaking all over. Caya jumped down from the altar once more. He danced into the fire. For a moment he stood there like a black Phoenix and then he stamped his way out of the flames and returned to the centre of the altar. The shaking girl flung herself down on the sand and rolled towards the fire. She rolled through it once and when Caya shouted she did it again, then she took off her dress and picking up a handful of burning coals ran them over her naked body. The beat of the master drum was steady, unchanging. A group of women stamped into position and danced in and out of the flames and after this cleansing ceremony they began trembling. One by one they passed out shouting strange words and frothing at the mouth. Their voices echoed and re-echoed over the swamps, more terrible than the cries of phantom slaves. When all of them were sprawled out on the sand like charred mango branches abandoned by a charcoal burner, Caya put down his drum and sang the ritual chant to Osein, the Shango god of virility. Doorne, his torso bright with sweat and the muscles of his neck standing out, began a contrapuntal chant to Moko, the father of black magic. Other sacrifices were brought to the foot of the altar – a white cock and six hens. Doorne ended his chant, seized the cock by its neck, bit the head off and spat it into the fire. There was a gasp from the onlookers as he held the neck to his mouth and drank the blood.

"He's a devil-man!" a woman sang out, and other voices joined in:

> "He's a devil man, a Moko-man
> a devil man, a Moko-man..."

Caya resumed his drumming and the chorus of drums quickened their tempo until it reached a peak of dissonance. Suddenly Tengar bounded into the open space before the altar. He was naked except for a loin cloth and a white flimsy cape trailing behind him. He moved with the speed and power of a jaguar, leaping, whirling, barely touching the ground. He snatched up the chickens one by one, wrung their necks and flung them into the crowd shuffling and stamping around him. His face was contorted, his eyes huge, white, luminous, his teeth bared. Two men flung lassoes around him and drew the nooses tight then they danced around him until he stood still, bound from shoulders to ankles with rawhide thongs. The two men knotted the thongs at his ankles and left him. Tojo and Basdeo came down from the altar and circled him beating their drums frantically.

Tengar strained against the thongs. They bit into his skin, deeper and deeper until with a bellow, he broke free. The thongs fell on the sand and he raised his arms to the moon. He leaped high four times drawing up his knees and flinging his arms wide and then he collapsed and lay still. He left a legacy of frenzy for the other dancers, for they closed in around him and began leaping and shouting until they too passed out one by one.

★   ★   ★

Hector found himself, laughing, shouting, sobbing. He broke away from the ceremony and headed for the swamps. He did not know how his legs had carried him there but when he caught himself he was standing outside Tengar's hut at Maiden's Head. The door was open and he walked up the steps and called out:

"Elsa! Elsa!"

"Who is that?" a sleepy, frightened voice enquired.

"It's me, Hector, I want to see you!"

"Is what you doing here at this time of morning? You must be crazy!"

"I want to see you, Elsa!"

"Suppose Tengar come and catch you, boy? Look I don't want no trouble you hear me."

"Tengar won't come. He's at the Shango fête and it won't finish until sun-high."

"Boy, you better go home. What happen, you drunk or what?"

"I'm not a boy any more."

"Then is all the more reason why you should have some sense in you' head. Why you don't go home, Hector?"

"I want to see you. I have fire burning all over me and it's no use my going home."

She ran past him down the steps and he grabbed her and held her against him.

"I don't feel like it," she said, pulling away, "let me go, boy!" She bounded away leaving a piece of her nightgown in his hand. She ran down the reef. He caught up with her and lifted her off her feet. She struggled so violently that he stumbled and fell on the sand. They lay together panting, and his laughter came out in gasps. Elsa drew his head down to her breast and he sucked at the nipple like a nursling. The warmth of her flesh comforted him. She burst out crying and sobbing and became hysterical and this chilled the fires in him. But when he tried to get up she clung to him. His mind was clear for the first time since he had left Honey Reef and he wanted to go home. Elsa, wrapped her legs around him and her animal smell attracted and repelled him in the same way it had done the first time he had laboured with her. She kissed him, using her tongue like a serpent's, and he knew that he did not want to escape her any more. When she had drained the sap out of him and he was feeling limp, he rolled away from her and vomited. She tried to put her arms around him and he pushed her away.

"Let me be!" he said roughly, and she held her face close to his so that he could see the venom in her eyes.

"Is so you talking to me, eh? Me is just a thing to use and cast aside just like your papa used to do. Well take a tip from me, brown boy, don't never come near me no more, you hear!"

"I didn't mean to hurt you, Elsa. I didn't know what I was saying or doing, don't be vexed with me," he pleaded, but she walked away and left him.

CHAPTER THIRTEEN

HECTOR returned home to find Sister up and fully dressed. The way she gripped the arms of her rocking chair, and her silence when he greeted her, told him more plainly than words that she knew he had been out all night, that he been to the wind-dance.

"Sister, why are you so angry with me?" He felt much happier when she was talking. Her silence oppressed him. He knew that his question would irritate her so much that she would have to speak.

"To think that I bring you up all these years to be a Christian young man! And all the gratitude I get for it is that you climb out of the window like a thief and go and beat you body about in the moonlight and the dew!" Hector knew that this was the prelude to a spate of trenchant reproof and he stood leaning against the wall saying nothing in his own defence. "You don't have pride or what, boy? The Bradshaws had they bad ways but en't never one of them who could say 'this one or that one didn't have no pride' because they was all prideful people. After this night I won't never be able to hold up me head and look nobody in the face in this village. The Lord knows I try to bring you up right, boy! I teach you to respect you'self, to fear the Almighty, to live so that no man can ever point a finger at you. . . but like I fail in me task, all I succeed in doing is bringing up a young savage who en't no better than the barefoot, good-for-nothing people in this village, people who act like they heeding the word of the Lord on Sunday whilst all during the week they heart black and bitter with the poison that drip-dripping into it from the devil's tongue." Sister had never spoken to Hector in this way before. She regarded his going to the wind-dance as a terrible betrayal. Through the years, she had carefully fashioned the mould that he should have fitted his life into, and now, just as she was about to sit back and admire what she had created, Hector had broken out of the mould. His rebellion was such a fundamental one, she knew that the whole pattern of authority she had established over his life was broken for ever. She had allowed Hector so much liberty only because she had been certain that she had no rivals for his love and his loyalty, and that he should betray her in this way was something she could not forgive. She had renounced Shango worship and adopted a new faith since she was seventeen, and because it was still close to her, because the sound of drums still echoed in her blood, because church bells had muted but had never silenced the invocations of Shango chants, she had embraced Christianity with a fervour bordering on fanaticism.

"I feel so much shame that it choking the love that I have in me old heart for you, boy. Is how you of all people can do this to me? Is how you can do this to me, me who rock you in me arms when you was so young you didn't have the strength to raise you' head off a pillow, me who stand vigil by your cradle all night long so that me could hush-a-bye you to sleep when you cry out?" She hugged her chest and rocked from side to side as if her shrivelled breasts were aching her, and tears ran down her cheeks. Hector went up to her and rested his head on her shoulder the way he had done the night his father had brought him back to Tarlogie.

"Don't cry, Sister, don't cry. . . it wasn't such a bad thing that I went. . . it only made me see how much I belong here. . . I don't even want to go away and study, I want to stay here with you. . . it wasn't a bad thing that I went. . ." He would have said anything to comfort her although they both knew that the time was coming for him to go and that he wanted to go. He was young and selfish and greedy for experience. Those who loved him and those he loved were like sticks that he used to grope his way through the half-dark, half-light world of his adolescence; when he broke out he would throw the sticks away and rush blindly forward. He embraced her and they wept together, he for his youth, the idyll that was slipping away and she for the life she had lived through him for a season.

160

★   ★   ★

La Rose arrived at eight o'clock and scolded Hector for not doing his homework.

"You're not going to matriculate in this way you know, the exam will be coming up in six months." The teacher began his geography lesson, "Where does the Ganges River rise?"

"In the mountains of the moon, Sir."

"What's come over you, Hector? You sound like a man in a trance. Pull yourself together, boy. Now name me four of the world's longest rivers!"

"The Ganges. . . the Amazon. . ." His eyes strayed to the window on his right, and he saw Tengar walking across the swamp towards Maiden's Head. "I'm not feeling too well, Mr. La Rose, I have a headache and my stomach's feeling upset."

"I'll have a word with Miss Smart, that you should see a doctor."

"No, don't tell her anything. . . I'll be all right in a minute. . . the Mississippi and the Nile. . . the Ganges is in India, the Amazon in Brazil. . ." he saw Tengar climbing up the steps to his hut.

"You're not well, Hector, and I'll have to talk to your guardian." La Rose always spoke of Sister in the most formal manner.

"I'm all right now, Sir. . . ." La Rose stood up and called Sister.

"Miss Smart! Miss Smart!"

"You want me, Teacher?"

"Yes, Hector's not very well, I think he should see a doctor."

"Hector, go to your bed, boy!" Sister ordered, "I think he must be tired, Mr. La Rose, he didn't sleep well last night. I will put him to bed and give him some castor oil." This was the medicine Hector hated most but he did not object because he felt that he was getting off lightly. "I'm sorry you had to come all this way in the hot sun for nothing, Mr. La Rose."

"It's all right, Miss Smart, if the boy's sick then it couldn't be helped."

"Have something to eat before you go, Teacher."

"I would prefer not, Miss Smart, I had breakfast just before I left home."

"He should be all right by tomorrow and if he en't better I will send Tojo to inform you, Teacher."

161

"Thank you, Miss Smart."

She watched him wheel his bicycle up the drive.

"That's a fine young man, eh," she said and added for Hector's benefit, "anybody would be proud to have such a son."

★   ★   ★

The mid-morning sun was heating up the swamps and there was a haze over the saffron, the weeds, the lilies and the birds feeding beyond Maiden's Head. A flock of herons, pink against the sun, was flying out to sea and pairs of parakeets screamed across the sky on their way to the mango groves on Honey Reef.

Sabgar, the Syrian pedlar had spread out his wares by the roadside and a crowd of villagers had gathered around him. He was a thin man with a body like a bent hairpin, a face as narrow as a blade of razor grass, and cunning eyes glinting like blue steel in his head. He strutted around his bright baubles like a sandpiker, encouraging reluctant buyers to take advantage of his cut-rate prices.

Tengar had passed the Syrian without pausing to look at his merchandise. He had promised to buy Elsa a new dress but he was feeling too dazed and tired after the Shango fête to bother about keeping his promise.

He found Elsa preparing lunch when he entered the hut.

"Well, Mr. Tengar, you had you'self a proper good time, eh? You stay out all night and make plenty bacchanal. I hope you en't planning to do this too often, man, because me en't good at staying home and waiting for me man to come home night after night. Me is the kind of plant that you got to water and fertilise often or else me don't take root."

"All me want to do now, gal, is to catch some shut-eye quick 'cause weariness killing me."

"All right, sleep all the sleep you want but don't forget what me telling you!"

"Elsa, you know I am a man who likes his yard and me don't stray from it, so why you want to heap quarrel on me head when me eyelid so heavy I almost need two-by-four planks to prop them up." Tengar stretched out on the floor. His eyes felt as if they had dust in them. He closed them and felt the weariness thickening his blood, turning it to molasses.

Elsa had not noticed the sky darkening and when a thunder-storm broke and white scythes of lightning made jagged cuts through black clouds, she rushed out to fetch her washing. Halfway up the steps the rain came down and drenched her. The roof was leaking and drops of water fell into the charcoal brazier, hissing and filling the small room with steam. Elsa moved the brazier and put an enamel basin in its place. Tengar was asleep breathing heavily. The rain stopped suddenly and the sun burst out. She went to the door and watched the clouds break up and scatter, the wind like a mad shepherd was chasing them over the western horizon. Tengar's loud breathing irritated her. It reminded her of how much trouble she had gone to preparing lunch and how, without bothering to eat he had thrown himself down on the floor and fallen asleep. She was growing more and more restive in Tarlogie. What she missed most was the excitement of many men lusting after her. She had tried to convince herself that living with Tengar would be enough but at heart she had remained a courtesan and her eyes were always straying towards new savannahs. After six years of living with Tengar she still felt unfulfilled. He was as strong as a mule and had sprinkled her days with delight but she was still dissatisfied.

She thought of her affair with Hector and shrugged away the memory of this small-boy from the big house who was beginning to smell his sweat and to feel the stir of sex in his limbs. She felt no guilt about having seduced him. "It was his own fault," she told herself, "the boy came into my hut challenging me with his lean brown self. What was I to do but make him dip his wick in the honey so that he could feel what it's like to be a man?" Elsa regarded sleeping with a man as something as natural as washing your bare feet at the bottom of the steps before you entered a hut. So long as a man was young and strong and his beauty was not too difficult she was willing to give him a try. The only reason why she had not been promiscuous in Tarlogie was because the village was too small, eyes were always watching her every move and tongues were always ready to start clacking. Picking on Hector had been a wise move. No one would suspect this dreaming bright-eyed boy from the big house, and no one would mind if they did. The Hingensens and Bradshaws had birthed many bastards in their time; this was a privilege to which their wealth and position entitled them. The villagers, whilst they were always quick to condemn the poor, were partial to prodigal sons who came from rich families.

Elsa went inside the hut and stood over the sleeping Tengar. His face in repose reminded her of old man Doorne's. The expression on the face was one of childish brooding. His mouth was open and his lower jaw hung loose with a trickle of saliva running down the side of his mouth nearest the floor. His big nose had nostrils which arched outwards and as he breathed, they palpitated. His forehead was wide and smooth and beaded with drops of sweat which looked like morning dew on waterlily leaves. Looking at him and listening to his breathing Elsa became conscious of the life force which was generated somewhere inside Tengar's Samsonian body, and she sensed that this life force was a volcanic thing crying out for release, that everything he had done so far – his trips to the balata forests, his snatching her away from Jojo in the Georgetown market, his church going, his shango worship, had been an attempt to come to terms with the wild urges, the choking impulses in his heart. She saw all this in swift intuitive flashes and she knew that if she could give herself completely to Tengar she would be able to help him.

But a man had cast a spell over her when she was fifteen. He had mashed and trampled down the green splendours of her youth and left her like a sea egg sucked dry by the sun. She had tried to break away from the memory of him by labouring under other men's sweating, eager bodies, but the memory had never stayed away for long.

She squatted on the floor beside Tengar, turning her back to him and looking through the open door at the bisi-bisi and wild cane reeds leaning away from the wind. Beyond the reeds, standing in the midst of a cluster of water-lilies was a governor crane holding its plumed head high and standing motionless on one leg.

Elsa remembered the black-faced, black-hearted man – he had seemed old to her even then – who used to sell milk. Her mother would send her to his cow pen in the early mornings. The very first time she met him he had frightened her. His leering, speculative eyes had pinned themselves on to her young body, weighing her limbs as if they were merchandise. The old man's eyes had made her feel like crawling into a hole in the ground to escape their persistent, lecherous probing.

"Ma," she had pleaded when she returned home, "Ma, don't send me back to that old man, I beg you, don't send me back 'cause that old man got a look in he eyes like a johncrow that waiting for something to die. I beg you, don't send me back, Ma!" But her mother wearied by the sun, the burden of work and poverty, had chased her away.

"The man selling milk cheap, en't nobody else selling it cheaper than he, so go 'long 'bout you business, gal, and leave me to me toil!" she had shouted.

Elsa had tried to get the neighbour's daughter to accompany her to the cow pen but the girl had opened her eyes so wide that they had looked like bowls of milk with black buttons floating in them, and said:

"That old man is a devil-man, girl, and somebody will have to use bush ropes to drag me near him!"

The old man never spoke to her but his eyes always left her feeling that there was something unclean in her body. One morning she was bending over her pail of milk when he came and stood close to her and the consciousness of his evil presence was so overwhelming that she began to shiver. After a while she felt his hands fondling the tight lumps of her breasts and she jumped away, crying out like a curlew startled in its sleep. She had snatched up her milk and fled and his deep, chuckling laughter had followed her. As she ran down the baked mud path she felt as if her head was spinning round and round on her neck. His laughter followed her all the way home. The feel of the man's thick, moist fingers persisted. If he had cut his hands off and glued them to her bosom they could not have felt more real. She wanted to confide in her mother but she was certain that he would kill her if she did. Obsessed with the secret, she became feverish and delirious and her mother had to tie her down to her bed. She was ill for a week and when she was well enough to return to the cow pen, she refused to go. Her mother, who had a heavy hand and a market woman's tongue, persuaded her to change her mind with a balata whip and rounds of abuse.

The look in the old man's eyes became more compelling, more venomous. She was trapped, and the old man's labaria eyes revelled in her torture as he watched her come and go. She grew to hate as well as fear him. She was certain that one day he would turn into a snake and coil and constrict her body, mashing up her bones and crushing her into jelly. It came to her suddenly that she had to kill him. One morning she wrapped a prospecting knife in a piece of cloth and tied it around her waist. When she reached the cow pen she avoided his eyes and walked up to him. He had spoken to her for the first time that morning.

"Elsa, gal, is what you got round you waist, gal?" he had asked, laughing a jackal laugh, "You got a knife? Well, if you want to kill me here is you' chance!" He had torn open his shirt, exposing a black chest with grey hairs growing between the pectorals. She pulled out the knife and held it poised to strike and he had come so close to her that she could smell the fresh perspiration on him.

"Kill me, gal, kill me! Ha, ha, ha!" Her hand trembled and she dropped the knife. He picked it up, "If you don't have the mind to do it then I will do it meself." He raised the knife and she, without knowing what she was doing seized his hand and begged him not to kill himself. He pushed her away and kept on laughing and laughing and she grabbed her pail of milk and ran away sobbing.

There was a thunderstorm one August night and the thunder and lightning had awakened her. She heard the old man's voice calling in the silence that followed an explosion of thunder.

"El-s-a-a-a-a! El-s-a-a-a-a-a!" Her mother was sleeping beside her on the floor of their hut and she turned to see if she too had heard the voice, but the old lady continued snoring rhythmically.

"El-s-a-a! El-s-a-a!" The voice was more insistent, closer to her. She got up and crept out of the hut, feeling dazed and following the voice like a dancer hypnotised by a Shango drum.

It was past midnight and the villagers were sleeping soundly under thatched and zinc roofs which muffled the rain's droning, and the noise of wind slashing across palm fronds and tamarind trees. The tree frogs having begged for downpours through a long dry season were silent.

"El-s-a-a, come, gal!" The wailing voice called out, and she hurried towards the old man's hut at the back of the village. As she approached she saw parallel bars of light shining through cracks in the board windows. She hurried past the giant silkcotton tree and walked up the steps. Lightning flashes illuminated the swamp and the grove of trees on the southern reef. She paused halfway up the steps and felt the rain pasting her dress against her body and the water running down her forehead and into her eyes. She closed her eyes and the next flash of lightning filled her mind with a vision of mounting staircases of surf up which the wind climbed noisily, of swamps where sleeping birds stood motionless with their heads buried in the feathers of their wings, of swamps over which the wind scattered fireflies like sparks, of white hills rising out of a black ooze, of forests where the branches of tall trees interlocked like the arms of lovers, of huts with dark interiors, some filled with warm vaporous breath and others housing dead men and women who lay twisted like rope on mud floors, and for a moment she thought that the dead, like lightning, had burnt out themselves to light the earth. She opened her eyes and the vision was gone and there was nothing but wind and rain and darkness around her.

The door was ajar and she entered. The old man was sitting on the floor with his back to her. There was a brass goblet in front of him and a thin spiral of smoke rose up from it.

"You was calling me and I come," she said, closing the door behind her. He stood up and came to her. Standing under the lantern, his eyes were hidden in shadows but she could feel them on her.

"I was waiting for you, gal. I was willing you to come and waiting," he said and he took off her dress and began to rub her down.

"Is what you want with me, old man?" she asked in a strangled voice.

"I want the youngness of you' limbs, the softness of you skin. . . all you' youth lock up and clench like a tight fist inside you. . . I want to tear it open so that it can fertilise me old bones. En't no one else in the village can give me what I want but you, gal."

He gave her a warm drink in an enamel cup with blue edges

167

and when she drank it she felt fires burning and swelling inside her. He embraced her, pressing her against him. His hard, knotted body was as rough as a lignum vitae trunk and the feel of it was so overpowering that her mind seemed to be breaking up and scattering itself into fragments of separate feeling. The urgency of her craving for him made her hysterical and she sobbed and whimpered like a sick baboon. They wrestled together and when she cried out with pain and ecstasy she remembered him telling her not to be afraid over and over again. Afterwards, she could remember little else besides his hot breath, and his grizzly chin bruising her face, her neck, her shoulders.

The storm had ceased at fore-day-morning and she woke up to find the old man standing over her, telling her to go home before her mother missed her. She had thrown herself at his feet, begging him to let her stay.

"You must go, gal, you must go now. You will come back again but you must go now," he said, and he had wiped the blood clots from her loins and she had gone home.

★   ★   ★

Elsa turned around and looked at the sleeping Tengar once more. For a moment he opened his eyes and looked at her.

"Tengar," she said, "if this thing hadn't happened to me, me could have did love you plenty, boy, but the man who cast this spell over me, who blight me young and juicy days, who knead me heart dry of all the things that does flower in woman's heart is you' father, that monkey-face man who always acting like he grudge every breath me breathe, he is you' own father, Ebenezer Doorne."

Tengar closed his eyes and turned over on his side. He did not hear her. After his exertions at the wind-dance only a loud explosion could bring his mind back to consciousness.

CHAPTER FOURTEEN

"HECTOR is why you don't go to your bed, boy?" Sister called out from her bedroom door. "Is after one o'clock and I can hear the morning crickets already."

"I'll go in a minute, Sister, I'm learning some geometry theorems and as soon as I finish I'll go." He could not keep the note of irritation out of his voice. "She's always getting at me about staying up late," he thought, "and the exam's only two months off. Why can't the old woman let me be. It's always, 'Hector, go to bed boy. Hector, you know how you're not too robust.' Hector, this, and Hector that, and since I went to the wind-dance she's been really crotchety and acting like I committed some kind of crime."

"You aiming to wreck your health or what, boy? The white-man books drive plenty folks mad – there is Prophet Wills, the schoolmaster, that man used to be nice and quiet, a proper gentleman until book-learning turn a screw loose in he head. And now what he doing? He traipsing up and down the coast talking crazy and saying that the end of the world is at hand – then there was Lawyer Brown, a tall samba man who could tickle a young-gal heart by just looking at she. What you think happen to he? He mumbling his days away in the Georgetown poor house. And is nothing else but the white-man book-learning that pin madness on he. I'm telling you, boy, if is so you got to sore up your eyes and wreck your health, the examination en't worth it."

"But I'm not wrecking my health, Sister, I'm feeling fine and anyhow Teacher La Rose told me that he stays up studying night after night and he looks all right to me. . ."

"Don't tell me about Teacher La Rose, boy, 'cause that young man is all skin and bone with the clothes flapping around he, with the hollows under he eyes so deep, it's a wonder that his eyes don't get lost away and drowned in them hollows. You would have to keep pumping food inside he for a whole year before he begin to look like a human being."

"Sister, why are you so vexed with me?" Hector had wanted to ask this question since the morning after the wind-dance.

"Vexed with you, boy? You mean about staying up late?"

"No, it's not about staying up late, it's about something else that you won't tell me. We were getting on all right, then suddenly you changed and it's just like if I've become a stranger to you these last few months."

"It's not me that's changed, boy, it's you. You're growing up, and growing up does make young people selfish. I'm the same Sister that your young eyes first light on the evening when your daddy bring you back to this village. I en't changed at all. I'm the same old black woman carrying a heavy load of memory, waiting for Mantop to come and carry me to the forest of the long night. Me skin might crinkle until it look like a map with plenty rivers, me body might get dry as a stick, but me old heart is full already, full of good things and bad, full of sorrow and laughing – so full that there en't no more room left in it for any kind of change to come about."

Hector knew that he wouldn't get anywhere with the old lady once she started to shield herself with words, so he changed the subject.

"You know, Sister, there are times when I feel that it would be a good thing for me to go away and study, to clear out of the village, but now that the time's drawing near sometimes I wish that I fail my exam so that I might go on staying in a place that I know. That last time that I went to Georgetown to visit my father I found the whole world full of strangers and I was frightened. At least if I had grown up in the city I wouldn't have been afraid, but I'm a country bumpkin, a muddy-footed peasant. . . I often wish I had grown up in the city, the only thing is that I couldn't have learned about hunting and fishing there, could I?"

"You would've learnt how to be a proper hypocrite in the city, boy, I can tell you that, city folk is a two-faced lot."

Sister pulled up a chair and sat at the table facing Hector. She was wearing an embroidered bed jacket over her white cotton nightgown and Hector noticed that the tassel hanging from her nightcap shook every time she spoke.

"I'm not two-faced now, Sister, and if I had grown up in the city I wouldn't have been two-faced either."

"I wasn't saying that you was two-faced, boy. Is where you get that idea from at all? You're not a city man and you never will be one, thank God. This coast has already given you something that, wherever you go, you will have strong memory to hold on to – the smell of the earth, the feel of the hot sun, the knowledge that when you stand facing the sea there en't nothing behind you but swamp and forest and the blue horizon – you can never tear them things out of your system even if your restless spirit carry you to the ends of the earth. And what you think the city would 'ave given you, boy? I will tell you: the memory of the bird-voice of that old harridan of an aunt of yours, of streets that the sun bake hard, with houses all around pressing down on top of you, of beggars and street preachers – that is what it would 'ave given you because the city don't have no heart to it. So let me pick up me old body and go and try to catch some sleep," she stood up and pulled her night jacket around her shoulders, "and don't be long, Hector!"

"No, Sister, I won't be long now."

Sister returned to her bed but could not fall asleep. She lay on her back looking at the ribbed dome from which the mosquito net spread outwards over her bed. A single mosquito had got inside the net and she heard it singing close to her right ear but made no attempt to drive it away. She had not been sleeping well of late. Old age was making her afraid to sleep, afraid that one night she would close her eyes and Mantop would ambush her. Recently she had found herself thinking about death quite often. She thought about it impersonally, estimating how much more time she had to live and going over in her mind the things she wanted to do before she died. The fear of dying in her sleep had come upon her suddenly, at the very time when she had convinced herself that she was unafraid, that she was a righteous, god-fearing woman who did not have much on her conscience to trouble her. The thought of Hector's having to go away had aggravated this fear.

"Once he leaves," she told herself, "I'll have to marry old man Galloway, because I won't be able to endure this Bradshaw big house when it's full of silences. I'll miss the boy when he's gone. I know that he'll forget all about me for a while because young people nowadays don't think about anyone but themselves, but the time will come when the loneliness and the strangeness of strange places will make him think back to the days of his youth, when old Sister was the rock on which he used to lean and all of a sudden he will feel close to me again, and the voices of strangers won't be able to shut out my voice. Still, I can't complain because the boy brought gladness into the house all these years and if the spirit move him to come back after his studies then he will bring joy to my old heart again. . ."

She heard Hector moving about the living-room, heard him bolt the front door and walk quietly to his room. She closed her eyes. For a moment she heard the wind singing in the po-boy and tamarind trees but it was such a familiar noise that she soon lost all consciousness of it. The sounds of wind and surf were like heartbeats in Tarlogie; you were only conscious of them when they threatened to die down or when they rose to a peak of fury.

She turned on her side and tried to sleep but could not. Thoughts rang in her mind like alarms every time she dozed off. She had denied that anything had come between herself and Hector when he had asked her the question outright, but something had intruded into their relationship. Part of it was the fear that his departure would leave her with nothing but the spectre of her old age grimacing at her. But his going to the wind-dance had forced her to accept that anyway as he grew older he was drawing further and further away from her. When his father had left him in her care she had sworn to herself that she would not become too fond of him. "I'm taking this on because of his mother," she had told herself, "she was a good woman but she was weak, and in her weakness I was the one person she could cling to. The boy en't responsible for how he come into the world, for the sin and shame and sorrow that was heaped around him when his mother birthed him. I bring him up but I will always remember that I was only a servant in the Bradshaw house when his mother, because I was the only person she had to talk to and confide in, made me housekeeper. I must always remember that I'm a black woman in a village behind God's back. Fitz Bradshaw would have thrown me out long ago if I hadn't known his family secrets – all the going's on and the treasons tied up with Hector's birth. So don't deceive yourself, old woman. Don't for a moment allow any make-believe to turn your head."

★　　★　　★

La Rose had been to New Amsterdam for ten days to sit for his final teacher's examination. He turned up at the big house the day after his return wearing a new suit and looking as if he was delirious. It surprised Hector to see emotion breaking through his impassive mask. But La Rose had worked towards a goal, a seemingly impossible goal and reached it. If he passed his final examination (and he was certain that he had) he could then become a schoolmaster. Normally it would have taken a village boy thirty years to achieve what he had done in seven. The villagers had laughed at him, criticised him, hinted to his mother that for a poor black boy he had been aiming to hang his hat too high. Now he was about to show the lot of them that they had been wrong.

"Teacher La Rose," Hector said, "I finished all the problems you set me before you went away."

"Eh, what? Oh, yes, the problems," he looked at the book and then at Hector and he saw that he had been allowing the boy to read some of his thoughts. "Tell me, Hector, what do you really want to do with your life?" he asked twisting his mouth so that Hector thought he was smiling but when he saw the glitter in La Rose's eyes he knew that there was a desperate intentness behind his words.

"I don't really know, Mr. La Rose," Hector said. The question put him on his guard, made him suspicious. Everyone had been asking him the same thing – Reverend Grimes, his father, Sister – the question was always designed to create an opening so that they could tell him what he should do with his life. He could never answer it honestly; they did not expect him to. Behind it was the assumption that he was too young to make independent decisions. "I don't really know," he repeated, hoping to absolve himself from any further responsibility to reply.

"You don't know, eh?" La Rose continued relentlessly, "Well look at me, I didn't have any choice. I did what I had to do, the only thing that was open to me to do. I told you before that I have brains – the kind of brains that makes a man pass examinations. I've been passing them since I was seven. The first one I passed entitled me to go to grammar school." His long, bony, black fingers kept toying with the pages as he spoke and this both annoyed and fascinated Hector. "Yes, I won a scholarship but couldn't take advantage of it because my mother couldn't afford either the clothes I needed or the fare to Georgetown. In other words it was just as if I hadn't won it. It's all right to go to school barefooted in a village but you can't do it in the city. Perhaps I didn't tell you why I'm saddled with a clock-work brain, didn't explain fully. I never had a chance to live life as it should be lived with plenty laughing and bacchanal."

Hector wilted under La Rose's malicious gaze. It was as though he was holding him responsible for what life had done to him. "If I had had a chance to live, really live, then the books and the exams wouldn't have castrated me. But I never had the chance, and look at you! You have all the chances. Sometimes when I sit here opposite you I suddenly feel like laughing and I ask myself, 'why should I for a couple of dollars help you to do all the things I missed?' You don't know what you want to do, hmmm! that's a fruity one, boy! You see, you can afford not to know. I knew since I was six. I had one of two choices – to be a ricefield yokel or to try to be a teacher. . . I chose to be a teacher knowing what it would mean, my mother did not want it, she said that there were too many mouths to feed in our household, but I set my heart against the land, and when my mother saw how strong my spirit was and how set my mind was, she gave in. . . . "

And Hector kept thinking, "Why is he telling me these things, I am a boy and he, is a man and there are so many things that men do that I do not understand. I can feel little sympathy for him and yet he is trying to wrench it out of me." For a moment he was unhappy that there was no pity in his heart for others. He could pity himself, that was so easy, but to feel deeply for others meant that he had to break out of the private enclosures of fantasy in which he lived and he was afraid to do this.

"You must think that I am mad to talk to you like this all of a sudden," La Rose continued, "but I want to tell you this; I've been wanting to say it to you for years now: you've got all the chances I never had. You didn't even have to win scholarships to start you off because your father could afford to pay a hungry black boy to tutor you. Boy, you were born with a jewelled spoon in your mouth, I can tell you that and I'm not going to hide it from you any more: I hated you every minute of it. I'm not an envious man by nature but sitting here opposite you year in year out caused my insides to knot themselves up with hate and envy. Why should you have all these opportunities? You're a weakling who would have been dead long ago if you didn't have women to pet and pamper you back to life. Who gave you the right to all the privileges you have? You came upon them just by the accident of having a father who is a robber-man and a bully. I'm wasting all this breath on you because I feel you should know these things, know and feel them in every curve and crevice of your belly, boy. If you walk out into the wide world without knowing who you are and what you are you will be lost!" The teacher's anger exploding in a rush of words frightened Hector. He felt the man's hatred sawing into unplumbed places of his young mind and he wanted to escape. He was embarrassed for La Rose. All along he had looked on this man as an idol and now, suddenly, he was breaking his stony mask and revealing the human face behind it. Hector fidgeted in his chair and tried to look away but La Rose's big reddened eyes pinned him down, compelling him to stay where he was.

"Make good use of your chances, Hector, make good use of them, boy, because if you don't there will be a curse on you, a host of black tongues like ladles dipped in poison will pour curses on you and the hot venom in those black tongues will blight your life. You hear me, boy? You hear me?"

"Yes, Mr. La Rose. . ."

"Then take what I've told you and let it sink in deep and don't ever let forgetfulness down it even while you're asleep, boy. You hear me?"

"Yes, Mr. La Rose." The teacher got up and paced up and down, and once he stood by the window and held his face to the wind. "Are we going to have more lessons today, Mr. La Rose?"

"Eh, lessons?" he sat down once more. "No, Hector, that will be all for today. I'll take your homework with me and mark it." He closed his eyes and opened them slowly. His lids could have had cement hardening on them the way he fought to keep them open. "And by the way, Hector, you're such a secretive person you should be able to keep what I told you between us. You're not a namby-pamby boy-child any more you know."

"I won't tell a word of what you said to anybody, Mr. La Rose."

The teacher arranged his papers and books into a neat pile and left quickly and Hector stood at the window and watched him pedal away on his ancient bone-shaker.

CHAPTER FIFTEEN

CAYA left for New Amsterdam one fore-day morning and no one knew that he had gone until the cartmen, returning from the Port Mourant market, reported that they had passed him on the road at sun-high and he had told them that he was going to visit Dookia. The villagers were well informed on what had happened to Dookia since the police cattle van had driven her away to New Amsterdam. Cartmen, bus and lorry drivers, itinerant beggars brought news regularly and it was passed from yard to yard, embellished with imaginative detail and stamped with the authenticity which comes with many repetitions. It was said that the Government had offered Dookia a lawyer to defend her and she had turned the offer down. The Tarlogians were for ever suspicious of anything the great ones of the city offered. They reasoned that if the Government paid a lawyer to defend you, it meant that the man's duty would be to ensure that you were hanged. They applauded Dookia's refusal to be trapped. After all, they said, Dookia has enough money to afford the best criminal lawyer in the country. She should get somebody like Lawyer Boodoo, a man with honey on his tongue, a man who, if he can't win the jury over with words, then he knows how to oil their palms.

They knew that Caya had gone to New Amsterdam to fix things up. He already had the backing of the village obeah-man and with the help of a good lawyer he would be doubly reinforced in his bid to make Dookia escape justice.

Caya visited the New Amsterdam prison circumspectly. He had done so many things to qualify him as an inmate rather than a visitor, that from the moment he passed the first guard at the gates he felt that a host of eyes were scrutinising his past. He walked across the prison compound with the caution of a man who expected craters to open under him at any moment. The sight of Dookia shocked him. She had not changed at all and did not seem to be the slightest bit concerned about her fate.

"Howdy, Dookia," he said. He had slipped a five dollar bill into the warder's pocket and the man was picking his teeth and looking out of the window opposite Dookia's cell.

"Howdy, Caya, how things going in the village, man?" Caya had expected to see a distraught, helpless woman and on his way to the prison, had seen himself as a hero coming to her rescue. Her composure was almost an affront to him.

"Things going fine in the village, girl, everybody's wishing you well and hoping that you'll soon be out and about."

"Not everybody, Caya. I know in me heart that some of them will be wishing that they hang me. I was born in that village and I know the folks in it." He noticed that she was looking rested and well fed. Her black eyes shone like polished adze but they gave no clue to what she was thinking and her skin had the clean, cool look of a star apple bathed in morning dew. She's so much in control of herself, Caya told himself, you will have to scrape her deep before you find any feeling.

"I brought some fruit and cooked meat for you," Caya said. She knew what he had come for and was masking her anxiety so that he would panic and say what he had to say quickly.

"The rum-shop crowd must be fretting and fuming now that they don't have no place to congregate in Tarlogie."

"They got to walk all the way to the rumshop in Saltan Village and they don't like it one bit, girl." Dookia's impassive façade had the desired effect for suddenly Caya asked, "You see the lawyer yet?"

"The Government send one to me, a brown man who had more talk than a river coming down a mountain. He come and straight away he start acting friendly and he ask me why I did this thing, and I say, 'how can I tell you why? You're a stranger, I don't know you and you don't know me. Tell me, Mister Lawyer, how I can begin to inform you how twisted up and tied up love between me and Chinaman was.' And anyhow, how can I trust a Government man?"

"You did well, Dookia. You did splendid, girl; wasn't no use trusting that man because all he wanted to do was to take the words out of your mouth and shape them into a rope to hang you. I got a plan and it's bound to work." Caya pressed his face closer to the bars, lowered his voice and continued: "Lawyer Boodoo agree to take on the case but, he say it will cost three thousand dollars. . ."

"Lord Almighty! All that money just to save me?" Dookia was alarmed and flattered at the same time.

"Your life is worth more than that, girl," Caya said gravely, making an objective appraisal of Dookia's value, taking into account the shop, the land, the kennels and the cattle that the late Chinaman owned.

"If you think that Lawyer Boodoo got enough magic in his tongue to get me off then go ahead and make the arrangements, Caya, you is the only person that I trust; I got some good-for-nothing family, a brother and a cousin, but I don't trust them," Dookia said, and this provided Caya with an opening he had been waiting for.

"I know this en't the right time to talk about something like this, girl. . ."

"Time's up!" the warder said.

"Give me one minute more," Caya pleaded.

"All right, old man, but don't stretch out the minute too far because the superintendent might be coming around this way any time."

"Dookia, I want to ask you something."

"Ask me then."

"I want to marry you if this heavy story blow over. You think I got a chance?"

"I won't say yes and I won't say no because there's a big if hanging over everything." She had been expecting the proposal. Caya had wanted to hang his hat in her bedroom long before Chinaman's death. She would not have minded but it would have been too risky with an impotent, suspicious old man watching and waiting for her to betray him.

"Tell me something before I go, Dookia, why did you do it?"

"I had to do it," she said, "I had to do it." She could not put into

179

words how the old man had been hanging on to her like a parasite orchid or how an unreasonable impulse had driven her to cut him down so that she could free herself of the tentacles of age and feebleness that were suffocating her, how he had shamed her before his friends, and blind votaries of love and hate had impelled her to break out of the oppressive, claustrophobic atmosphere surrounding their lives in the two small, dark rooms at the back of the shop.

"I got to go, Dookia," Caya said, "and when Lawyer Boodoo come to see you, you must take heed of his words and you must repeat everything he tell you to say at the trial."

"I will take heed of his words if my heart can shape them and me tongue can speak them."

Caya hustled away after thanking the warder. He had not visited New Amsterdam since he was a boy and on his way to the lawyer's chambers he stopped to look at a few shop windows, thinking that with Dookia's money behind him he would be able to buy all the things that he imagined a shop owner should have – velour felt hats, two-toned shoes, colourful shirts and doeskin flannels.

Lawyer Boodoo's chambers were on the ground floor of a big two-storeyed house. A greying Negro clerk, dressed in a white drill suit and wearing steel-rimmed spectacles, opened the door in answer to his knock.

"I want to see the lawyer," Caya said.

"Have you got an appointment?"

"How can I have appointment when I come all the way from Tarlogie?"

"You could have written."

"I can't write, mister."

"What's your name?"

"Caya, just tell the lawyer that Caya is here; he will know the name."

The clerk looked him up and down, slanting the look down the wide bridge of his nose.

"Don't you have a Christian name and surname like everybody else?" he asked wearily.

"I'm not a Christian so I don't have no Christian name and I'm

180

not a SIR so I don't have no surname either. Just use the name Caya; I've been using it for thirty-six years and it does fit the tongue all right, man."

The clerk led him inside.

"Sit down, Mr. Caya," he said, pointing to one of the benches facing the door to the lawyer's office. There were half a dozen other clients in the waiting-room. At the other end of the bench on which Caya sat was a grim, bony East Indian woman who was breathing open-mouthed, showing a single yellow tooth in her lower gum. She was staring straight ahead, never taking her watery, near-sighted eyes off the door in front of her. The clerk reappeared and told Caya that the lawyer would see him and he hitched up his trousers and walked into the office. The lawyer stood behind a big desk which was bare except for a plain sheet of paper in front of him. Lawyer Boodoo was a tall Madrasee Indian with narrow, hunched up shoulders and an incongruously big head. He had bushy brows, a large beaked nose and cheeks which looked as though he was constantly sucking them in.

His face was one which could have served a witch doctor, a general or a politician to advantage.

"Sit down, Caya," he said, offering his hand. A handshake was a courtesy that he extended to all his clients since it was a good way of allaying their initial suspicions and putting them at ease. The Negro clerk kept hovering behind him until he sat down and dismissed him with a wave of his hand.

"Is our client willing?" he asked Caya.

"She say that you can go ahead with preparing to defend her, boss."

"Hmmm! It's not an easy case you know, and the prosecution lawyer is as sharp as a blade of razor-grass." He said this more to himself than to Caya and kept looking down at the sheet of paper before him all the time. He raised his head suddenly and twisted his lips into what was meant to be a smile but looked more like a leer. "You think she'll be able to afford my fee, Caya?"

"Dookia's got a pile of money salted away, boss. Rum-shop business is a paying business and, Chinaman, Jesus rest his soul, was not the kind of man who used to allow money to pass through he fingers like water."

"I see you've got a more than average interest in this case, Caya," Boodoo said rocking backwards and forwards in his swivel chair.

"I'm interested in the rope missing Dookia's neck, boss."

"I've defended over a hundred murderers in my time and the only case I ever lost was the one in which my client died from heart failure during the trial, and that you must admit was unusual. But nevertheless this case is a tricky one. . ."

"Sound as if that case that you lose was one where there was powers outside of the law loading the dice 'gainst your client, boss."

"There's no such thing as forces outside the law, Caya; the law embraces everything."

"Yes, boss, I suspect that it does."

"I'm going to frame my defence like this: I'm going to make the jury see Chinaman as a monster, a brutal, inhuman creature. The thing is, Caya, I can't make a man out to be too much of a monster, the jury tends to disbelieve me, so I'll start out by making him out to be a good man, a responsible husband, and then I'll show how by taking to the bottle he became the depraved individual who drove his young and faithful wife to the extremes of human endurance. You can't imagine how a jury enjoys being told about a man's downfall; it makes them feel so virtuous. And speaks more eloquently than the currency of the realm. . . and that reminds me. . . I need a thousand dollars to start with, I want it paid in a week from today."

"I don't understand all you was telling me, boss, but I understand the money part of the story and you will have the thousand dollars in your hand by next week, God willing." Caya rose to leave and Boodoo shook him by the hand once more.

"I'll do my best, and my best is always worth investing in," he said, ringing a small hand bell to summon the Negro clerk.

CHAPTER SIXTEEN

HECTOR met Elsa by accident late one afternoon when he was on his way back home from the foreshore. He had only taken the route across Maiden's Head because Sister had told him that Elsa and Tengar had gone to Port Mourant for a few days. Elsa had emerged from the dark interior of the hut unexpectedly and called out:

"Well, well, if it isn't the young master! What strange wind blow you this way, sir? Because you was avoiding me like a leper. I'm not vexed with you because, after all, you have the right to do whatever you feel like doing with we village folk and then to drop we when the spirit move you."

"I wasn't avoiding you."

"Chu! Don't come to me with that ballad, boy, every time you see me during these last few months you been dodging and hiding. What you 'fraid of, young master? You en't the only fish that swim in my pond, you know."

He couldn't squirm out of it, she had him trapped. There was something in her words like the humming of wind through high tension wires and he sensed that if he did not handle her with a certain amount of finesse she would make things unpleasant for him.

"I wasn't avoiding you," he repeated, suddenly picturing Elsa coming to his home and making a scene, an act he was sure that she was quite capable of, and one that he had to forestall, "it's only that I had to study for my exam and I haven't been going anywhere."

"Don't come to me with that ballad, boy. I know you and I know your papa and both of you can lie faster than a deer can run.

What I want to find out is who you think you are at all? Who tell you that you can treat me like if I is a nobody?" For the first time in his life Hector was being caught up in the web of a woman's emotional frenzies, a woman with whom he had slept. Since the night of the wind-dance, he often found himself lying awake at nights, feeling his body burning with hot desire. Elsa had sparked a need in him which he knew would last for the rest of his life. He did not feel that it was a sinful need. He had tried to, but although his life in Tarlogie had been an isolated one, it had also been wild and free. The sun had planted seeds of desire in his blood and they had germinated and exploded.

"What do you want of me?" he asked Elsa, and she came close to him and said:

"Treat me like if I'm a flesh-and-blood person." She was talking to him as if he was a man and not a boy and this pleased him although it in no way lessened his fear of what she might do. In some ways he was still a boy but he did not lack resources of cunning and deception.

"I want us to be friends, Elsa," he said, and she laughed her uninhibited nigger-yard laugh in his face.

"You sound just like your papa," she said; "the two of you is birds of a feather." This angered Hector, he couldn't stand anyone laughing at him.

"I've got to go," he said, "Sister's waiting for me." He had been waiting for a chance to escape and she had at last provided it.

"You think you can walk out just like that?" She was playing a cat-and-mouse game with him. It was good for her ego that she should have Bradshaw's son like clay in her sensuous hands. "I don't want nothing much of you, boy, 'cause you en't got nothing much to offer. Is you who get the most of everything so far." Hector kept looking out for Tengar because he didn't want him to come and find them together. "Don't worry, Tengar's safe and sound in Port Mourant," she said, as though she had been reading his thoughts.

"I've really got to go, Elsa."

"Go on then, who stopping you, boy?"

"Why do you have to go on this way, Elsa, to keep making me feel so badly?"

"It's good to feel bad sometimes, boy, you can't go on in life living with you' head in the clouds. Everything come so easy, eh? Even the first woman to cross you path, you didn't have to fight for she. When I was you age, I was already scuffling about to live and nobody ever give me anything except I had to offer something in return. . ."

"Tell me what I must do then! Tell me!"

"Stop treating me like if I am dust in the air, something that you must hold your nose against before you pass by. I got feelings like everybody else you know." It was only at this point that he understood that he had hurt her pride.

"I treated you badly, Elsa, but I swear I didn't mean to." He wanted genuinely to reassure her. There are some creatures like the three-toed sloth which live perpetually in the upper branches of tall trees in the forest and never come close to the earth until the trees are cut down or a storm uproots them. He had been living like that in Tarlogie, shut away in a nest with an old woman, two servants and a tutor. He had never had to come to grips with a grassroots human relationship until Elsa webbed him into her life. She suddenly felt sorry for him and wanted to mother him.

"You so young and foolish, boy!" she said, and they sat down on the warm sand and he laid his head in her lap. The dusty fabric of cloud and sky was bright with stars and a noisy sea wind bounced over the surf before it wheeled and tumbled across the swamp and the reefs. Hector stayed with Elsa as long as he dared. He could not overdo it or Sister would think that he had met with an accident. She could always be trusted to think up the most imaginative disasters befalling him.

"I have to go, Elsa," he said. He was lying on top of her and the feel of her warm black body was a drug.

"You could have been my son," she said, and she chuckled and added, "the son of a whoring cantankerous woman. Is better you're not me son 'cause a son must feel proud of he mother and you wouldn't have feel so proud of me; you would've did grow up cussing the day I birth you."

"At least I would have known who my mother was, I'm not so sure that I know now. . ."

"You better go, Hector, or the old woman will start to fret and fume, and don't try to see me unless I send word to call you."

★　　★　　★

Hector returned home to find an angry Sister waiting for him.

"So you courting, boy! You chin en't grow a single manly hair and the scales hardly fall from you eye and you courting another man's woman."

"I went to see Tengar, Sister."

"Don't come to me with no ballad about going to see Tengar. I know he en't nowhere around this night. What's the matter with you, boy? Is what devil you got inside you plaiting evil around you young heart? I try me best to bring you up in a God-fearing manner, to teach you to uphold the word of the Lord in thought and deed. I never say this before, and to tell you the truth it will cause an aching in me soul to say it, but the sooner you clear out of this village the better it will be. I would rather see you dead than bringing shame to me doorstep, boy. After all the sacrifices I make for you, boy, this is all the thanks I getting? But is my own fault. I should have known better what to expect after that night you go and shame you'self by dancing like a savage in the moonlight." Hector took the tongue lashing in silence. To try to defend himself would only make things worse.

"You got to learn to fight against the powers of darkness, boy. You got a bad habit of drifting into things and then acting like you not responsible for what develop. Look here, you breaking away from my authority step by step, but you must realise that from now on you must know that whatever you do you will have to answer to the Redeemer for you' actions. From this night on I swear that I'm giving up all responsibility for you, go whichever way your spirit move you to go, but don't ever look back to ole Sister to lift a finger to help you. The Prophet in the Good Book say: 'When I became a man I put away all childish things.' Carry these words in you' heart, boy!" She sat in her rocking chair spitting the words out at him, pressing her hands together to keep them from trembling. Hector stood well away from her, waiting for the high wind of her anger to die down. The atmosphere in the room was charged, oppressive. He had thought of many things to say whilst she was berating him. The statements formed themselves in his mind very clearly – I am a man. . . I've been a man for a long time but you never would admit it, you kept on treating me like a boy. . . you gave me freedom but you only did it so that you could bind me closer to you. . . I don't want you to shut yourself away from me for your old dried-up body is the one rock I have to lean on. . . Someday I'm going to be rich and powerful and I'll come for you and take you away from Tarlogie – several times he was on the verge of uttering the words that sounded clear as birdcalls in his mind but they never passed his lips and because he had hesitated too long he could say nothing.

He went to his room and sat on his bed, assuming a posture of deep sorrow which he did not really feel. He was tired but he would not go to sleep. He kept hoping that Sister would come in, and seeing his apparent remorse, feel sorry for him and they would embrace and things would be back on their old footing. He waited and waited and when she did not appear he felt that he should make the first move, go out to her and say that he was sorry, that he would never again flaunt her wishes; but he knew that he could not act out this contrite role convincingly enough. He hated the thought of having to live through the next few weeks, of having to face Sister in the morning, of pretending to Tojo and Clysis that nothing had gone wrong. He wondered if he had ever really loved anyone in his life, if he would have loved his mother and she him. Perhaps the habit of loving had evaded him entirely. Sister's reproofs had left him with no sense of guilt. The things he had done did not seem to merit her anger. There was an invincible innocence about him which an ocean of wrongdoing could not destroy. This innocence acted like an emotional buffer against his ever being too deeply involved. Tanta Bess, his neighbour had once described him as "Mr. Bradshaw's hot house flower." Everything he had done and felt would have to be repeated in the world outside his hothouse before he could lay claims to brotherhood with other men. He heard Sister watering the plants and closing the jalousies and afterwards he heard her footsteps approaching. She stopped outside his room and he could picture her standing still and listening. Just as he was sure she would enter, she walked away slowly. He sat listening to the wind and surf, the dogs in Dookia's kennels pulling at their chains and barking and the carts rolling by on the public road.

★   ★   ★

Sister sat in the rocking chair beside her four poster, inert as the darkness outside her window. She was sorry that she had roughed up "her boy". After all, she thought, he was a young man-child with contrary urges constantly surging through his growing limbs and his unformed mind. Even she sometimes felt these urges echoing through her desiccated body, so why should she obstruct the boy while he was groping and crawling and jostling his way out of the confused interlude between boyhood and manhood? He was a strange boy, a wild boy, a dreaming boy who often gave the impression that most of his life was being lived in a fantasy world where he spent his time climbing up and down a ladder which joined his private heaven to his private hell. And yet, she had to admit, he had an earthy, physical side to his nature as though the land had breathed the smell of mud and swamp water into his being. You only had to watch him eating, shovelling his food down as if he was afraid that someone would snatch the plate from before him, to know that he had some of the peasant in him, or watch delight brightening up his face when he returned with trophies from a hunt to know that despite his book learning he was a young animal. She had tried to build moral fences around his life, but could she in all fairness do this in Tarlogie?

"It's me own pride that's hurt," she said to herself; "and pride is a creature standing on one foot on top of a tall tree so the slightest breeze can make it tumble down. It's not what the boy do that hurt me, it's how he do it, all on his own without me having any part in it. I en't no better than his old harridan of an aunt because is same way so she would have been vexed, and same way so she would have put the blame on him and not on she-self. What if he go sporting and frolicking with a no-good village girl! Is same way so I would have sport and frolic when I was his age if my mama did give me half a chance.

She remembered the first moonlight night they had sat out on the front porch, she sitting in her rocking chair and he beside her crouched up into a tight ball to keep his meagre body from shivering. He had spoken to her freely that night, told her about

188

his sisters and Martha and Laljee, about the games he used to play in the front garden, about the day he had tried to run away and how he had met the old beggar, about the way Martha used to cook him special titbits behind his aunt's back – he had confided in her as if she were a playmate because she had made him feel safe within himself for the first time.

Sister's reverie was so pleasant that she dozed off and would have fallen asleep in her chair but Hector's voice broke in:

"Sister! Sister!"

"What you want, boy?" She looked around in the darkness, expecting to see him beside her for the voice sounded close. She listened, straining her ears, but she only heard the wind in the po-boy trees and the surf booming like laughter out of the deep throat of the sea, and she realised that she had been dreaming. She got up and prepared to go to bed and while she was undressing, decided to make things up with Hector. "I'm an old woman," she mumbled to herself, "with one foot in the grave and the other one on a banana skin. What's the use of carrying on a vendetta with a young strip of a boy whose face en't beat against enough years to even give it a definite shape yet, and besides he got to sit for his exam soon and is a bad time to upset him. He's young and foolish but he don't bear malice; after couple mornings he will forget all about what pass between us this night."

CHAPTER SEVENTEEN

PREACHER GALLOWAY paid his usual visit to the big house after his Wednesday night prayer meeting, but Sister was not there. She had gone to New Amsterdam to give evidence in Dookia's trial. Hector wondered why the preacher had come. Galloway knew that Sister was away. He had even offered to accompany her but she had not taken kindly to his suggestion.

"Although I thank you for your offer," she had said with a severity which she seemed to reserve specially for him, "I'm a single woman and I won't be seen in a distant place with a man who en't me kith or kin, nor a man who en't tied up with me by marriage." This rebuff had upset the preacher profoundly. He had caught on to the barely veiled implication and knew that there and then he should have proposed, but his habit of silence on the subject of marriage had been established over forty years and he could not find the words to break it.

Hector was sitting at the table reading, and Tojo and Clysis, released from Sister's disciplines for a few days, were giggling and tumbling behind the bamboo curtains. The preacher's unexpected appearance silenced them and they went downstairs to their rooms.

"I just dropped in to see that everything was all right," Galloway said, "I promised Miss Smart that I would." Hector knew that the preacher had come with something else in mind because while Sister was away, old man Doorne was sleeping in the kitchen and Galloway never crossed Doorne's path if he could help it.

"Everything's all right, Mr. Galloway," Hector said, and the old man drew up a chair and sat opposite him.

"Miss Smart told me that you might be going away if you pass your examination, Hector."

"Yes, to England."

"When you're gone, Miss Smart will be left all alone here, boy."

"I'll write to her often," Hector said.

"She's getting old and she'll need someone beside her," the preacher said quietly. "Fancy her being in this big house all by herself! With the loneliness greyhairing her head and not a chick or a child to keep her company." It was only at this point that Hector realised the preacher had come to confide in him, to disclose a secret intention.

"You're her best friend in the village, Mr. Galloway, and you can help to look after her." The preacher pretended not to have heard him.

"I've known Miss Smart since she was a small girl with her hair plaited like bush rope and falling down behind her neck. Old Reggie Smart, her brother, was my good friend." He looked at Hector slyly, "I always had a soft spot for Miss Smart, always," he said firmly, as though he expected the boy to contradict him on this point. "She was a fine girl, a properly fine girl and she grow up to be an even finer woman. Why I never asked her hand in marriage I don't rightly know. . . but she was always so sharp with me that the words would get knotted up at the tip of my tongue whenever I try to say them. I want you to do me a favour, boy," the preacher leaned forward and lowered his voice, "I want you to sound out the situation for me. . . I mean to say, you can act casual-like one day and get round to the subject of Preacher Galloway. Ask her what she think about me. . . Mind you, don't tell her that I ask this of you, don't even tell her that I visited tonight. . . just ease round to the subject softly-softly and whatever she say, you come and tell me, and if the news is bad don't be 'fraid to tell it to me straight out. You think you can do that for me, boy?"

"I'll do it," Hector said, feeling very important being entrusted with this mission.

"You'll be doing me a mighty favour, boy, and old Preacher Galloway won't forget it," he said, getting up and leaving hastily.

Doorne came in shortly afterwards and said, "Like you had visitor, Master Hector?"

"Visitor?"

"Yes, I saw that serpent-tongued man, Galloway, going through the gate couple minutes ago."

"Oh, the preacher? He must have made an attempt to come in and changed his mind because I didn't set eyes on him," Hector said, thinking that he would have to warn Tojo and Clysis to keep quiet about Galloway's visit.

"Just as well he didn't come in. I don't know why he got to be prowling round here when he know full well that I'm looking after the place."

*　　*　　*

Sister returned in triumph. She was convinced that she had been entirely responsible for Dookia's acquittal. She described every detail of the court proceedings to a houseful of awed listeners. The whole village converged on the big house before she had time to take the big black hatpin out of her Sunday hat and to settle down in her rocking chair.

"We hear the news, neighbour. Lord, it must 'ave been something to witness!"

"Sister, you fortunate that the Almighty spare you to go and help poor Dookia in her travail!"

"When I think 'bout what you had to face, Sister, me belly turning like cartwheel and me eye starting to swim!"

"Tell we 'bout it, Sister! We can't stand the anxiousness!"

"Neighbour Smart, you're a properly brave woman to go into the white man's court and look the judge in the eye. They tell we that you act like a general from beginning to end."

Sister sat down and fanned herself.

"The journey fatigue me," she said, "and Boysie's bus is not the most comfortable bus in the country you know."

"Tell we what happen!" they asked all together.

"The rope barely miss Dookia, I can tell all you that. It was close, properly close. Lawyer Boodoo do his very best, he talk like the roof of his mouth was made of honeycomb, and Caya buy some useless magic from the obeah-man but the judge and jury still keep looking on stony-faced. It was only when I step into that witness box that things change for the better. . ." There was an admiring gasp from the crowd. "When I stood up and fix me old eyes on the all of them, and tell how Chinaman was a rascal-man, a drunken good-for-nothing man with a tongue so dirty and vile that even if you did scrub it with carbolic soap you couldn't scrape off all the dirty words on it. I tell say, that not only Chinaman was a bad man, but his father before him was the same. . . The lawyers ask me plenty of questions. I didn't like the way the prosecution lawyer was talking to me and I tell him so, 'Young man,' I say, 'I'm old enough to be you mother so don't talk to me like that!' and he had to tone down and change his tune. To cut a long story short I knew from the time I step down from that witness box that no rope wasn't going to necklace Dookia's throat and the worst that could happen to she was that they would lost she 'way for a couple mornings for manslaughter. . . ." For the villagers, the court was a stage where life was dramatised for their entertainment. They envied Dookia her short spell of glory. As far as they were concerned, the act of chopping down her husband merited no moral condemnation. Chinaman had gone out of his way to call down murder on his head. The great ones in the city might live by their mechanical laws and statute books but the villagers lived in a community where secret tensions built themselves up under calm surfaces, dictating their own stresses and relaxations, creating drama to relieve the strain of a monotonous destitution. Dookia's trial had provided the village with a vicarious excitement which left everyone with the same satisfaction that an audience feels after seeing a good play.

Hector had watched Sister's performance from behind the bamboo curtain. When she had finished he sat by the window overlooking Dookia's back yard, waiting for the guests to leave. It was a hot, humid day and dark billowing clouds were labouring across a grey sky. The rainy season, three months overdue, was at last approaching. The water level in the ricefields had been falling steadily, and the water, nearing the roots of rice stalks and rushes, was taking on the rusty, reddish colour of the mud under it. Another month of drought would have meant disaster for the farmers. It was only during the last week or so that the air had become heavy with the promise of rain.

Hector heard Sister scolding one of her guests for coming into her house with cattle dung on his feet, and another for keeping his hat on. This was a hint that the show was over and the audience should go home. She called him when the living-room was empty of its chattering, murmuring visitors and he went to her and embraced her. They had been reconciled before she had gone to New Amsterdam but there was a lingering uneasiness between them.

"Everything went all right when I was away, boy?"

"Yes, Sister, everything was fine but I missed you just the same."

"I so glad to be back in my yard! The town is such a confusing place, I couldn't sleep at night for the noise. Them godless folks in the town like they don't have nowhere to rest they head when night come. Is twenty odd years since I set foot outside this village the last time, and all the folks I used to know die out or gone away – there was Miss Trim, the lady my brother used to court and never marry, Mantop came for her couple months ago; then there was Paul Slowe, the contractor, they tell me he living in Georgetown now. I didn't know a living soul in that town no more."

"Everything was quiet here; Doorne was sleeping in the kitchen but I hardly ever saw him, he used to come in late at night and leave at foreday morning for the cow pen."

"And how about La Rose?"

"Oh, he came every day as usual and you could set the clock by his comings and goings."

"I'm glad to be back," Sister said, holding her face up to the wind, "it was so hot in the town!"

"When is Dookia coming back?"

"Any time now. She tell me that she can't bear the town because everywhere she turn the boldface town folks keep looking at she like if she was some kind of criminal."

Hector wished that he had been called on to give evidence at the trial. "After all," he said to himself, "I was the only person who witnessed the murder, I alone saw the whole thing." Now that everything was over he could have his dreams about how he would have conducted himself before the judge and jury. On further thought, however, he decided that his evidence would most likely have made the rope necklace for Dookia's neck and he would not have wanted to be responsible for that.

There had been many murders on the coast. Sister, Doorne and Tengar had told Hector stories about them – of how Ramgobin the cattle dealer had shot a policeman by the hairpin bend where the road turned into Kiltearn Village; how Longman Daniel, the Negro farmer had returned from the war to find his wife living with another man, and how he had locked up the doors and windows of his hut and chopped down his wife, her lover and the children she had borne him with a cutlass which he had spent a week sharpening; how Tanta Bess' husband, Lion, had been murdered by a neighbour whose pigs he had stolen. Somehow Hector did not regard murder as something unnatural on the coast. The swamps were too vast and silent not to have violence lurking in the depths of their quietness, and the long nights of dungeoned darkness too full of the voices of dead slaves calling out for vengeance not to breed terror. The swamps were vast, but people lived huddled together in villages, colliding like tadpoles in small ponds. The villagers were islanded in small enclosures, living too close to one another, sharing their dreams, their frustrations, their awe of the unknown, each individual knowing too much about his neighbour's life for the other not to hate him. Explosions of anger were a necessary relief from the tensions of living like crabs in a barrel.

Hector left Sister in her rocking chair and sat out on the front porch. The crowd which had poured into the big house to hear Sister's story of the trial had broken up into small groups outside the rum-shop. Further down the way, Roopnarine the fisherman was drying copra on zinc sheets spread out in his front yard. Between fishing trips he made coconut oil in a small dark shed behind his hut. One of his sheep stood by his fence scratching its back on the barbed wire whilst, in his back yard, pigs were rooting around his latrine. Roopnarine was unconcerned about Dookia's triumph. He was a man who kept to himself and what happened between his neighbours Dookia and Chinaman was their concern.

"Hector!" Sister called out, and he got up and went inside to her, "you had any visitors whilst me was away, boy?" Hector looked at her suspiciously. Was she trying to find out if Elsa had come around, he wondered.

195

"What kind of visitors, Sister? Nobody came around."

"Not even Preacher Galloway, boy? I thought that being such an old friend of the family the least he could do was come around and see that everything was going all right."

"He must have known that Doorne was staying here," Hector said.

"He should 'ave come just the same, Doorne or no Doorne!"

"I always thought that the preacher was something of a scamp, you know what I mean, Sister?"

"Is so you will talk disrespectfully 'bout a man old enough to be your papa, boy! Your eyes en't pass Preacher Galloway's yet, boy, but even when they do don't try to mauvaise langue that old man before me. I know him long and he's a faithful friend. I'm not saying that he don't have some contrary ways, but all in all, there en't another one like him from New Amsterdam to Orealla. Trouble and me meet face to face plenty times, but there wasn't an occasion when Mr. Trouble pin his eyes on mine that old man Galloway wasn't around to help me out."

"I was only making mirth, Sister. I hadn't any intention of running down the preacher." She grumbled to herself, and once or twice she looked at Hector trying to fathom what was going on in his mind. Hector sat in a Berbice chair and picked up a copy of Dumas' *Count of Monte Cristo*. He had read and re-read this novel until he knew parts of it by heart. He thumbed through the pages waiting for Sister to go. Once she was safely in the kitchen, he could slip out and run to Preacher Galloway with the news of what Sister had said about him.

Monte Cristo and *A Tale of Two Cities* were his favourite novels. He liked books with daring, romantic heroes. One of the books he had to read for his examination was Hardy's *Jude the Obscure* and he had found the atmosphere it conjured up too heavy, the characters too sombre, their lives weighed down by too much brooding and melancholy. La Rose reminded him of Jude, they were both men who had no room for laughter in their lives. He could identify himself with Charles Darnay or Monte Cristo, live through them, share in their exploits. Reading about them, he was transported from the wild coast into a world so unlike his that his imagination could embrace it completely and he could enjoy a delicious loneliness roaming up and down this fantasy world. Jude's world was too much like his own and Jude was too much like a flesh-and-blood man. He knew no one like Monte Cristo or Darnay and this enhanced their appeal.

When Sister got up to go into the kitchen, he pretended to be absorbed in his book. He waited until he heard her scolding Clysis and Tojo for neglecting to scrub the kitchen floor, and he tiptoed out.

He found Preacher Galloway reading the papers on his veranda. The old man was dressed in his Saturday afternoon uniform – a three piece serge suit, high collar, a black tie with a diamond pin stuck in it and spats. He was very strict about his dress on Wednesdays, when he conducted the prayer meeting and visited the big house, on Saturdays, when he took an afternoon stroll as far as Saltan Village and on Sundays. He was wearing steel rimmed bifocals that had such thick lenses they looked like window panes washed by rain.

"Good afternoon, Mr. Galloway," Hector said, looking fascinatedly at the preacher's eyes as they swam behind his glasses. Galloway folded his paper carefully and laid it aside.

"You came sooner than I expected, boy."

"I brought up the subject like you told me and Sister talked a lot about you."

"You didn't let on that I put you up to this I hope?" the preacher asked severely, pressing his lips together and turning his head from side to side as though his collar was too tight.

"I didn't say a thing about your coming, Mr. Galloway. Sister asked me if you had come around on Wednesday night and I told her that you hadn't."

"So how did you bring up the subject in question, boy?"

"She was saying that you should have come around as usual even if Doorne was there. . . and then I said that I thought you were a scamp. . ."

"A scamp, boy!" he straightened up and one foot tapped on the floor disapprovingly. "Hmm! And what happened then?"

"I was only saying that to make her say what she thought about you, Mr. Galloway."

"Go on then, tell me what she said!"

"She said that there isn't another man like you between New Amsterdam and Orealla. . ."

"And what else, boy? Tell me the whole story word for word."

"She said that you were the best friend she ever had, that you're a very noble man, that she used to admire you since she was a small-girl. . . she said that you were shy but behind the shyness you were a big-hearted man, somebody she could depend on all the time. . ."

The preacher had been keeping up a grim front for as long as he could but before Hector finished he was smiling all over his face.

"I won't forget this, boy, I promise you, and when Galloway gives his word he means it, every bit of it."

"I must go now, Mr. Galloway, I don't want Sister to miss me." The old man slapped him on the back affectionately.

"You're a good boy, Hector, a fine boy, and if you were old enough to toss down some grog with me we would have clinked glasses and drank to your health. I can see an outstanding career marked out for you, mark my words, you're going to be the only distinguished Bradshaw."

Hector felt good, not so much about the compliments the preacher had lavished on him, but over the fact that the old man had treated him like an adult. As fellow conspirators, questions of age and protocol had become irrelevant.

★　　★　　★

Caya and Dookia returned from New Amsterdam that evening and celebrations at the rum-shop lasted until dawn. A few of the senior patrons made welcoming speeches but the rank-and-file regulars showed their appreciation by drinking pints of free rum. The sergeant-major who had taken charge of the police station just after the murder, and Mark-a-book and his subordinates were some of the first arrivals at the boisterous fête. Caya was not by nature the kind of man to throw money away on this hard drinking, loud-mouthed crowd but what he was doing was encouraging his guests to make a loud enough din to drive away Chinaman's ghost. He didn't want a phantom to be sharing his new life with Dookia. Soon after the fête had started, Caya gave his version of the trial. He sat behind the counter on a high stool and said:

"Lawyer Boodoo is the greatest lawyer who ever warble to a judge and jury, he put on a performance in that court that make me hair stand up straight on me head. The man I kept looking at all the time was the foreman of the jury, he was as stony-faced a black man as you ever did see, wasn't he Dookia?" He turned to his woman. She was sitting in the doorway leading to the stock room. Caya wanted to show his guests that he wasn't going to treat her the way her late spouse had done, that she had become a part of him and would share in all his activities.

"Yes, Caya, he was a stony-faced man, I never did set eyes on a man with a face like that," she said from the shadows.

"Well, Lawyer Boodoo talk and talk, he use words the way an obeah-man does use magic. But whilst he was hypnotizing the jury you could see, and it was clear to all to see, that the foreman wasn't going to budge. Man, I'm telling you that man had ropes hanging in he eyes and if Jesus Heself did preach the Sermon on the Mount to he, he wasn't going to budge. What happened after the first couple of days was that Lawyer Boodoo see that words wasn't the thing that was going to change that stony-faced man, so he try money, and I can tell all you this, friends, the language of money does sound more sweet than a piper owl singing, because the foreman face change from stone to clay. On the last day when Lawyer Boodoo was really talking to earn his money, he end up by saying" – Caya got down from his stool to give an imitation of the lawyer – "'My Lord, ladies and gentlemen of the jury, this is how the case stands, but before I leave you to make your final decisions, I ask you once,' and at this junction the lawyer point one finger straight at the foreman of the jury, and somebody tell me afterwards that this was a signal to show that he was offering a hundred dollars for Dookia's life. Well the foreman keep looking straight through he as if he was made of rain water; so the lawyer add another finger and say: 'I ask you twice,' but still the foreman keep looking through him because two hundred dollars wasn't enough. 'I ask you three times!' the lawyer shout, and the way he say it the foreman knew that he wasn't bidding no higher, so the foreman bow he head down in acceptance and the lawyer continue: 'Think well on what I have told you so that you will not send a sorely tried citizen who has already paid a heavy penalty in suffering to the gallows!'" Caya resumed his position on the stool, pausing before his finale. "After that," he said, "the jury retire, and after they waited for what look like a proper time, they come out again, and when the judge question he, foreman look he straight in the eye and say, 'Not guilty, my Lord!'"

"But I hear that is after Sister say she piece that things change for the better," a man said.

"I en't saying that Sister didn't make a good showing, pardner, but take my word for it, what win that case was the magic the obeah-man put on the judge and the money the lawyer pass on to the jury."

"Let we all drink to Dookia and thank the Lord that she return to we safe and sound!" Mark-a-book shouted, and the other guests banged their mugs on the counter, cheered and downed their drinks. Dookia sat in the shadows acknowledging this boisterous tribute impassively. Caya gave her a drink and when she swallowed it, she shivered as if someone had walked over her grave.

CHAPTER EIGHTEEN

NEITHER Doorne nor Tengar were present at the celebration. They had not been asked and they were both too proud to attend uninvited. Caya wanted his relatives to know that his good fortune was his own and he did not intend to share it. He had been scrambling for crumbs all his life and now that he had hogged a full repast he was as greedy as a maipuri leopard over it. Placed in the same position, his father would not have acted differently. Doorne understood his eldest son and having expected nothing of him, was not disillusioned. Tengar, however, remembered the days when he had saved Caya from starvation and he complained to Elsa about his brother's ingratitude.

Tengar and his woman had been quarrelling like tomcats since the night of the wind-dance. She was determined to return to the city and he was stalling. He argued that he had settled down for the first time in his wandering life and didn't want to uproot himself again. Elsa needled him and nagged him and stung him like a queen bee trying to stir a drone into activity.

She sat on the step above him watching at the outlines of his torso, an inert blob of darkness which was darker than the night that was settling around them. Above them, rain-clouds chased by the wind, were winnowing stars. The occasional flicker of lightning silhouetted the arc of courida and mangrove trees that curved around the foreshore and the surf sounded muffled. Elsa resented Tengar's inertness and she wanted to prod him with her foot so that he could show some sign of life. Tengar must have sensed her resentment for he turned round and said:

"Looks like we'll be in for a hell of a rainy season. When you hear the surf growling and probing up the beach like that, is a sure sign that rain's going to pelt down like fire for months on end."

"I hope to God that I can clear out before the rains come, because the rainy season is the worst one, it does lock you up inside a smelly hut night and day and every time you turn around, you does be stumbling over the pigs and sheep and chickens that living with you. I'm telling you for the last time if you don't make up your mind soon, you will drift in here one day and find me gone."

"Why you don't go, Elsa?" Tengar asked the question quietly. He had been searching for a solution for months, and although this one had occurred to him several times before he had not dared to mention it.

"So you want to get rid of me, eh? It was you who bring me here you know. It was you who break into my quiet life like a robber and upset everything. The next man I take on will have to be rich, I can tell you that, he's not going to be no big, black man who is going to sit down like a lump of mud watching time pass by." Tengar was no match for Elsa in an argument. Her nimble mind could take anything he said and twist it into a whip to beat him with. Although she had still a certain fondness for Tengar she did not love him any more, but she needed him as a protector whilst she was setting herself up in the city. The kind of men she hoped to sell herself to would be ageing roués like Fitz Bradshaw who would be flattered to think that their rival was a black giant like Tengar. Men often measured the worth of a woman by the kind of man who had already won her. Tengar, in his innocence, did not know what Elsa was planning for him. She had sworn never to go back to whoring and he believed her. She was planning, once they got to the city, to keep him just as she had kept Jojo and her other saga-boys. She was so convinced of her absolute hold on him that it never occurred to her that he might object to the role she had decided he should play.

"Tengar, boy, you at home!" a voice called out from the swamp and the two listened and heard the sound of feet splashing through the mud and water.

"I wonder is who coming here at this time of night," Elsa said; "it sound like your father. . . but it couldn't be!"

"Aye, aye, who is that!" Tengar called back.

"Is me, Doorne!"

"Is some kind of trouble that old man bringing to we doorstep," Elsa muttered, and they waited until the old man had parted the darkness at the bottom of the steps and he stood looking up at them with his eyes bright as moonshine.

"What breeze blow you this way, old man?"

"I want to talk to you, boy," Doorne said, and the way he said it Tengar knew that he was expecting him to ask Elsa to leave them alone.

"Don't listen to he, Tengar," Elsa said fiercely; "when that old man not brewing bush rum he does be brewing mischief."

"Woman, you got a tongue like a sword! You don't have no respect for your man's father? These young men nowadays does allow woman to lead them with bridle and bit. . ."

Elsa turned on Tengar angrily: "Is so you allowing your family to come to we house and insult me!"

"Old man, if all you come here to do is to insult me woman, then the same breeze that blow you here had better blow you back to you' own yard. . . Besides, all these years I living here you never so much as cross me doorstep to say good morning, how d'ye do or kiss my arse."

"Is your woman I come to talk to you 'bout, and what me got to tell en't nice to hear."

"I don't want to hear nothing about she. I done hear enough already; this village already make up so much story about Elsa that there can't be nothing left to say."

"He only want to make strife fester between we, Tengar; don't listen to he. He old and dried up and he hate young folks, young folks is he kinnah." Elsa was baffled. She couldn't imagine what the old rascal-man had come to talk about. It wasn't he who had a hold over her now, it was she who had one over him. Her words stung Doorne and he had to hold back his anger before he spoke again. Tengar went inside the hut, lit the storm lantern and hung it on a nail over the doorway then he came down the steps and sat beside Elsa.

"The night of the wind-dance I followed a certain young man to Maiden's Head," Doorne said, and his voice was as harsh as two boughs rubbing together in a high wind. . . .

★   ★   ★

Hector had been waiting for Elsa's message. He had kept hoping that she would contact him while Sister was in New Amsterdam but Tengar had returned from Port Mourant unexpectedly and it would have been too dangerous. He was glad that Tengar had not come around since his return and after Sister had come back from the trial, his dread of having to face his friend had increased. He knew that they would have to meet but he preferred that it should happen when he was fully prepared. He had often thought of going to Tengar and confessing. He was sure that the heroes in the novels he had read would have done this, and challenged their rivals to a fight to the death. There were even times when he saw himself wrestling with Tengar and defeating him. The life that he lived out in his fantasy was always more real, more satisfying than the reality of his mundane existence in Tarlogie. In his make-believe world, the image he created of himself was bigger than life, fearless, noble and benevolent towards the weak mortals who surrounded him, but the gap between fantasy and fact was too vast for him ever to bridge it.

Then one night he suddenly decided that he would visit Tengar and Elsa. He would go and face his rival in the presence of the woman they both loved but who only loved him. He would treat him with a haughty disdain and Elsa would beam her admiration at him.

He told Sister that he wanted to go for a walk to clear his brain and she warned him not to go too far because she could smell rain in the air. Once outside his front driveway he headed towards Maiden's Head. The wind was blowing straight at him and when he was halfway to the reef he heard angry voices. He tried to identify the voices but the surf was too noisy. He walked through the swamp as silently as he could and approached the hut from the western end of the reef. He crept forward in the darkness until he was able to see Tengar, Elsa and Doorne clearly in the yellow light of the storm lantern. Doorne was standing at the foot of the steps, looking as puffed up as a bull frog, and he was saying:

"I follow this young man in question across the public road, over the swamp and when I see he heading for your house I say to meself: 'Doorne, this business don't look right, man...'

"Tengar, don't listen no more to this old man, he's a devil! He

204

don't sleep when night come, he does stay up like a bakuman hatching plans to eat up innocent people's soul. Don't listen to he!"

Hector edged backwards involuntarily. He was glad that the darkness was so thick, that the clouds were too loaded with rain for the wind to part them and let the stars shine through.

"Why you so upset, Elsa girl?" Doorne taunted her. "You' conscience, if you got any such thing left, must be eating you up. . ."

"Tengar, you going to sit here and let this old devil heap a mountain of insults on your woman's head!"

"Old man, I don't want to hear nothing else and if you don't fetch you'self away from me yard I will have to make you go!" Tengar was sure that his father had some Judas motive behind his story. The old man had never liked Elsa and he knew from long experience that when Doorne didn't take to someone, he took a venomous delight in scandalising their name. Suddenly Elsa rushed at Doorne and spat in his face screaming:

"You nasty whore-dog! Ruction devil-man! I going to tell you' son the whole story 'bout you' goings on!" She began clawing at and pummelling the old man until Tengar dragged her away and forced her to sit down:

"You better go now, old man," Tengar said, but Doorne stood rooted by the fury inside him. Tengar was still holding Elsa and she shrugged his hand away and said,

"I'm all right and I'm going to say what I started to say, then this old demon can tell you anything he like. You know why this old man, your father, don't like me, why he would turn the earth I walk on into burning coals if he could? I will tell you here and now: he is the man that start me out whoring. . . it was he who take me maidenhead when I was a girl of fifteen. . . this same black-hearted, black-faced demon you see standing before you had me under such a spell that I had to go to an obeah-man and pay him to break it. . . he had me in his power until he could mash me up like an ant under his foot and he used to beat me and plant he dried up seed inside me night after night. . . but for the obeah-man I wouldn't have been here to spit in this old devil face tonight. . ." She would have rushed at Doorne again if Tengar had not restrained her.

205

"Is true what she say, old man? You is me father and I is your son, but if you lie to me I will carry you to the cross. How come you was taking advantage of a young girl when you had two sons who you left to weather the seasons like grass!" The old man moved out of Tengar's reach and began laughing a terrible, demonic laugh.

"You don't see that the man is mad," Elsa said, "that he mad with the evilness that festering like yaws inside he devil's heart!"

Hector crept away and the old man's racoon laugh followed him. He set out for home from the far side of the reef so that they could not hear him. Because he was crossing the swamp by an unaccustomed route and it was dark, he stumbled in mud holes which water buffaloes had made and all the time he thought he could hear the old man following him. He fell several times and by the time he reached the public road he was wet and mud spattered. He kept cursing himself for being a coward, telling himself that he should have stayed at Maiden's Head and made sure that Doorne wasn't going to expose his goings on with Elsa. And how was he to explain to Sister where he had been? He could tell her that he had gone to visit Tengar without explaining what had happened, but this would mean having to cover up later on if Tengar visited the house and asked him why he had been avoiding Maiden's Head. Perhaps it would be better to tell the truth but Hector, despite the preaching, the moralising he had been subjected to by Aunt Hanna and Sister, had an aversion to telling the truth. The few times he had tried doing it he had only got into trouble. Telling lies was for him a secret game in which he could twist his imagination like a liana. It was a game that gave him as much pleasure as hunting.

A rainstorm caught him a few hundred yards from home, one of those apocalyptic storms which the villagers say is the result of the devil and his wife fighting. When Hector arrived drenched and shivering, Sister rubbed him down with coconut oil, gave him a drink of rum and sent him to bed.

*   *   *

"Oh, God, me own father!" Tengar kept chanting over and over again. He was standing with his legs wide apart and rocking from side to side. This was his way of working up his anger and the movement and the chanting were almost ritualistic.

"I come to tell you about the carryings on of your woman and you only acting like you gone crazy," Doorne said, "the woman must 'ave put magic on you."

"Go away from me sight, old man! Go away!" Tengar shouted, and Doorne braced himself, expecting his son to spring on him.

"Go 'way devil-man! You're a black-hearted, black-faced Satan!" Elsa said, and the old man turned and walked away quickly, laughing his loud, crazy laugh until the rainstorm broke. And when the thunderclaps cannonaded in the sky, they seemed to be echoing his mad mirth. A wild, inchoate anger possessed Tengar completely after the darkness and the rain had swallowed up his father and when it burst out of him he bellowed like a red howler.

"Tengar! Tengar, you gone mad, man!" Elsa said. She was frightened. She had never seen her man angry before, and part of her fear came out of not knowing and not understanding why he should be so enraged about something that had happened so long ago. She tried to press herself against him but he shoved her away and ran inside the hut. She fell on the wet sand and lay there wondering what he would do next. "Tengar! Tengar!" she kept calling out, until the accumulated tensions inside her found a release in tears. She heard the loud thumpings of his footsteps inside the hut, the clatter of pots and pans as he flung them through the doorway and afterwards he came down the steps carrying the canister in which they kept their belongings.

"What you doing, Tengar?" she asked.

"We leaving the village this very night," he said.

"In all this rain and storm?"

"This village is a cursed place and I don't want morning to catch we here. I will hire a donkey and cart and we can start out." He sat beside her on the sand and the rain pasted their bodies together. In the aftermath of his anger he felt bewildered, weary and when he tried to recapture what had just happened, his thoughts floundered in emptiness.

Dayclean found Tengar and Elsa on their way to Georgetown. They had hired Ramjohn's donkey cart and travelled by it as far as Port Mourant. Tengar had met Tanta Bess at the market and asked her to take the cart back to Tarlogie and then he and Elsa had caught Boysie's bus on its early morning run to New Amsterdam. They crossed the Berbice river on the midday ferryboat, boarded the train at Rosignol and arrived in Georgetown by nightfall.

When the villagers woke up and began preparing to set out for the ricefields and provision farms, a few of them noticed that Tengar's hut had collapsed. They would have gone across the swamp to Maiden's Head to investigate but Ramjohn told them that Tengar and Elsa had left the village during the night. There wasn't much speculation about why the giant had gone so unexpectedly because everyone knew that he was a balata worker and whenever it looked as if money was getting too scarce, he would go to the balata forests for a season. As for his woman, they had never taken to her nor she to them. She had come to Tarlogie as a stranger and after years in the village had left without having ever changed.

Before Tengar left, he had knocked away the stilts from under his hut, and sold his chickens and pigs to Ramjohn.

★   ★   ★

Preacher Galloway paid his usual visit to the big house after presiding over his Wednesday night prayer meeting. As soon as he entered, Hector knew that the old man had come to do the thing he had been postponing for forty years.

Galloway's cotton wool hair was brushed and oiled and he was wearing his biggest and highest white collar, a red velveteen suit with waistcoat to match, black boots and spats which were freshly blancoed. Sister stopped rocking back and forth in her chair for a moment, looked the preacher up and down and said:

"Like you going into your second youth, Mr. Galloway! I can't remember seeing you rigged out in this kind of fancy dress before." This made the old man so uncomfortable that he nearly stuck the bowl of his clay pipe into his mouth by accident.

"I'm getting old, Miss Smart, and I thought that I'd better wear out the few pieces of clothes I possess before they use them to deck me out in my coffin."

"From the looks of it, you got a long time on this earth yet, Mr. Galloway, before they stop up your mouth with earth; they will stop up mine long before they do yours, I'm sure of that."

"The Good Lord will decide that in His own time, Miss Smart; in the meantime we'd better make the most of the days of grace that He grants us. When the grave chooses to yawn under you and the long sleep tumbles you inside it, won't be a thing that me and you can do about it."

Hector stayed on for a few minutes after the preacher had arrived and then he complained of having a headache and went to his room.

"The boy's fulling up he head with too many books," he heard Sister saying after he had shut his door behind him.

Sister's intuition told her that Galloway had come intending to say something important and she encouraged him to say it by talking irrelevancies – about her trip to New Amsterdam and the things she had bought, how Roopnarine was smuggling cattle across the Courentyne River into Dutch Guiana, the way in which old man Doorne was skulking about and avoiding everybody of late, how the price of rice was lower than it had ever been because the Government (without thinking about the poor people in the villages) had imported rice from Burma, and although Burmese rice was cheap, nobody had money with which to buy it, how Tanta Bess' daughter had taken ill again and her mother had taken her to a city doctor who treated her for hookworm and cured her in a week.

"Miss Smart, I have a matter to talk over with you," Galloway interrupted her, clearing his throat several times before he continued; "this matter was like a lump in the pit of my heart for forty odd years, Miss Smart. . ."

"Yes, Mr. Galloway?"

"Because of this, Miss Smart, it's hard to find the words I need. . . it's like this, Miss Smart, I would very much like you to do me the honour of giving me. . . yes, of giving me your hand. . ."

"Hand, Mr. Galloway? My old dried up hand?"

"Yes, your hand in marriage, Miss Smart."

"You take me breath away, preacher," Sister said, fanning herself with her hand and looking everywhere else except at her reluctant suitor, "you certainly rob me of breath." The preacher saw that things were going in his favour and he went up to Sister boldly and took her hand.

"Is your answer negative or positive, Miss Smart?" Even at this moment of crisis he was unable to relax his formal, Victorian manner, his stilted speech.

"Positive, Mr. Galloway," Sister said in a quiet voice, and when the preacher tried to embrace her she held him off, and had her complexion not been a midnight one he would have seen her blush.

"What will the children say if one of them comes in and catch us. . . two old people like us acting like young lovers," she said, but the preacher was not in a mood to be deterred and he pressed forward and kissed her over and over again. Afterwards, the two old people sat down in silence, each trying to measure the long span of years since they had first met with dusty memories, until Galloway said:

"Sister. . . I think I have the right to call you, Sister, now. . . how soon you think the event can take place?"

"Not before the boy goes away. I owe it to his dead mother to wait; she was good to me, preacher, and before the Good Lord call she away, she make me promise to look after the boy's interest as long as there was breath in me body and marrow in me bones, so I will wait and see him go off to study for a profession like his papa promised he would, after he pass his examination."

"I hope it doesn't take too long, Sister, because the clock's ticking away our last days, the twilight and the darkness near to us, whilst the day just cleaning for Hector."

"It won't be long, preacher. It won't be long, and yet. . . me, too would like it to be soon because I was waiting so long for this that the waiting turn all heavy inside me bosom."

CHAPTER NINETEEN

A LONG dry season had followed the June and July rains. Hector had taken his examination and returned to Tarlogie to await the results. Life was gushing over at the rum-shop once more and the nightly sessions were more boisterous than ever. Dookia was with child and some malicious tongues were clacking out gossip, saying that Chinaman planted his last seed in her but Caya was strutting about and saying that time was on his side because it would show from which pod the ripe seed had fallen. Ramjohn was drowned in a gale off the coast and when his body was washed up three days later, bloated and roasted by the sun, it had to be buried on the foreshore. Dodo, the beggar, stopped in at the big house on his way through the village. He was using the cheap bus service to go farther afield because of competition by younger and stronger rival beggars in the city. He brought news of Tengar, said that he was working on the docks, and his strength was the talk of the waterfront. An Englishman had offered to take him to Britain so that he could join a circus and get paid for showing off his muscles and his blackness, but Elsa wouldn't let him go. She didn't think that there were folks anywhere who would pay good money just to see a naked black giant.

Dodo also said that Hector's father was still keeping Dela and the talk in the nigger-yards was that she had obeahed him and sucked his guts out so that all that was left of him was a shell. Dodo had slept under the backsteps and left at foreday morning well rewarded for his news.

Sister was acting like a young girl, preening herself before a mirror for hours on end and getting Clysis to massage the wrinkles out of her face at nights before she went to sleep. She was so nice to Hector that he was uncomfortable and he wondered every now and then whether he had done the right thing in acting as a go-between. Preacher Galloway too, had changed; his hot gospelling about hell fires had cooled, and on Sundays he sermonised about gardens of Eden and heavens alight with black faces, mostly the faces of Tarlogians, the lists of whose sins the Good Lord had torn up.

Aunt Hanna had been writing regularly to Hector since he was sixteen, writing those querulous, carping letters. The boy felt sure that she was hoping he would fail his matriculation, that if he passed it would represent a victory for Sister and his aunt wanted to cheat her of this. La Rose was due to start his schoolmastering when school reopened in September and if Hector failed he would have to go to Georgetown for a second try at the examination. Hector didn't know if he had done well or not. He had nearly crammed himself sick in the two months before the exam and during this time he had memorised much and learnt little. La Rose had accompanied him to New Amsterdam and during the two weeks they had spent there, had made him recapitulate in detail the answers he had written down in the examination room. Hector couldn't help feeling that the answers he had given La Rose were better than those he had written down a few hours before.

One day early in October the postman delivered a telegram to the big house. It was addressed to Hector but Sister answered the knock at the door and received it. Tojo had seen the postman wheeling his bicycle up the drive and had announced his coming. He always delivered the mail from Georgetown on Tuesday mornings, and since it was Thursday his presence suggested some very unexpected and dramatic news. Tojo had felt it his duty to alert the household and had done so with zest. Sister signed the chit the postman handed her, then she balanced the envelope, in her hand, held it up to the light and tore it open, slowly, deliberately. Hector stood by, impatiently, feeling a superstitious dread. The postman lingered in the doorway. He already knew what was in the telegram and was enjoying the drama. It was not every day that he delivered a missive like this.

"You waiting for something, Mr. Barnes?" Sister asked, and she gave him such a sharp look that he left hurriedly. "That man does stick his black nose in everybody's affairs. I'm going to complain to the postmaster. . ."

"What does it say, Sister?" Hector asked. He was sure that someone had died.

"Lord ha' mercy! It's good news, boy." She handed him the telegram and it said:

"You have matriculated. . . congratulations from us all. . . Fitz."

"I'm proud of you, boy," Sister said, "I always did know that you had it in you. You're the only Bradshaw who ever had any brains and you get it from your mama's people. Her two brothers who went to the States was both brainy men and she herself wasn't nobody's fool."

"I wonder what my daddy's going to give me," Hector said, "he promised me something special if I passed."

"That's all you can think about, boy?" Sister asked. She had expected him to be sorry at having to leave her. He saw the disappointment on her face and said:

"I'm glad I don't have to take the exam again, Sister, because if I have to go away from you I prefer to go far away not just to Georgetown."

"What you mean by that, boy?"

"I mean. . . if I'm near to you. . . suppose I had to stay in Georgetown to sit for the exam again I would just pick myself up and come back to you," he said and she was all smiles.

"You better run along and share the good news with La Rose because is he you got to thank more than anybody else."

"But he left Saltan village a month ago, Sister. Remember? He came to tell us goodbye before he went away."

"I can't 'custom meself to that young man's going, boy. I get so accustomed to his coming here day after day that it's hard for me to realise that he's not coming no more, that he take to schoolmastering."

★   ★   ★

The rainy season came early and the rice farmers had to work night and day to save their crops. Hector was marooned in the big

213

house, listening to the downpour swishing and drumming on the galvanised iron roof like a monotonous fanfare. One day when he could no longer stand the damp twilight of the house, he walked through the rain to the edge of the swamp beyond his back yard. Passing by Doorne's hut, he called out to the old man but there was no answer although he was sure he had seen a blob of shadow in the window for a moment. When was the old man going to come out of his spell of sulking, he wondered. Perhaps it was true what Elsa had said: Doorne was a vampire-man who had to fasten himself on to someone and bind them to him by magic, perhaps even now he was plotting to enmesh his next victim.

Hector stood at the edge of the swamp watching the raindrops tap-tapping upon the lotus lilies and running off the wide lily leaves like quicksilver. Behind him he heard the raucous caw-cawing of carrion crows which were bunched together on the palm fronds. A party of villagers, two women and four men, walked past him. They were carrying sacks of ground provisions on their heads and because of the weight of their loads were leaving deep footprints behind them. They greeted him and their dark forms tunnelled through the wall of rain and disappeared. Water trickled down his forehead and into his eyes and the white slanting rain, the swamp carpeted with weeds, lilies and a host of small yellow flowers, fused and shimmered as though he was viewing the landscape through frosted glass. He began to feel cold and ran all the way home.

Whilst he was washing the mud off his feet at the foot of the back stairs, he heard his father's voice inside the house. Sister was standing in the doorway looking angry and upset. He expected her to scold him.

"What's the matter, Sister?" he asked, and she clicked her tongue the way she always did when her vexation was too much for her.

"Go inside and see," she said. His father was sitting in a Berbice chair in the living-room and he went up to him and kissed him on the forehead.

"I thought I'd come and stay for a couple of days and then take you back with me, boy. Congratulations, I'm proud of you. . . the stone that the builders rejected, eh! Your aunt couldn't believe it when we heard the news. . ." His father laughed a strangled kind of laugh that ended suddenly. Hector, standing over his father and looking down at him, noticed that the old man's face had changed. The cheekbones jutted out above hollow cheeks and the eyes were slightly out of focus with dark crescents under them. It was only after his father had spoken to him that he noticed the Indian woman squatting in a corner of the room. Fitz's eyes followed his son's and he chuckled and said, "That is Dela, I brought her along with me." Hector was considering if he should say something to the stranger-woman when Sister came in and said:

"You don't have no respect for yourself, Fitz Bradshaw, or for your son? I don't think you're quite right in the head, man. Busha Bradshaw did plenty in his time but I don't think he ever cast his self-respect to the wind this way. What you aiming to do at all? To heap shame on you' poor children's heads before they even start out in life?" Hector expected the old man to explode but he didn't seem to mind Sister's reproaches, and he turned to his son and said:

"You know about the woman already, they must have told you about her. Well, I'm getting old and tired of pretences. Dela's looked after me well during all these years I've known her. . . she doesn't love me, doesn't even care for me, but she's loyal, one hundred per cent loyal, more so than any blood relation will ever be."

"It's your house, Fitz Bradshaw."

"Yes, my house – a house full of ghosts. That's why I brought Dela with me, she can exorcise the phantoms, drive them out of my life for good." Dela kept staring at him and her face could have been a mora carving with inset eyes of quartz. Hector couldn't understand it all and he kept wondering what had happened to his father.

"If the house have ghosts is nobody else but you responsible for that," Sister said; "ghosts can't trouble them who have a clear conscience."

"You have to go away and battle it out on your own soon, Hector," Fitz said, turning once more to his son, "and it won't harm you to know the kind of father you have. I exiled you on this coast, acted like I was never responsible for your existence, boy, and you know something? I never lost any sleep over it, I'm a son-of-a-bitch of a father. . ."

"The man's going mad!" Sister said. Laljee was hunched up in the corner opposite Dela and it was only after he coughed that Hector became aware of his shadowy presence.

"You growing tall as a coconut tree, Master Hector," he said, as though he had been unaware of the tensions in the room.

"I must go and help with the dinner," Sister said, disappearing behind the bamboo curtains. Tojo came into the living-room to light the lamp but Fitz sent him away, saying that he preferred the darkness, that it made him feel as if he were hiding in a cave under the rain. Hector was glad for the escape that Laljee's remark provided him with.

"How's the car running these days, Laljee?"

"We had to leave it in New Amsterdam and come by bus, Master Hector, she couldn't stand up to the road in this rainy season."

"I brought a present for you, boy," his father said, and Laljee got up and took a radio out of a large cardboard box. "It's for passing your examination." Hector would have been enthusiastic about his gift if the woman had not been there with her brooding, overwhelming presence. Her silence was so formidable it had even defeated Sister. "You see how my boy doesn't even thank me for giving him the magic box, Dela?" Fitz asked, and he was not put out when she said nothing. He was accustomed to talking to her for hours without her showing any sign that he was either boring or interesting her.

"Thank you very much, Daddy," Hector said.

"Go on and look at it then! It's yours and Laljee can show you how to fiddle around with the knobs."

Hector approached the radio cautiously. He would have preferred to have had it in his room where his father and the woman could not laugh at him if he did something wrong. Tojo, who had been looking on from behind the curtain, joined him and they admired the radio without touching it. Laljee switched it on and after a few moments a blare of Latin-American music filled the room. Sister emerged from the kitchen to see what was happening and after Fitz explained that he had brought the radio for Hector she said:

"It's just like you, Fitz Bradshaw, you think that money can

216

compensate for all the years you neglect your one-son. Why you didn't think of giving young La Rose a present too? Come to think of it you should have gone to him and thanked him in person because some of what he give you' son is more than you can pay for with money and gifts."

"Old woman, don't weary me with your preachifying; I had enough of that from the boy's aunt and now I'm getting old and tired and want a rest from it all. I said already that I was a hopeless father – I evaded the responsibility of bringing up my own son – I exiled him up here and now I'm sending him abroad into another exile. Blame me all you like but it isn't going to make me lose any sleep, I had too much blame pinned on me already; if I piled it up it would rise higher than Roraima of the red rock. You know what I like best about Hector? He's never tried to blame me. . ."

"He never set eyes on you long enough to do that," Sister said, and he ignored her and continued:

"And, Dela here, she's never blamed me for anything. . ."

"Don't talk to me about that Buck-woman, Fitz Bradshaw! You bring her here in all you' shamelessness and tell me 'bout how is your house. Well let me tell you my part of the story; if it wasn't for the boy I would 'ave pack up me few belongings and cleared out. I have a duty to this boy and I en't going to leave him in the lurch. . ."

"Duty or no duty, you're enjoying every moment of the drama, old woman, and as for Dela, you can say what you like about her, she has a habit of not understanding what she doesn't want to hear, isn't that so, Dela?" The woman heard him and looked up and the sudden way in which she did this reminded Hector of an ocelot alerted to danger.

"Light the lamp, boy!" Sister said to Tojo. "You can turn it down after you light it but we en't goin' live in no darkness in here." Tojo obeyed hastily, avoiding Fitz's eyes as he struck a match and afterwards, regulated the flame. Hector, seeing Dela clearly for the first time was surprised that she looked so young. Her smooth moon-face could have belonged to a girl of fifteen, but with it she had a woman's body. Her shoulders were wide and thick and her breasts, which from the way the nipples were thrusting out you knew were unsupported by brassières, were full and firm. Her hair, coarse grained and black as a marudi's wing, was swept back and a single long plait fell down her back. She stared at Hector, and he, unable to endure the impenetrable blankness of her stare, smiled stupidly, excused himself and joined Sister in the kitchen.

"Your papa's going crazy," Sister said as soon as he came into the kitchen. "Notice how his eyes does look glassy and how his mouth does tighten up all of a sudden. I see plenty madness in me time, it's a thing me can recognise when I see it. And you know who responsible for his craziness? That woman, she sucking he substance out like a vampire."

"But she looks innocent, Sister," Hector said, and what he meant was that he thought her beautiful. The only other young woman he had known was Elsa and she had a sensuous ugliness.

"Don't tell me 'bout how she innocent, boy! You too young to know if a woman is an angel or if she is the devil's wife. There's something about that Dela that does make me skin crawl. You notice it, boy?"

"I only noticed that she looks so young and her eyes look like swamp water when there's no wind blowing over it."

"I'm telling you, boy, that woman bring something evil into this house, she got more evilness inside her than Delilah ever had, that's why your papa acting crazy like a moonstruck monkey."

"She looks all right to me, Sister, I can't see anything bad in her."

"You're too young to see these things I tell you, boy. You're blind with youth, you got eyes to see and yet you can't see. Life's got to tear away the scales from you' eyes first. Elsa was a good for nothing girl but she didn't have no evil inside she. Elsa was one of God's children but that flat-faced woman is a child of Satan."

Dela ate her dinner in the kitchen with the servants and Fitz did not object. He sat at the table with Hector and Sister. They ate in silence until, towards the end of the meal Fitz said:

"We can switch on the radio after dinner, the reception is much better at nights."

"Can Dela use a knife and fork, Daddy?" Hector asked, unaware of his indiscretion.

"She eats with her fingers," Fitz said, without bothering to look up from his plate, "and she's very clever at doing it." Sister grunted loudly but didn't say anything.

Tojo told the villagers that the magic-box was going to call music and voices out of the sky and despite the rain a crowd gathered outside the big house. Laljee placed the radio on a low table on the front porch and Tojo hung a storm lantern over it. For most of the onlookers it was their first glimpse of a radio.

"All you think a small box like that can catch any voices out of the sky?" a woman asked, and her question sparked off a general discussion.

"That boy, Tojo, was always a rascal-boy and me sure he bring we here so we can make fools of weselves."

"Is where you born at all? Black Bush? The thing all you seeing there en't no magic-box, they call it a radio and all the high-and-mighty folks in the town got them and you does hear music and talking coming out of them all day and night."

"Since you know so much 'bout it, Mr. Man, then tell we how it does catch the voices and the music? Tell we that?"

"Maybe the Good Lord does store up all the things that people does talk about and lock them up in a corner of Heaven."

"Then some smart-man must 'ave found the key, eh!"

"But is why all you black people so foolish, you don't know. . ."

The murmur of voices ceased when Hector and Laljee appeared on the porch. Laljee, conscious of the attention focused on him, switched on the radio with a flourish. There was a loud humming and crackling and the crowd tittered. Someone said, "I tell you all that that thing can't catch no voices out of heaven!"

Laljee kept tuning in until a stranger's voice shouted:

"Is that Berlin?. . . Is that Berlin?" over and over again, and the suddenness with which this alien voice burst upon Tarlogie caused the crowd to stumble backwards. Laljee turned the knobs once more and silenced the voice, and there was a scream and whine of static until he tuned in to some dance music. The music was less disturbing than the foreign voice and the villagers listened and marvelled, oblivious of the gusts of wind stinging their faces with raindrops.

★　　★　　★

219

Someone was pacing up and down the living-room and the noise woke Hector. At first he thought that it was Sister but when he listened he knew that the footsteps were too heavy to be hers. He heard his father's voice and after a while realised that the old man was talking to himself. He lay still for a long time, listening to the wind and the rain and the footsteps and then he decided to get up and go to his father. The living-room was dark and he paused in the doorway until his eyes adapted themselves to the gloom. His father, dressed in a sallow nightshirt, kept up his pacing and mutterings and Laljee, stretched out on the dining-room floor was snoring.

"Are you all right, Daddy?"

"Can't sleep, boy, can't get a wink of sleep. The nights here are too long, this is a house of long nights and when I try to sleep it's as though I have bright electric bulbs inside my head, and the glare wakes up all my sleeping memories and sends them marching like crabs in August, endlessly."

"Go to bed, Fitz Bradshaw," Sister said. She too had been disturbed by the noise and had come out to investigate. "If sleep and you turn enemies, then get down on you' knees and pray to God and ask Him to wash you' conscience with hyssop."

"Go away, old woman, I'm tired of scoldings and women sermonising about what I have done and what I should do! Go away and let me be! Why are you all against me? Why can't even one of you understand that my heart is ailing and sick with the weight of piled up confusions until I feel like a snake that has lost its head in a maze of coils!" The fury and the anguish with which his father said this moved and startled Hector; it reminded him of the baying of a wounded beast.

"Daddy, what's wrong? What's the matter?" Hector asked, and when he put his arms around his father the old man leaned heavily against him, and the physical contact with this man who had all along been a stranger to him made him conscious of his own youth and strength. "You must try and get some sleep, Daddy." He led his father into his room. The woman was on the edge of the big four poster with her face turned towards the wall. Hector heard her breathing and could smell the strong, stale odour of her sweat.

"Wake up, Dela!" Fitz shouted. "You can't have peace all through these long nights whilst I can find none!" Hector helped him into the bed, and the woman woke up and held the old man against her, and she rocked gently and cooed to him, making a wild rhythmic noise which came from deep inside her. She acted as though she was unaware of Hector's presence and the boy crept out of the room and closed the door behind him. For a moment, he thought he heard his father sobbing but the rain was drumming too noisily on the roof for individual sounds to define themselves. Sister was waiting for him in the living-room.

"He's in a bad way," she said.

"What's wrong with him, Sister? It's just like if he's lost contact with everybody and everything around him."

"Jesus in his mercy knows, boy. When I think of that same Fitz Bradshaw as a young man, bright with the promise that the Saviour does give to so few people, it does make me heart crinkle up and weep blood inside me."

"I would like to help him, Sister, but what can I do? All I really know about is what happened to people in books."

"For all you' contrary ways, the Lord give you a wiser heart than you' papa, boy, and the wisdom in you' heart should save you from a lot of folly, and yet I don't know what you can do about Fitz Bradshaw; things gone too far for anybody to do anything else but watch and pray."

Hector returned to his room and sat by his window looking out into the darkness, and all he heard was the droning and hissing of the rain and the wind's insistent lisping. He thought about his life in Tarlogie, about the wild and carefree idyll it had been. It was as though for most of his youth he had drifted down a broad river. At times the river had been swift, at times turbid, and now, suddenly he had run into cross-tides of sorrow, and he could no longer drift along, he had to steer a course or drown.

While he was sitting at the window he heard the rain change its tune. It was no longer drenching the earth but pattering on flood water. He leaned out of the window and saw water churning around the tall pillars that supported the house.

CHAPTER TWENTY

THE heavy rains which had been falling up country caused the Canje River to overflow its banks and to top the watershed between the Canje and Courentyne rivers. The coastal plain stretching east and west of Tarlogie was mostly below sea level, a shallow bowl rimmed by the Atlantic on the north and terraced rain forests to the south. The great volume of water pouring down from the hinterland soon filled the bowl and the encroachment of swollen Atlantic tides augmented the flood. The flood had crept up on Tarlogie like a thief. There was no rush of waters, no high winds. The villagers woke up one morning and found themselves living in stranded arks. Many of them lost all their livestock overnight and life only continued because of the charity of the poor to the destitute. Because of the quiet way in which the flood had come, the devastation seemed more terrible. The rain had been falling so monotonously that the villagers ceased being conscious of it. Like the surf bursting along the foreshore, it was only echoing faintly in their minds. They woke up to a pale dawn to see water halfway up the stilts that supported their huts.

Rain was still falling up country but it had stopped on the coast. They woke up to a drowned calendar when day melted into night and anaemic sunlight probed into the twilight of small rooms whilst outside the light seemed to expand and contract in new cycles of time. Like symbols of survival, fires blazed in miniature hearths and blue wood-smoke spiralled above the roofs of huts. Plaintive, despondent voices shouted across placid wastes of water telling of the loss of crops, of livestock and even those who had possessed nothing complained of having lost much. Caya's rum-shop, although perched high above the water, attracted few customers. The Tarlogians saw so much water around them that they lost the taste for drink.

After a few days swollen carcasses, surrounded by faeces from the latrines floated past the huts. Overhead, bloated carrion crows wheeled and soared indolently before returning to feast on the dead things below them. Old man Doorne, who was always a jump ahead of any disaster, rented out a fleet of ballahoos to the villagers so that those who did not own these flat-bottomed punts could ply up and down. Some of the villagers whose huts had been built too low, took refuge in the schoolroom opposite the police station. Tojo and Clysis had to abandon their downstairs room and sleep in the kitchen. The branches of the tamarind and po-boy trees provided a sanctuary for Sister's chickens and Hector and Tojo went out in a canoe in the mornings and fed them. Some of the chickens caught cramp and fell into the water and waiting alligators snatched them up. Hector sat at the kitchen window in the afternoons and shot at the alligators and those he killed floated up on their backs and joined the cortege of dead things that the ebb tide pulled towards the foreshore. One night Tanta Bess called out to say that Marajin, an old East Indian woman, was stranded in her hut and unless somebody fetched her she would die of starvation. Hector was always glad of a chance to get out of the big house. His father was getting worse, complaining that everyone was against him; saying that his food was poisoned, that Sister had tried to murder him in his sleep.

Hector and Tojo paddled their canoe to Marajin's hut. She was curled up on a table with the water all around her. They carried her to the police station moaning and whimpering and clutching her belly to ease the cramp in it. At night it was very quiet in the village. No dogs were barking and the piper owls had no melodies to flute to the pale moon.

CHAPTER TWENTY-ONE

THE third Sunday of the flood was Harvest Sunday and Sister wore her best dress to go and hear old man Galloway preach. Hector accompanied her without his usual objections. Both he and Sister were happy to get away from the oppressiveness of the big house. They left Fitz sitting in his Berbice chair and Dela and Laljee squatting in their corners. Dela and Laljee had become shadow-people living in the twilight world of Fitz's madness. As Tojo paddled the ballahoo towards the church, Hector noticed that there was an air of febrile gaiety about Sister, she chatted and laughed a great deal. When they were nearing the church she turned to Hector and said:

"You know what's matta with your papa, boy? He fighting to break out of the dying forest of his flesh – that is what the all of we trying to do, me and Preacher Galloway and your papa. Only thing is that some of we en't fighting so hard in weselves to do it. One day you going to have to fight the same fight, boy, but you got time. . . you will have to wait you' flesh start to tighten itself around the hollow log of bone that age does turn all old people's bodies into. When the time come, boy, I hope you will have enough peace nesting inside of you' heart to ease the strain of the fight."

"Why are you talking so strange, Sister?"

"Don't worry, boy, don't worry, you will find out in God's good time."

The church was full and some of the congregation who couldn't even find standing room stood up in their punts outside and looked through the windows so that they could see and hear what was going on. Preacher Galloway was dressed in his red velveteen suit and a blue waistcoat and his collar was so high that it gave him little room to indulge his habit of screwing his long neck from side to side. He bowed to Sister and she nodded formally and took her place in the front row. There were many palm leaves but few harvest gifts around the altar and the preacher began his sermon saying:

"Brothers and sisters, this is a time for lamentation for this year we have had a harvest of flood, the skies have wept a deluge of rain and left us with empty hearts and months of weeping and sorrow. I will ask you all this, and you must think about it: cast aside your sorrowing and complaining for a while and think! Is there one God of the poor and another of the rich and the high-and-mighty? I don't know, brothers and sisters, many a time I turned my ole eyes inwards and looked into my own heart for an answer. . . but I never found it. All I know is that there are many barefooted ones and plenty ragged shirted ones who live under the stars in this village and when drought or flood comes it is they who suffer. When I look outside the church windows on this, the Lord's day, all my eyes can see is water, muddy water and all the green things that give us life are sleeping under the water – the cassava and the corn, the young rice and all the sprouting things we accustomed to nurse and cherish. And who is to blame for this? Tell me that. Because if all you know the answer then the Lord must have spoken to you whilst He must have lockjaw every time He looked my way. All I know is that we're a patient people, a waiting people, we going to live through many more droughts and floods until one bright day we will shout with a mighty voice and the sky will shatter like the walls of Jericho and we will give fallen stars to our children to make playthings out of them, and when that day comes the road to the Land of Promise will stretch wide in front of the all of us and all the powers and principalities and the powers of darkness won't stop us then. Many of us here won't live to see that day, brothers and sisters, but it will come just the same, it will come." The congregation murmured and Sister shouted:

"It will come, brother! Praise the Lord, it will come!"

After the service a woman said:

"Me didn't understand what he was getting at, but it did sound good and the words roll off he tongue and catch fire inside me belly!"

Sister left immediately after the service, complaining that her head was aching. She went straight to her bed when she got home. Hector had never known her to be ill before and the look in her eyes and the way her skin seemed to be stretching tight around her skull, troubled him. He sat on the edge of her bed and tried to massage the pain out of her head. Her body was seized by a succession of spasms. When she spoke it was as though her tongue had grown too big for her mouth and Hector had to move close to hear her.

"Boy, I know you want to go and call a doctor. . . What I want you to do is to send message to call the preacher 'cause Mantop breathing the breath of death all over me and I en't going to leave this bed alive, I know it." Hector looked around the room. He felt that there was a strange presence with them. "I can see by you' face that you know Mantop is here, boy, so send and call the preacher for me. . . Lord, ha' mercy on Galloway, this young boy and the madman in this house!" she said.

Preacher Galloway and Hector remained at Sister's bedside all through the night, listening to her breath forcing itself out of her lungs and rasping in her throat. Fitz paced up and down the living-room muttering to himself or going to the window and shouting challenges to imaginary assailants. Who-you birds called out from the surrounding trees and their calls echoed over the water. The other people in the house could not sleep because they knew that Death's messenger-boy had come for Sister. The morning sun flared out above the water and the mist and it was the brightest sun that had appeared since the rains had started falling two months earlier. Sister had not spoken since she had invoked God's mercy for Galloway and Hector. She saw the sunlight coming through the window and she raised herself up and smiled. Her smile reflected all the love that had been stored up in her heart for nearly fourscore years. Galloway helped her to sit up and she died in his arms with the sunshine on her black face. Tojo and Clysis came into the room and found the old man and the boy weeping.

★　　★　　★

The flood waters had fallen two feet but there was still no dry land on which the dead could be buried. Doorne and Caya, having got permission from the police said that they would bury Sister under the po-boy tree in the back yard. She had always wanted to be buried there and they knew that her spirit would not rest anywhere else. They built a greenheart pen, caulked the seams, bailed the water out and dug a deep grave. The burial took place in the afternoon and the whole village turned out for it. Caya had made a coffin out of crabwood boards lined with galvanised iron. It was watertight and so heavy that it took four men to lift it. When the villagers had gathered around the ten-foot high pen in their canoes and ballahoos, Preacher Galloway stood up and began the burial service. Fitz Bradshaw and his woman looked on from the kitchen window. Galloway was proud that since he had been unable to marry Sister, at least he could bury her. These ceremonies were of equal importance in his eyes. Hector stood beside the preacher, holding on to a branch to steady the boat. His spirit was overloaded with grief and he heard little of what Galloway was saying. In the midst of the burial service, a chicken fell out of a tamarind tree and an alligator caught it and swam away. As the preacher read out the lesson his faltering voice gained strength and deepened:

"Man that is born of woman hath but a short time to live and is full of misery. . ." The voice carried across wide stretches of water, dying away in disembodied echoes. Hector felt as though it was all a daydream and when he heard Galloway say, "Dust to dust, ashes to ashes, may her soul find eternal peace!" he looked down expecting to see dry land and feel earth under his feet. Doorne and Caya heaped mud on top of the coffin and they roofed the pen with palm leaves.

★   ★   ★

Three weeks after Sister's death the public road reappeared twisting like a vandal brush-stroke across a muddy landscape. The flood waters had retreated and deep footprints were weaving crazy patterns in the muddy yards. The villagers avoided the big house. They said that it was a nest of madness and death, and that the radio harboured frenzied spirits from outer darkness. Some of them had seen Fitz's demon-face at the window and heard his ranting at night. Others spoke in whispers about the mute woman who, since the day she arrived, had not gone outside the big house.

One afternoon Fitz got up from his Berbice chair and announced that he was going for a walk.

"The old woman's spirit is oppressing me," he said, "it's all over the place and I can't breathe. Sometimes I can feel her black hands reaching inside me to stop my heart from beating."

"I will come with you, boss, and on the way back I can stop in at Caya's shop and have a drink. I en't had a drink so long me throat feeling like it lined with dead leaves," Laljee said, and Hector was indiscreet enough to add:

"Both me and Laljee will come with you."

"I'm going by myself," Fitz said, looking from one to the other suspiciously. "I don't want any shadows trailing behind me. Look at what Fitz Bradshaw's come to, eh! Got to have people hounding him down everywhere he goes!" He walked out of the room and when he reached the top of the driveway Hector and Laljee followed him. The old man went to the police station and reported that Laljee, Hector and Dela were scheming to poison him so as to get hold of his money and his estate. After that first visit, Fitz began calling at the station daily to spin out a fantastic web of accusations. Mark-a-book would listen to him composedly, pretending to be writing down what he was saying. The Sergeant was glad for the diversion Fitz's visits created. The villagers were too busy wresting a living from their devastated lands to commit even minor crimes and the intervals between visits to the rum-shop were long and boring. On the other hand, Fitz got a macabre satisfaction out of being able to slander those closest to him to a stranger.

Hector consulted Laljee on what should be done about his father.

"You think we should carry him back to Georgetown, Laljee?"

"What-for carry him back, Master Hector? Him happy here with the woman and if he go to the city your auntie will grab the chance to take control of the whole family. All she will have to do is to ask the Law to certify the boss, then she will get hold of the money and the estate, and once she do that then she wouldn't walk and tell dog howdy."

In the weeks after Sister's death, Hector began to realise more and more that his father's madness had turned him into a child again and that he, the son, had now to father the old man. This realisation made him feel very protective towards Fitz.

"I think my daddy should go back to Georgetown, Laljee."

"Why, Master Hector? Why?"

"It's the place he knows best. Laljee!"

"Yes, Master Hector."

"What is this thing that has crept inside my daddy, this madness thing?"

"Is a peculiar thing, Young Master, it does coil round your heart like a black snake. It does cloud you' spirit like morning mist, it does darken you' vision outside and brighten it inside, it does cut you off from you' kith and kin and send you sailing down a river of night where the current does be so strong that is hard to turn back without drowning."

"But why did it have to happen to him?"

"This life we living full of luck and chance, Master Hector, and all of we got madness tethered like a wild ram-goat to we heart and sometimes the goat does break loose and the hooves does keep pounding inside we head night and day."

"You think it will happen to me, Laljee?"

"It can happen to anybody, Young Master."

"Do you think that Dela's mad too?"

"Dela got the gift of quietness, Young Master, and the quietness wrap around she so thick that madness can't never break in."

"I wish she would teach me how to wrap this quietness around me."

"You got to have it in you' blood, Young Master."

"Did you ever hear her talk, Laljee?"

"Plenty times, Master Hector; she got a brother who does live with she and she does talk to he all the time. It's just that she don't talk outside of she language. In any case, she is a woman and when talk was sharing womankind get a bigger share than anybody else."

"Laljee, you know. . . somehow I feel that my daddy wants to tell me something. . . the few times we've been alone he kept looking at me in a strange way. You must leave us alone this evening and tell Dela to go for a walk or something."

"I will try and fix it up, Master Hector."

★   ★   ★

Fitz Bradshaw sat in his Berbice chair listening to the wind and the surf and watching at the bats flying swiftly in and out of the circle of light around the front porch. Laljee and Dela had gone out and this delighted Fitz. He could sit there by himself and gloat over their impending downfall. "I exposed them all to the police," he said aloud, "the Sergeant's going to arrest them all tonight. I told him how Hector's scheming to get hold of my money, how Laljee keeps a knife hidden in his bosom and how I caught him the other night standing over my bed with the knife in his hand ready to stab me, how Dela puts poison in my food, and she knows all kinds of poisons that the doctors can't trace in your bloodstream. . . They hang fireflies over my bed at nights, fireflies big as bumblebees, and they wink over me and keep me awake. . ." He heard footsteps and waited, terrified that someone had been spying on him, reading his mind.

"It's quiet in here," Hector said, and the boy came and sat opposite his father in a cane chair.

"Quiet? In here?"

"Is it all right if I sit and talk to you for a while?"

"Talk to me? Too many voices have been talking to me of late, boy." The old man looked around the room suspiciously. "Who sent you to talk to me?" Hector got up and put a hand on his father's shoulder.

"Daddy, are you listening to me? Because I want to ask you something."

"Ask me, boy!"

"Tell me about my mother?"

"Your mother?" He laughed from deep inside him and Hector could feel his whole body shaking. "Your mother? She was a fine one, she died and left me to face it all. They kept her shut up in this damned tomb of a house and she broke loose and ran away by dying. . ."

230

"Who was my mother?"

"She had an affair with one of the farmers in the village and they sent him away and locked her up in here. . . the old woman was her jailer. . ."

"Daddy, I don't understand what you're trying to say! Tell me who my mother was?"

He shook off Hector's hand and shouted: "Blast your soul in hell! All you want to do is to get hold of my money!" For a moment Hector thought that his father was going to strike him but he only leaned back in his chair and began chuckling.

"You've got to tell me who my mother was. I've got to know! You sent me away to grow up here, you wanted me out of the way because I was always getting sick or because I kept reminding you about something you wanted to forget. . ." The words took hold of Hector and he hardly knew what he was saying, "What was I reminding you of, tell me?"

"Reminding me of? I'll tell you who you remind me of!" His father stood up and faced him, "I'll tell you who you are!" he laughed his crazy laugh right in Hector's face, coming so close that the boy could feel and smell his breath, "Your mother was my wife's sister. . . it was all her doing. They sent away her lover and she had to even up scores with them – with her sister and with Hanna and with the old woman – she came to me one night and said 'I want to have a baby' and I planted the seed in her. . . and afterwards, she couldn't face up to what she had done, they were too strong for her, so she just willed herself to die. . . and all the blame had to be rained down on my head. . . you can't win in a fight against those women! You think I'm mad, eh? You think so? You and Laljee and all the rest of you get together and talk my name and say I'm mad. . ." He laughed again and sat down, and looking at his father Hector could see that his mind had suddenly wandered away and that it was no use trying to reach him with words any longer. And yet he did not want to leave him alone. The news about his mother had not shocked him. She had always been a phantom-woman and words could never evoke a flesh-and-blood image of her. It was Sister who had mothered him and his memory of the old woman was a living one which drew strength from a multitude of associations. He could only picture his mother in relationship to Sister, the tall, old woman, zealously loving her God and seeing to it that all those around her lived by her tenets.

"How is it outside?" Fitz asked, although he could see for himself from where he sat.

"The sky is full of dark clouds, dark, dry clouds like dust," Hector said.

"What's that noise I'm hearing, boy? Is it the wind singing?"

"It's the people at Preacher Galloway's prayer meeting. It's their thanksgiving after the passing of the flood."

"Where's your teacher, boy? Doesn't he come to visit you now and then?"

"He's schoolmastering in Essequibo, Daddy," Hector said, and Fitz hummed to himself and tapped on the arm of his chair with his fingers. A night hawk cried out sharply and a gust of wind rocked the lantern and filled the room with dancing shadows.

★   ★   ★

Laljee and Dela walked towards Saltan Village, parting the darkness and enjoying the feel of the cool wind. They walked on the verging grass because the road had too many muddy puddles. The grass was wet where passing buses and lorries had splashed it with dirty water. They stopped at the bridge which spanned the canal separating Tarlogie from Saltan Village. A mule dray rumbled past. The driver, sitting upright and holding the reins, was fast asleep.

Laljee and Dela leaned over the rails and looked at the dark, running water. It was ebb tide and the koker gate by the foreshore was open.

"I'm going to New Amsterdam tomorrow for the car," Laljee said, and Dela looked at him and smiled. "Everything going to break up once we get to Georgetown, 'cause once the boss sister take over won't be no place for me or you, gal." Dela nodded her agreement vigorously. She understood, but like Laljee she had put aside enough money while the going was good and she was not worried. If Fitz still wanted her she would remain in the cottage. The strange, demonic spirits that had possessed him neither dismayed nor frightened her. They were not evil spirits, it was only that they spoke with the tongues of dead prophets. If

232

the spirits caused a wide river of indifference to flow between them, then she and her brother would return to their tribal lands and live in plenty on what she had saved up.

"We better be getting back," Laljee said.

On their way past the rum-shop a man called out:

"All you come and see the child of silence who the master harbouring in the big house!" and his companions left their drinks and came out to have a look. A drunken voice said:

"Is she bring death to ole Sister. . . they say she's a vampire woman and she does turn into a ball of fire when night-time come!"

"If all you don't mind you' own business I will put the police on you!" Laljee shouted, and someone pelted him with an empty bottle. It landed on Dela's shoulder and made her stagger. Laljee picked up the bottle and hurled it at the crowd on the rum-shop veranda. The bottle crashed against the veranda rail scattering fragments into the crowd. There was an enraged muttering and the men rushed at Laljee and Dela. A bottle caught Laljee in the small of the back and felled him. Dela bent down and picked him up. She ran towards the driveway with the old East Indian in her arms. A group of villagers, on their way home from the prayer meeting, rushed up to see what was happening.

"What's the matter?"

"What happen?" they asked.

"It's the vampire woman!" The anger which had come like a cloudburst out of a clear sky swept the newcomers along and they too began stoning Dela and the unconscious Laljee. The furore brought out the whole village. The terror in Dela made her shriek like an Esquimo curlew.

Tojo burst into the living-room. Hector was sitting under the lamp trying to read and his father was enjoying his distracted reveries. The windows and jalousies facing the road were shut and Hector thought that the noise he was hearing was coming from the rum-shop where a fight had broken out.

"They killing Dela!"

"Dela. . . Who?"

"They chasing she and Laljee down the road and stoning them!"

233

"The clouds are dark and dry like dust," Fitz said. Tojo stood looking at Hector, waiting for him to do something and Hector felt ashamed because he didn't know what to do. He only felt fear tightening up his insides.

"Where are they, Tojo?" he asked, and his voice sounded like an echo in an empty barrel to him.

"You got to do something, boss, or they will kill them two!" The fear fragmented itself and scattered like bats caught in the light. He ran out of the house and up the driveway towards the angry voices. The clouds had drifted away and stars were hanging low and bright. The animated silhouettes by the roadside seemed to belong to a monster which had emerged out of the swamps. By the time he reached the bridge, the crowd had caught up with Dela. She was down on her knees stooping over Laljee. Men and women were kicking and cuffing her and beating her with sticks. Hector broke through the crowd and stood over her and the blows that fell on him drove away his fear and filled him with fury.

"Leave her alone!" he shouted and his voice was that of his pristine manhood. It silenced the crowd and those nearest him backed away. He had come upon them so suddenly that he had taken the initiative away from them. The crowd might have turned on him if Caya and Doorne had not joined him. Doorne had his shotgun under his arm.

"Go 'way! Go and creep back to all you' smelly rooms! You should be 'shamed of you'selves carrying on like wild beasts, and some of you just come from prayer meeting," Doorne said, and the crowd drifted into and mingled with the waiting darkness.

"I sorry this happen, boss," Caya said, "me didn't know what was happening 'til Dookia alert me." Hector helped Dela up and led her towards the house and Caya picked up the old East Indian and followed them. Dela had a cut at the back of her head and blood was running down her neck and soaking the back of her dress. She was breathing unevenly and biting into her lip. Between them they washed and bandaged her wounds and Laljee's and afterwards Hector gave Dela a shot of brandy and sent her to bed. Laljee came to and started swearing.

"If only me did have a gun with me I would have showed them nigger-people what lead does taste like. . ."

234

"You all right, Laljee?" Hector asked.

"This old coolie-man tough like seasoned takuba, boss," Doorne said; "he got more lives than two cats put together."

Fitz was sitting in the living-room, oblivious of all that had passed. No echo of the crowd's exploding anger had pierced the shield of his madness. When Hector told him that it was time to go to bed, he allowed the boy to lead him to his room, undress him and help him into bed and for the first time in weeks he did not pace up and down the living-room during the night.

Sleep did not come easily to Hector. He lay in bed gazing at the canopy of his mosquito net, and when thoughts were about to form themselves in his mind the noise of the surf would crunch them up and bury them. He did not hear Dela enter his room, he only saw her approaching, wraithlike from halfway between the door and his bed. He closed his eyes and waited, thinking that she would hear his heart thumping since it sounded like master drums to him. He was conscious of her bending over his bed and then she put her thick, moist hand on his forehead. He waited and the hand was withdrawn, and when he opened his eyes she had vanished. Her gratitude, shown in this strange way, was somehow an endorsement of what, in the last few days he had come to know and to accept – that his initiation into manhood was now complete. Lying there, he had a vision of himself standing on a beach, a speck, facing the aloneness of wide spaces, at the mercy of the wind and the surf.

★   ★   ★

The next morning Preacher Galloway came around to the big house to explain that he had remained in the schoolhouse long after the prayer meeting.

"I would have scattered that crowd like leaves and poured God's anger on all of them if I was there," he said.

Laljee had recovered and had gone to New Amsterdam for the car, and when Hector told the preacher that they were leaving Tarlogie in the afternoon, the old man said: "I will look after the old lady's grave, Hector, I promise you that, and if you don't mind I want to plant a ring of po-boy trees around her; she was always one for listening to them singing in the night wind."

"You know I wouldn't mind, Preacher Galloway, plant them

so that the wind can't reach her when it's wet with dew, then she can sit and listen to the singing without feeling chill."

"God bless you, Hector. Go well, boy."

Mark-a-book turned up at mid-morning wanting to know if Hector would press charges against the villagers.

"I'm vexed with them, Sergeant, but what's the use of charging them," Hector said.

"I so vexed with them that I not going to have a drink in Caya's shop for a whole week," the sergeant said. Hector knew that this was hardly a sacrifice, since Doorne had supplied Mark-a-book with enough bush rum to last him for months. "Don't say nothing 'bout what happen in Georgetown because if the great ones hear I will be in big trouble."

"I won't say a word about it, Sergeant."

★   ★   ★

Hector left Tarlogie in the late afternoon when the tide was rising off the foreshore. The surf was pounding up the dark brown sands, and the wind coming out of a bellows of sea and sky was singing through the po-boy tree over Sister's grave. He led his father up the driveway towards the waiting car and heard Dela's shuffling footsteps behind him. Doorne and Caya and Tojo waved them goodbye from the front porch. The sun, big and yellowing, was nearing the dark groves of courida trees that rimmed the wild coast, and the people in whose midst he had spent his youth looked on from the darkness of their huts.

ABOUT THE AUTHOR

Jan Carew was born in 1920 in the village of Agricola in Berbice, Guyana. When he left Guyana in 1945 to pursue his education he began what he described as 'endless journeyings' that involved periods in the UK, North and South America, Africa and Asia. He lived in Jamaica between 1962-66 with his then wife Sylvia Wynter, moving to Canada for some years before settling in the USA. He taught at Northwestern University and at Princeton and was at the heart of developments in African American studies.

His first novel, *Black Midas* was published in 1958, in the same year as *The Wild Coast*, both set in Guyana. *The Last Barbarian*, set in Harlem, USA was published in 1960, and *Moscow is Not My Mecca* (1964) took a Caribbean student to disillusion in Soviet Russia. Jan Carew has written several books for children, a number of plays, and a collection of poems.

In his retirement to Kentucky, Jan Carew has resumed his old love of painting.

CARIBBEAN MODERN CLASSICS
Spring 2009 titles

Jan R. Carew
Black Midas
Introduction: Kwame Dawes
ISBN: 9781845230951; pp. 272; 23 May 2009; £8.99

This is the bawdy, Eldoradean epic of the legendary 'Ocean Shark' who makes and loses fortunes as a pork-knocker in the gold and diamond fields of Guyana, discovering that there are sharks with far sharper teeth in the city. *Black Midas* was first published in 1958.

Jan R. Carew
The Wild Coast
Introduction: Jeremy Poynting
ISBN: 9781845231101; pp. 240; 23 May 2009; £8.99

First published in 1958, this is the coming-of-age story of a sickly city child, sent away to the remote Berbice village of Tarlogie. Here he must find himself, make sense of Guyana's diverse cultural inheritances and come to terms with a wild nature disturbingly red in tooth and claw.

Neville Dawes
The Last Enchantment
Introduction: Kwame Dawes
ISBN: 9781845231170; pp. 332; 27 April 2009; £9.99

This penetrating and often satirical exploration of the search for self in a world divided by colour and class is set in the context of the radical hopes of Jamaican nationalist politics in the early 1950s. First published in 1960, the novel asks many pertinent questions about the Jamaica of today.

Wilson Harris
Heartland
Introduction: Michael Mitchell
ISBN: 9781845230968; pp. 104; 23 May 2009; £7.99

First published in 1964, this visionary narrative tracks one man's psychic disintegration in the aloneness of the forests of the Guyanese interior, making a powerful ecological statement about man's place in the 'invisible chain of being', in which nature is a no less active presence.

Edgar Mittelholzer
Corentyne Thunder
Introduction: Juanita Cox
ISBN: 9781845231118; pp. 242; 27 April 2009; £8.99

This pioneering work of West Indian fiction, first published in 1941, is not merely an acute portrayal of the rural Indo-Guyanese world, but a work of literary ambition that creates a symphonic relationship between its characters and the vast openness of the Corentyne coast.

Andrew Salkey
Escape to an Autumn Pavement
Introduction: Thomas Glave
ISBN: 9781845230982; pp. 220; 23 May 2009; £8.99

This brave and remarkable novel, set in London at the end of the 1950s, and published in 1960, catches its 'brown' Jamaican narrator on the cusp between black and white, between exiled Jamaican and an incipent black Londoner, and between heterosexual and homosexual desires.

Denis Williams
Other Leopards
Introduction: Victor Ramraj
ISBN: 9781845230678; pp. 216; 23 May 2009; £8.99

Lionel Froad is a Guyanese working on an archeological survey in the mythical Jokhara in the horn of Africa. There he hopes to rediscover the self he calls 'Lobo', his alter ego from 'ancestral times', which he thinks slumbers behind his cultivated mask. First published in 1963, this is one of the most important Caribbean novels of the past fifty years.

Denis Williams
The Third Temptation
Introduction: Victor Ramraj
ISBN: 9781845231163; pp. 108; 23 May 2009; £7.99

A young man is killed in a traffic accident at a Welsh seaside resort. Around this incident, Williams, drawing inspiration from the *Nouveau Roman*, creates a reality that is both rich and problematic. Whilst he brings to the novel a Caribbean eye, Williams makes an important statement about refusing any restrictive boundaries for Caribbean fiction. The novel was first published in 1968.

Roger Mais
The Hills Were Joyful Together
Introduction: tba
ISBN: 9781845231002; pp. 272; October 2009; £8.99

Unflinchingly realistic in its portrayal of the wretched lives of Kingston's urban poor, this is a novel of prophetic rage. First published in 1953, it is both a work of tragic vision and a major contribution to the evolution of an autonomous Caribbean literary aesthetic.

Edgar Mittelholzer
A Morning at the Office
Introduction: Raymond Ramcharitar
ISBN: 978184523; pp. 208; October 2009; £8.99

First published in 1950, this is one of the Caribbean's foundational novels in its bold attempt to portray a whole society in miniature. A genial satire on human follies and the pretensions of colour and class, this novel brings several ingenious touches to its mode of narration.

Edgar Mittelholzer
Shadows Move Among Them
Introduction: tba
ISBN: 9781845230913; pp. 320; December 2009; £9.99

In part a satire on the Eldoradean dream, in part an exploration of the possibilities of escape from the discontents of civilisation, Mittelholzer's 1951 novel of the Reverend Harmston's attempt to set up a utopian commune dedicated to 'Hard work, frank love and wholesome play' has some eerie 'pre-echoes' of the fate of Jonestown in 1979.

Edgar Mittelholzer
The Life and Death of Sylvia
Introduction: Juanita Cox
ISBN: 9781845231200; pp. 318; December 2009, £9.99

In 1930s' Georgetown, a young woman on her own is vulnerable prey, and when Sylvia Russell finds she cannot square her struggle for economic survival and her integrity, she hurtles towards a wilfully early death. Mittelholzer's novel of 1953 is a richly inward portrayal of a woman who finds inner salvation through the act of writing.

Elma Napier
A Flying Fish Whispered
Introduction: Evelyn O'Callaghan
ISBN: 9781845231026; pp. 248; February 2010; £8.99

With one of the most delightfully feisty women characters in Caribbean fiction and prose that sings, Elma Napier's 1938 Dominican novel is a major rediscovery, not least for its imaginative exploration of different kinds of Caribbeans, in particular the polarity between plot and plantation that Napier sees in a distinctly gendered way.

Orlando Patterson
The Children of Sisyphus
Introduction: Geoffrey Philp
ISBN: 9781845230944; pp. 288; November 2009; £9.99

This is a brutally poetic book that brings to the characters who live on Kingston's 'dungle' an intensity that invests them with tragic depth. In Patterson's existentialist novel, first published in 1964, dignity comes with a stoic awareness of the absurdity of life and the shedding of false illusions, whether of salvation or of a mythical African return.

V.S. Reid
New Day
Introduction: tba
ISBN: 9781845230906, pp. 360; November 2009, £9.99

First published in 1949, this historical novel focuses on defining moments of Jamaica's nationhood, from the Morant Bay rebellion of 1865, to the dawn of self-government in 1944. *New Day* pioneers the creation of a distinctively Jamaican literary language of narration.

Garth St. Omer
A Room on the Hill
Introduction: John Robert Lee
ISBN: 9781845230937; pp. 210; September 2009; £8.99

A friend's suicide and his profound alienation in a St Lucia still slumbering in colonial mimicry and the straitjacket of a reactionary Catholic church drive John Lestrade into a state of internal exile. First published in 1968, St. Omer's meticulously crafted novel is a pioneering exploration of the inner Caribbean man.

Austin C.Clarke, *The Survivors of the Crossing*
Austin C. Clarke, *Amongst Thistles and Thorns*
O.R. Dathorne, *The Scholar Man*
O.R. Dathorne, *Dumplings in the Soup*
Neville Dawes, *Interim*
Wilson Harris, *The Eye of the Scarecrow*
Wilson Harris, *The Sleepers of Roraima*
Wilson Harris, *Tumatumari*
Wilson Harris, *Ascent to Omai*
Wilson Harris, *The Age of the Rainmakers*
Marion Patrick Jones, *Panbeat*
Marion Patrick Jones, *Jouvert Morning*
Earl Lovelace, *Whilst Gods Are Falling*
Roger Mais, *Black Lightning*
Edgar Mittelholzer, *Children of Kaywana*
Edgar Mittelholzer, *The Harrowing of Hubertus*
Edgar Mittelholzer, *Kaywana Blood*
Edgar Mittelholzer, *My Bones and My Flute*
Edgar Mittelholzer, *A Swarthy Boy*
Orlando Patterson, *An Absence of Ruins*
V.S. Reid, *The Leopard* (North America only)
Garth St. Omer, *Shades of Grey*
Andrew Salkey, *The Late Emancipation of Jerry Stover*
and more…

All Peepal Tree titles are available from the website
www.peepaltreepress.com
with a money back guarantee, secure credit card ordering
and fast delivery throughout the world at cost or less.

Peepal Tree Press is the home of challenging and inspiring literature
from the Caribbean and Black Britain. Visit www.peepaltreepress.com
to read sample poems and reviews, discover new authors, established
names and access a wealth of information.

Contact us at:
Peepal Tree Press, 17 King's Avenue, Leeds LS6 1QS, UK
Tel: +44 (0) 113 2451703 E-mail: contact@peepaltreepress.com